Jackie gripped the flashlight in fingers grown icy with remembered fear.

There was no way for her ex-husband to find her again after all this time. She'd covered her tracks carefully. Hadn't she?

She fought her sudden surge of panic, knowing she wouldn't be comfortable until she checked every room in the house.

As she reached the long, low dresser in her bedroom, a brilliant flash of lightning sizzled through the room with eerie clarity. Her eyes lifted to focus on the mirror. Her heart stopped completely.

In that instant she saw the body—dressed in an elf costume—lying sprawled across her bed.

ABOUT THE AUTHOR

Dani Sinclair began her official writing career when her sister caught her between jobs and asked her to write a romance novel. Dani had been creating her own stories since she first learned to read, so she agreed. A latecomer to the romance genre, having grown up on action-adventure, Westerns and later science fiction, Dani quickly plunged into this wonderful realm. She combines her love for romance with her need to write suspense.

Dani and her family reside in Maryland outside of Washington, D.C. An active volunteer in writers' groups, she is a member of Romance Writers of America, Washington Romance Writers, Virginia Romance Writers and Sisters in Crime.

Books by Dani Sinclair

HARLEQUIN INTRIGUE
371—MYSTERY BABY
401—MAN WITHOUT A BADGE

Don't miss any of our special offers. Write to us at the following address for information on our newest releases.

Harlequin Reader Service
U.S.: 3010 Walden Ave., P.O. Box 1325, Buffalo, NY 14269
Canadian: P.O. Box 609, Fort Erie, Ont. L2A 5X3

Better Watch Out
Dani Sinclair

Harlequin Books

TORONTO • NEW YORK • LONDON
AMSTERDAM • PARIS • SYDNEY • HAMBURG
STOCKHOLM • ATHENS • TOKYO • MILAN
MADRID • WARSAW • BUDAPEST • AUCKLAND

For Roger—husband, friend, lover and helpmate. Thanks for always being there.

And for my mother, Ruth Ann Shaughnessy, who always made Christmas a magical time.

ACKNOWLEDGMENTS

Heartfelt thanks to Barbi Richardson, Vicki Singer, Jacki Frank, Linda Lou Mercer, Robyn Amos and Barbara White-Rayczek. Thanks, friends.

ISBN 0-373-22448-6

BETTER WATCH OUT

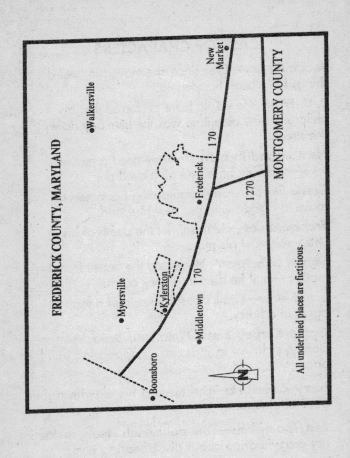

FREDERICK COUNTY, MARYLAND

- Walkersville
- Myersville
- Boonsboro
- Kylerton
- Middletown
- Frederick
- New Market

I 70

I 270

MONTGOMERY COUNTY

All underlined places are fictitious.

CAST OF CHARACTERS

Jackie Neeley—Ever since she moved in, weird things have been happening.

J. D. Frost—He would have preferred that his children's new playmate was the little boy down the street.

Heather and Todd Frost—They need a mother's love—and they have one all picked out.

Bessie Starnes—She's liquidating her assets to move to Florida with her new husband.

Frank Starnes—He hasn't let the death of his wife's son slow his plans.

Donnie Leiberman—He rented the house from his mother—until he died in a fiery crash.

Seth Bislow—Frank's best friend, and a loan agent in a hurry.

Oggie Korbel, Steve Pinta and Brad Volmer—Donnie's closest friends are disappearing one by one.

Larry Zalewoski—Did he find his ex-wife again after all this time?

Ben Thompkins—This policeman deals in facts not crazy stories about disappearing elves.

Aunt Dottie—She loves her nephew's children, but she's addicted to soaps and talk shows.

Prologue

"Hello?"

The sleepy response filled his ear. Nervously, his eyes swept the backyard through the uncurtained window. Nothing moved, but his fingers gripped the telephone tightly.

"It's me," he said. "We've got trouble."

"Hey, man, it's four o'clock in the morning."

"Never mind the time check, will you listen up? We've been made."

The voice suddenly snapped awake. "Cops?"

"No. One of the places we hit. The dude's crazy. He wants his stuff back. Says he'll slit our throats if we don't come through."

"Wait a minute. How come he didn't go to the cops?"

Did that shadow out by the garage just shift? He stared until his eyes ached. "Look," he said, trying to keep the fear from his voice, "we gotta meet."

Yes, there it was again. A small movement, but enough to make his throat go dry.

In his ear his friend was saying, "Okay, man, chill. I'll be right over."

"No! Don't come here!"

"Hey, man, what's wrong?"

The shadow lengthened, taking on exaggerated proportions in the moonlight. He couldn't swallow past the fear that clogged his throat. "I'm on my way!"

He dropped the phone in its cradle, grabbed his jacket and keys and fled down the hall to the front door. That cold voice he'd heard earlier and the echo of those softly spoken threats chilled his blood. The dude was crazy.

Crazy enough to kill.

He ran for the car, got inside and slammed the door. The frost that rimed the windshield obscured his vision, but he couldn't wait for the defroster to kick in.

He turned on the wipers and made it out of the driveway before he powered down the window and stuck his head out to watch for parked cars and the Stop sign at the end of the street.

To think only an hour ago he'd been pleasantly buzzed. Why the hell had he answered that telephone? And that voice, that chilling voice.

Maybe they should just disappear for a while. Let the guy break in and help himself, take whatever he wanted. They could lay low, play it cool, maybe take a vacation somewhere. Yeah. Not a bad idea.

What was wrong with the car?

The steering felt funny. Man, that's all he needed, a car problem at this hour.

He glanced in the rearview mirror, but he couldn't see a thing out the back window. His gaze returned to the tiny circle the defroster had created on the windshield.

By then, it was much too late to worry if he was being followed.

Chapter One

The watcher was back. Jackie tried to slow her breathing. She must not scare the children.

"Jackie, here's another red one."

She pushed her glasses back up the bridge of her nose and accepted the sparkly red ornament from the little girl's hand, proud that her fingers weren't shaking. Only her insides were doing that. She glanced around the brightly lit store, wishing she hadn't let Angel go home early. There were no customers inside the ice-cream parlor at this hour. Only the two neighborhood children helping her decorate the tree in the front window.

"Jackie," the exasperated young girl said, "you already have a red one right next to that."

"It's okay, Heather, I'll fix it in a minute. I have to get down right now." She scurried down the ladder, heart hammering against her ribs.

Ten-year-old Heather followed her gaze to the window. "Uh-oh."

Her younger brother looked up from the tiny plastic reindeer he'd placed on one of the crowded bottom branches. "How'd it get so dark already?" Todd found the clock prominently displayed on the holly-draped wall. "It's still early."

"Looks like a storm," Heather told him. "Aunt Dottie

says this is the craziest weather we've had in years. We'd better get home. Aunt Dottie'll be mad."

"Naw, she'll still be watching that talk show."

Jackie drew her eyes from the shadowed figure at the back of the parking lot, almost indistinguishable from the evergreen trees. For the first time, she took note of the weather. A rumble of something that sounded suspiciously like thunder rolled across the sky.

Jackie looked back to where the watcher had been standing, unsurprised to find him gone.

"Heather, Todd, get your things together. I'm going to run you home."

"Now? What about the store?"

"Yeah. It's too early to close," Todd argued.

Jackie shook her head at the nine-year-old boy. "Not tonight. Hurry up. Go into my office and get your stuff." She couldn't fight the sudden feeling of urgency. She had to protect these children.

No doubt, her apprehension came from finding the damaged teddy bear the previous morning. A garish yellow teddy bear just like the one Larry had won at the carnival nine years ago. A teddy bear she couldn't find today.

Carefully, Heather placed a green-and-white ornament back in the box. "What about the tree?"

"We'll finish it tomorrow."

Todd's face mirrored his confusion. "But..."

Heather watched Jackie closely with a solemn expression. "Come on, Todd."

The little girl had immediately picked up on Jackie's distress. It wouldn't do to frighten the children.

Was the back door locked? Hadn't Angel used it when she went home?

Jackie skirted the booths and the tables whose chairs

hadn't been straightened yet for the night, and hurried to the rear of the store.

The back door was unlocked. She threw home the dead bolt and brought down the steel bar that went across the door. Her eyes swept the dimly lit storeroom, fastening on the walk-in freezer next to the bathroom. Shut, but not locked—she wouldn't allow a lock on something so dangerous. Opening it, she flicked on the light and peered inside. No one hid in the freezer.

She poked her head in her brightly lit office as the children ran toward her. Empty, thank God. She started to feel foolish. There were lots of reasons why someone might be loitering in the parking lot the past few days. But not one of those reasons explained the appearance or the disappearance of the yellow teddy bear tied to the front door of her store yesterday morning. A teddy bear whose eyes had been plucked from his fuzzy face.

Jackie swallowed her fear. Larry couldn't have found her again after all this time. He couldn't have. But there had been that menu stuck to her windshield the day she moved from the apartment. The menu had come from a local Chinese restaurant with dinner items for two circled in red ink. Items that just happened to correspond to the last meal she and her ex-husband had shared.

If only she hadn't thrown the menu away. That had been a stupid reaction born of fear and denial. But the bear was another matter. She'd resisted her first impulse to toss it away, as well. There was always the chance that it wasn't the same bear Larry had given her, but one some child had lost—a child who had plucked off both black button eyes.

Jackie shuddered and glanced around as the bell tinkled over the door out front. The sound sent adrenaline racing through her system.

Someone had entered Sundae Delights.

"Stay in here," she whispered to the children. "Shut the door." They looked at her with luminous eyes, and Heather hurried to obey.

Jackie told herself to stop scaring the children. She told herself it was just a customer. Fear told her otherwise.

She reached the counter in time to watch a large, lean man move through the small shop with a predator's supple grace. His dark eyes missed nothing as he took in the white walls and the cool blues and greens of the furniture along with the multitude of holiday decorations that added a festive air.

Fear trickled away, leaving her shaken. She had never seen this man before in her life. A customer, after all.

"Okay, where are they?"

For a moment, Jackie could only blink in astonishment. The deep, gravelly voice didn't frighten her. Friendly exasperation rather than menace lay behind the words. Still, her fingers reached under the counter, seeking the reassurance of the ice pick she kept there. She was very conscious of her vulnerability in the face of such a strong masculine presence.

"May I help you?" Her voice sounded amazingly calm, but it was the only part of her that was.

"Where's Jackie?"

She tried to swallow, but the acrid taste of fear filled her mouth. This was not a customer. She drew back her shoulders as her fingers found what they sought. "I'm Jackie."

"You are?"

She stood completely still as those dark eyes swept over her. If he thought her helpless, he was mistaken. "I'm closed for the day, so please state your business."

The underlying aggression she sensed in him disappeared in a heartbeat, replaced by sudden wry amusement. "According to the sign, you're open until six."

Her voice was amazingly steady when she answered him. "The sign's incorrect. Today I close at..." she glanced at the clock, "ten past four."

"I won't beat them, you know," he said, eyes twinkling, inviting her to share his humor.

"What?" Her hand loosened on the ice pick beneath the counter. He was an impressive man. Handsome in an assertive way. The sort of man no doubt used to women doing whatever he suggested.

"Tempting as the idea might be at times, I'm not into child abuse. I just wish they weren't into parental abuse. At the rate they're adding gray to my hair, I'll only need a beard and some padding to play Santa next year."

Confused, she could only stare at him. "What are you talking about?"

"I've come for my children. My aunt just informed me that they think they work here now."

She released both her tension and her fingers on a long sigh of air. This was "poor Daddy"? This was the downtrodden father who slaved night and day to keep his family afloat? Talk about having the wrong image entirely.

Jackie saw his eyes flick to the spot below the counter where her hand had been.

"Were you planning to shoot me?" he asked, nodding to the area out of sight.

"Only as a last resort."

All trace of humor disappeared. His brows furrowed in concern. "I don't like the idea that my children are around a loaded gun."

"Me, either. You shouldn't have one."

He shook his head. "I meant yours. I don't own a gun."

"Neither do I."

"Were you planning to shoot me with your finger?"

Jackie pulled out the ice pick and shrugged. "Whatever

works.'' She didn't have to lift her head far to look him in the eyes, and she thought she saw a trace of respect there. Good.

Thunder rumbled overhead. The sky had turned a sullen dark gray which even the store lights had a hard time staving off. Jackie hated storms. Her gaze went to the window and the parking lot beyond. She couldn't see the watcher from here.

The man shrugged beneath his expensive-looking topcoat. ''Look, as delightful as this inane conversation may be, I want to get my children home before it starts to rain.''

''Good idea.'' She pushed at the wide lenses of her glasses and stared at his handsome face. She'd seen that same wavy dark hair on his daughter, and no mistaking those eyes. Todd often looked at things with that exact assessing expression. She'd thought he'd grow up to be a heartbreaker. Now she knew her instincts had been right. How could she possibly have pictured this man as some mousy accountant?

The lights flickered without warning. Her body jerked, head swiveling toward the window as rain began to batter the pane.

''It's only a storm,'' he said quietly.

''I know.'' The lights flickered again. Jackie heard the door to her office open.

''Jackie?''

''Come out here, Heather,'' the stranger called before Jackie could respond to that soft cry.

''Uh-oh,'' she heard Todd say.

Jackie caught the briefest trace of amused exasperation before the man hid it behind a stern expression. ''I'd say that sums things up rather nicely,'' he agreed in that quiet, gritty tone of his.

The children came around the corner looking submissive. Having never seen that particular expression on either child's face, Jackie watched them closely for any signs of fear.

Heather took the lead, as usual. "Hi, Dad," she chirped brightly. "What are you doing here?"

"I think that's my question, don't you?"

"We're helping Jackie decorate," Todd explained. "I did the bottom of the tree all by myself." He gestured toward the far end of the store and the heavily decorated lower half of the pine tree that stood there, its fragrant scent discernible even from here. "Heather did the middle and Jackie's doing the top 'cause she won't let us on the ladder."

"Smart woman," the man muttered.

"We been helping her put up all this neat stuff," Todd continued. "Isn't it great, Dad?"

His gaze traveled from face to face, landing squarely on Jackie's. She stifled an urge to shift under that penetrating stare.

"They do good work," she told him almost defensively.

"I can see that." He smiled wryly at his children.

Her pulse rate picked up at that smile and the two dimples it cleaved on either side of his face. The man had a terrific smile. Then, he turned it loose on her.

"The store looks very nice. The problem is, they aren't supposed to be here. I told them they weren't allowed to hang around the shopping center."

"We aren't hanging around, Dad," Heather protested. "We're working. Tomorrow we're gonna make some pine-cone centerpieces for the tables. When Christmas is over, Jackie's gonna show us how to turn them into bird feeders. Right, Jackie?"

Todd's small head bobbed in quick agreement. "Yeah, Dad, and we got your permission to play with Jackie."

"That was when I thought Jackie was the little boy who moved in at the other end of the street."

"No, Dad, Jackie's a lady," Todd corrected.

"I can see that."

His masculine appraisal trapped air in her lungs. Jackie felt her skin heat under that look. He couldn't possibly be interested in her. She wore baggy clothing and heavy framed glasses with her hair pulled back in an uncomplimentary ponytail. There was nothing remotely appealing about her looks. She'd made sure of that.

This man, on the other hand, would have many women making fools of themselves to garner his attention. His expensive dress coat covered a classy dark suit, and his bold tie probably cost more than the contents of her entire closet. She wouldn't be at all surprised if his shirt was monogrammed. He wore the clothing well, too well for her sense of comfort.

The lights flickered once more.

"I think you'd better go if you want to beat the rain," Jackie told him. She wanted his unnerving presence out of her ice-cream parlor as quickly as possible. She went to the register, withdrew four quarters and passed them to the children.

"What's that?" he asked.

"I pay my help."

"But we didn't finish," Todd protested.

Jackie met the dark eyes of his father. "I think you did for today."

A loud clap of thunder splintered the air. The power flickered and died with the burst. Startled, Jackie jumped back so abruptly she knocked the snow-cone display over.

Todd ran forward and threw his arms around her hips. "It's okay, Jackie, it's only thunder," he murmured in a high, shaky voice.

His fear acted as a balm to her nerves. Jackie drew

herself erect with an unsteady breath and stroked the top of his head as the lights came back on. "I know. I just didn't expect it."

Conscious of Todd's father absorbing the scene, brow pleated in concern, Jackie withdrew from the comfort of the small arms and tried to smile. "You guys better get home before we lose the lights permanently. I need to lock up here."

"What about the tree?" Heather asked.

"Just unplug it for now and I'll finish in the morning."

"But I thought you were going to let us help."

"Heather, Todd." At their father's tone, two faces lifted, Todd's in mutiny and Heather's in resignation. "Outside. The car is sitting right in front. I left it unlocked. We'll talk when we get home."

"But you have to let us come back, Dad," Heather pleaded. "Jackie pays us."

"Yeah, Dad. We got real jobs so you won't have to work so hard all the time."

Pain flitted across his features. "Get in the car. I need to talk to Jackie for a minute."

Jackie smiled at the two. "Your dad's right. You should all leave now. I want to get home before the storm gets bad, too." She just knew he wouldn't take the hint. With forlorn goodbyes the children trudged for the door, leaving their disturbing father standing by the counter.

"I'll wait for you to close up," he stated. His assertive tone immediately raised her hackles.

"That isn't necessary."

"I think it is. We need to have a talk."

"The children—"

"Will wait in the car," he told her firmly. "I can see them from here."

Lightning breached the darkness and Jackie stopped arguing. She hadn't done enough business to bother with the money drawer, even though she knew she shouldn't leave it in the register. He might be the children's father—and dressed in clothes that didn't come from the racks of any of the stores she favored—but he was still a stranger, and she wasn't about to open the safe with a stranger in the store. She turned and clicked off the revolving sign and the overhead menu.

"Can I help?" he asked.

"You could leave," she suggested. The words were rude, but his presence disturbed her more than the watcher and the storm combined.

"We need to talk for a moment."

"Look, I'm sorry, but I don't need to find myself in the middle of a family controversy." Jackie continued the shutdown procedures with fingers that trembled slightly. She heard him sigh, but she didn't turn around.

"At least let me introduce myself. I'm J.D. Frost."

"You have nice children." She busied herself checking the lid to the nut container.

"Do you have a last name, Jackie?"

"Yes." She walked back into her office, grabbed up her oversize coat and purse and set the alarm. She shut off the light, and coming briskly back out front nearly collided with the man. He had lifted the bridge and started behind the counter toward her.

Fear flicked to life once more. She gazed up at him, taking a half step back. "We have ten seconds to get out the front door or the alarm will trip." She was proud that her voice only quavered a little bit.

With a frown, he turned and started back the way he had come. Jackie breathed easier, casting a last look around as she hurried after him. He held the front door open and she motioned him through. Jackie flipped the sign to Closed and turned to lock the door behind her.

The rain had already tapered away to nothing, but the

sky continued to darken. The temperature was dropping with amazing speed beneath the stiff, cold wind.

"I think we got off to a bad start here," he said. "I didn't mean to scare you."

"You didn't."

He obviously saw past that lie, but didn't argue.

"Look, Miss…"

"Ms. Neeley," she said, pausing on the concrete sidewalk to dart a nervous glance at the tree line. The watcher had not returned.

"Ms. Neeley," he said, with a slight nod. "I'd like to talk to you about the children."

"Another time." The watcher could still be nearby. "I have a lot of things to take care of tonight and your children are waiting."

J.D. frowned, tossing a glance at his imported sedan and the two small figures inside. "They really like you."

"The feeling's mutual. They're welcome to continue to come to the store after school for a few hours, but only if you approve. If not, that's between you and them. And Aunt Dottie," she added with a trace of disapproval she couldn't quite hide. Heather had told her J.D.'s aunt had come to live with them after Heather's mother died of an aneurysm several years ago. "They do their homework when I'm busy, and I let them sweep and help with minor chores," she hurried to add. And then, because the situation bothered her so much, she added, "It gives them a break from soap operas and talk shows."

Dark eyes focused on her face. "What are you trying to say?"

Jackie backed down quickly. It wasn't her place to question the way he chose to raise his children. "I am saying, you are their father. You set the rules—"

"They aren't supposed to walk up here to the shopping center."

"Fine. If you change your mind, have them bring a note. Otherwise I'll send them on their way." She let him make the inference that maybe home wouldn't be where the children would go if she told them to run along. She reached into the pocket of her coat for her car keys.

"Wait a minute." He laid a restraining hand on her shoulder.

Jackie pivoted, breaking the hold, her stance defensive and ready for trouble. Apparently, that gave him pause. Surprise replaced his anger.

"Mr. Frost, I'm sorry, but this is between you and your children. I have to stop by my other store, and I'm running late as it is. Good night."

She strode to her nondescript white economy car, unlocked the door and slid inside. She could feel his eyes on her the whole time. It took her three tries to insert the key in the ignition, but he still stood on the sidewalk when she pulled out into traffic.

JACKIE DROVE SLOWLY, fighting a maelstrom of emotions. Mostly, she felt like a fool. Talk about overreacting. She braked gently on the wet pavement.

Nightmares from the past had her on edge. Still, she should have stayed and talked about the children. She would miss them if their father didn't let them come back, but J.D. made her uneasy in unexpected ways.

"He's just a man," she told the windshield wipers. "All right, a strangely compelling man, but just a man all the same." The light changed and she eased her car forward, feeling the hesitation as the tires sought traction.

The children talked about J.D. constantly. Aunt Dottie supervised them while he worked—which was apparently most of the time. From their comments, the woman lived for her television shows, basically ignoring them.

The children had stolen Jackie's heart the day they

walked into the store and counted out pennies to buy an ice cream they could split. One thing had led to another and now they earned their treats sweeping floors and wiping tables.

Rain sprinkled across her windshield, mixing with sleet. Jackie changed her mind about heading for her other store in Frederick. She turned around at the next intersection as the icy rain fell faster. She didn't really need to go there to talk to her partner. She would call Bessie after she got home. The roads were turning too messy to drive anywhere tonight. She gripped the steering wheel more tightly, glad she lived only two blocks from the store since her move four days ago.

She turned down her street and pulled into the driveway of the two-story house that would soon belong to her. The frame building suddenly loomed large and sinister in the growing darkness. Her attention went to the upstairs windows. She stared hard for several seconds, but nothing moved.

"Of course nothing moved. Unless I have mice, there's nothing inside there to move," she scolded herself, listening to the sleet batter her car. "The past is over."

But was it?

She couldn't quite shake the sensation of eyes peering down on her from behind the unlit windows. She scanned the quiet neighborhood carefully. She might not feel so isolated if she'd lived here long enough to meet some of the neighbors.

Lightning splintered the sky to mock her thoughts. Thunder rolled overhead, driving rain mixed with sleet before it. Really crazy weather. Jackie scrambled from the car and sprinted across the grass toward the shelter of the front porch.

She fumbled with the key, nearly dropping it before she got the door open and stepped inside. Switching on the hall light, she peered around. Bessie had offered to include all the furniture in the sale of the house now that her son was dead. The offer seemed a godsend, even if the furniture wasn't exactly to Jackie's taste. Her budget wouldn't have stretched to furnishing a four-bedroom house in its entirety otherwise.

She set her purse and keys on the hall table and shot a nervous glance at the darkened dining room. Nothing moved, of course. She proceeded straight ahead to the kitchen. This was her favorite room. A large, bright haven after a long day. She went directly to the stove to put water on to boil, trying to ignore the prickly sensations playing havoc with her nerves.

The old house creaked and groaned with the increasing rush of the wind. Having spent most of her adult years in apartments, Jackie couldn't get used to all the strange sounds that accompanied a large house such as this. Mentally, she scolded herself for being jumpy, but she continued to listen hard all the same.

Removing the unnecessary eyeglasses from the bridge of her nose, she set them on the countertop. Another blast of thunder rattled the windows. From overhead came the creak of what sounded like a floorboard. Was that a footstep?

The shrill cry of the teakettle almost sent her into cardiac arrest. The house complained again as it shifted under the storm's assault. Thunder rumbled overhead. The lights flickered in response. Jackie reached for the flashlight in the drawer next to the stove.

A floorboard protested above her.

Saliva vanished from her mouth. She stared at the ceiling while her pulse pounded erratically.

"There's no one up there," she whispered.

But visions of the past crowded her mind. There'd been a storm that night in Indiana, too. A summer squall had moved across the town. And Larry had waited silently in the bedroom for her to step inside.

Jackie shivered, gripping the flashlight in fingers that had gone icy with remembered fear. There was no way for her ex-husband to find her again after all this time. She'd covered her tracks carefully. Hadn't she?

She fought the surge of panic, knowing she wouldn't be comfortable until she checked every room in the house. Jackie snapped on the light in the dining room as she went past. The heavy oriental motif gleamed dully. The furniture in here held little more appeal than the art deco stuff in the living room, but Jackie carefully scanned every nook of both rooms.

Switching on the hall light, she mounted the steps. The sky split with an earthshaking roll of thunder that ripped a gasp from her throat. The lights winked out completely.

Her fingers fumbled for the flashlight. The dim orange beam barely illuminated the top step. Another flashlight sat in her dresser drawer, and those batteries were fresh.

The house groaned as another crash of thunder made her jump. A creaking sound came from the room on her right at the end of the hall.

Her mind cried for light, so she hurried for her bedroom. As she reached the long, low dresser, a brilliant flash of lightning sizzled through the room with eerie clarity. Her eyes lifted to focus on the mirror and her heart stopped completely.

In that instant, she saw the face behind her, twisted in a hideous grimace that froze her where she stood. Open eyes met her stare in the second immediate explosion of lightning. Dressed as an elf, the body lay sprawled across her bed.

It didn't move.

Chapter Two

A raw scream tore from her throat, suffocated by the powerful clap of thunder directly overhead. The flashlight fell from her nerveless hand and rolled on the carpet.

Jackie pivoted on legs that no longer felt attached, and ran for the hall in blind terror. Lightning danced eerily through the windows. A shadow at the end of the hall seemed to detach itself from the doorway and move forward.

Her screams joined the cacophony of thunder as she pounded down the staircase, nearly falling in her mad haste. She expected to be grabbed from behind at any moment.

The front door refused to open. Sobbing cries scraped her throat as she fumbled for the latch and forced it back. She flung the door open and hurtled down the wooden steps, heedless of the pounding rain and sleet and the lightning that pierced the night sky with jagged spears. She ran blindly for the house next door and raced up the steps.

No one answered her hammered blows.

She looked back toward her house and the crazily gaping doorway she'd left to the mercy of the gusting wind. A shape, barely discernible in the darkness, stood there.

She fled across the empty porch, running almost without conscious will. One leg followed the other over the railing. She leaped from the porch to land unevenly in a clump of bushes below. Her ankle twisted as she struck the hard ground.

Ignoring the sharp stab of pain, she sped across the next driveway and dodged into the shelter of a wind-whipped pine tree. Pain lashed her cheek when a branch smacked her in the face. Her breaths came in ragged gasps, so loud she couldn't hear anything above them. Had he followed? Had he seen where she went?

Jackie looked over her shoulder. A shadow moved in her yard. She fled in terror, unaware of the raging storm surrounding her.

J.D. HAD TO ADMIRE THE clever resiliency of his two children. They'd gotten around the issue of the shopping center rather neatly by asking him, in front of Aunt Dottie, if it was okay to visit Jackie. He certainly couldn't blame her for letting them go there after he said yes. And while they shouldn't have tried to trick him, what child could resist the lure of an ice-cream shop?

He turned his windshield wipers to full blast as the icy cold rain grew heavier. What a night to be outside. Anyone with half a brain was staying safe inside. He must have been nuts to suggest picking up a pizza at their favorite place when the lights went out. He should have called someone who delivered.

He never saw the figure until it was suddenly there in the middle of the rain-slicked street, arms waving wildly. J.D. stomped on the brake, knowing he would never be able to stop in time. Even as the antilock brakes kicked in, his car plunged forward, heading directly at the ghostly figure.

Time slowed. He watched the pale white face help-lessly. A woman, he realized, as she perceived her danger and attempted to twist to safety. She slid several feet, barely catching herself against the side of a parked mini-van. And somehow, unbelievably, he was past her, coming to a halt more than a car length away.

For an instant, he just sat there, drawing air into his starved lungs. He'd missed her. Unbelievably, he'd missed her. Then he threw the gear into park and fumbled for his seat belt.

He'd nearly killed the damn fool woman!

She leaned against the dark van, one bare hand splayed white against the metal as she shuddered for breath. She wasn't even wearing a coat, he realized. Anger drained from him as the wind tossed her ponytail across her face. Her desperation was palpable.

Stunned, he recognized her. "Jackie? Are you all right? I didn't hit you, did I?"

Reaching for her, he was unprepared when she twisted and launched herself at him.

"He's dead! We have to get help!"

Her disjointed sentences ran together as she gripped his topcoat in both fists. He covered them with his gloves. "Who's dead?"

"The man on my bed."

Her words punched his stomach. "What man?"

"I don't know." Her voice wavered, high and shrill. Sleet beat against her pale white face. "There's a body on my bed. Someone was hiding in the other bedroom. He followed me."

She twisted in fear to look down the empty stretch of sidewalk. J.D. followed her gaze, but no one was there.

"We have to get help," she continued. "The police!"

J.D. scouted the rain-swept street. The entire neighborhood was pitch-dark.

"Come on." Bracing Jackie's spent body against his side, J.D. guided her back to his car.

She didn't fight him when he half urged, half shoved her inside. He removed his topcoat, wrapping it around her huddled body and turned up the heater. She was wet clear through, he realized. Her hair lay plastered against her face, eyes tightly closed. He reached for his car phone.

"Give me your address."

She hesitated, then pushed the words past teeth that chattered. She waited in silence as he spoke to the police dispatcher.

He clicked off the phone and turned to her. "We'll meet them at your house."

She huddled deeper into his coat, her haunted eyes staring up at him in the dim light reflected from the dashboard. Though the car felt suffocating to him, the heat didn't seem to be penetrating the chills racing through her slight form.

He forced himself to drive slowly. "Whose body is it"

"I don't know."

"There's a dead stranger in your bed?"

"Would it be better if we were friends?" she snapped.

J.D. acknowledged the foolishness of his question with a nod as he turned the corner onto her street. Lights suddenly twinkled on everywhere. He didn't need to ask which house was hers. Only one had a front door gaping open with every light in the downstairs blazing a welcome.

He slid into her driveway, one wheel coming to rest on the lawn as the car lost traction. A thin sheet of ice coated the ground. Jackie didn't even notice. She peered around apprehensively as she reached for the door handle. J.D.

laid a restraining arm across her body. "Wait for the police. We don't know who else is inside."

"But the body—"

"Isn't going anywhere," J.D. assured her, "and you said someone else was inside."

She subsided almost gratefully.

They didn't have long to wait. A cruiser pulled to the curb behind them, disgorging a large, burly figure. J.D. recognized the officer at once. "Wait here," he told Jackie as he stepped from the warm car.

"Frost? What's going on?" Officer Ben Thompkins demanded.

"The lady says there's a body on her bed. The killer may have followed her out of the house. She flagged me down two blocks over. I was on my way to pick up a pizza for the kids."

Thompkins reached for his gun, his other hand going for his radio. "Get back inside the car, both of you."

J.D. had never seen Ben in his policeman persona before. The transformation was surprising. His good-natured softball buddy had been replaced by a hard-edged professional. J.D. turned back to find Jackie at his side.

"He's on my bed," she told Thompkins. "Upstairs."

"Get her in the car," Thompkins ordered as a second cruiser pulled up behind his.

Jackie hesitated, and he saw the fear staring starkly out of her expressive eyes.

"Let them do their job," J.D. advised gently, guiding her back to his car. The two officers conferred briefly before mounting the porch steps.

The sleet abruptly changed to large, fat snowflakes. Nerves kept them standing beside the car. Jackie handed J.D. his topcoat, but he shook his head.

"Put it on yourself before you catch pneumonia. I've got a suit coat on."

"I'm fine," she whispered, but obediently wrapped the coat around her like a blanket and stood staring anxiously up at the house as they waited. Snowflakes, interspersed with sleet, continued to pelt them.

Thompkins suddenly appeared on the porch and beckoned. J.D. and Jackie picked their way carefully across the grass. The porch steps were icy and Thompkins came forward to help Jackie mount the last couple.

"Show me where you were when you saw the body," he requested.

Jackie headed for the steps, limping slightly. J.D. sent Thompkins a questioning look that was met without expression. Puzzled, J.D. followed Jackie upstairs to where the second officer waited. Jackie turned left and entered the softly lit bedroom on the right.

The room was simply furnished, dominated by a double bed—a tidy, neatly made bed—with a smooth, undisturbed comforter spread across it.

Jackie rounded on them. "Where's the body?"

Thompkins stared balefully.

Nerves tightened in J.D.'s stomach. "No body?"

"No body at all," the officer confirmed without a trace of humor. "The entire house is clean as a whistle."

Jackie lifted stricken eyes. "No! He has to be here!" She raced to the closet and flung open the door. Clothing hung neatly, but there wasn't a lot of it, J.D. noticed. She whirled toward the connecting bathroom and darted inside. She returned, looking harried. Her breathing came hard and fast, as if she had just run a marathon.

"He was here! Right there on the end of the bed! Look underneath," she commanded. "He has to be somewhere!"

Thompkins coughed, then dutifully stepped forward, raised the bedspread and peered under the bed.

"Not even any dust bunnies," he told her.

"He was right there!" She aimed a shaking finger at the neat bedspread. A strand of wet hair fell forward against her cheek, but she ignored it. "There was a dead elf right there on my bed," she pronounced slowly.

J.D.'s stomach clenched tightly.

Thompkins didn't even flinch. "An elf," he echoed without inflection.

"A man dressed as an elf," she corrected. Her voice vibrated with emotion.

"There's no sign of forced entry," Thompkins said quietly. "No sign of disturbance anywhere in the entire house, unless you count the front door being wide open."

She pointed to the dresser. "I was standing right there in front of that mirror. I keep a flashlight in that drawer. When the lightning flashed I saw him."

"The dead elf," Thompkins said levelly.

J.D.'s gaze slid to the perfectly smooth expanse of her aqua bedspread. A military cot wouldn't be neater.

Here he'd been thanking his guardian angel that Jackie was a harmless, friendly shopkeeper instead of some pervert. Now she was turning out to be a fruitcake, he thought morosely. And just in time for the holidays.

"Was he small?" Thompkins asked.

Jackie's eyes narrowed in fury.

"It's a reasonable question, ma'am," Thompkins continued. "You did say an elf, and elves are—"

She squared her shoulders. "He was a man," she enunciated carefully. "A full-size man dressed as an elf."

"Full-size as in five feet? Six feet?"

She faced them with a regal glare of contempt.

"I have no idea how tall he was. I didn't take the time

to measure him. He lay crumpled on my bed right there, near the end.''

Thompkins lowered his hand to the spot indicated. ''The bedspread isn't warm and it isn't damp.''

Without a word, she hurried from the room and threw open the door across the hall. ''He has to be here somewhere.'' The room was empty except for the furnishings. ''Someone else was down the hall over there.''

In the direction she indicated, the hall was dark—even with lights on. Shadows loomed, probably because all the doors were closed. She flung open the door on her right. The room inside held a daybed, desk, computer and filing cabinet.

''I'm not crazy,'' she stated.

Thompkins's face held no expression whatever. J.D. didn't know what to say. He didn't know this woman or anything about her. They watched her open the closet, revealing nothing but empty hangers and a second computer system on the floor.

''Was there blood?'' Thompkins questioned. ''Any sign of a weapon?''

''No.'' She pushed past him, crossing the hall to check inside another bathroom.

''We checked all the rooms, ma'am,'' Thompkins said impassively.

Jackie whirled. ''He has to be here! I know what I saw.'' Angrily, she swiped at the strand of wet hair on her cheek.

''How old was he?'' Thompkins asked impassively as Jackie darted past him to open the final door.

''Young, I think. It was hard to tell. His face was all distorted.''

J.D. frowned. ''Distorted how?''

Jackie paused. ''A grimace. You know—like one of

those Halloween masks? His eyes were bulging and his tongue stuck out—''

"Could it have been a mask?" Thompkins asked.

"No." Her growing distress was obvious. "He looked dead. His eyes were open and staring and he didn't move." She entered the last room.

Unlike the rest of the house, in here there was organized chaos. Boxes, bags, men's clothing and miscellaneous items littered every available surface. She shouldered aside a stack of boxes to open the closet, then shoved aside some bags and got down to peer under the bed.

Thompkins turned to J.D. "Did you see this elf?" he asked.

J.D. raised his shoulders, dropping them quickly. "No, but—"

"Didn't think so."

"He has to be somewhere," Jackie insisted. J.D. noticed she was trembling.

"Did you take any medication tonight, ma'am?"

Jackie's eyes glittered and her face flushed with fury. For a second, J.D. thought she might slap the policeman. Instead, she drew in a ragged breath. "I don't take medication. Not even aspirin."

Thompkins didn't apologize. "Ma'am, we went through the house and there's no body. Was the second man dressed as an elf, too?"

Her lips tightened while her hands formed fists at her sides.

"Ma'am, I'm simply trying to find out what went on here tonight. You said one man was dressed as an elf. What about the man who chased you?"

J.D. saw the flash of fear she quickly buried beneath a show of bravado. Something had happened here tonight. Her fear, at least, was real.

"Could someone be playing a trick on you?" J.D. asked before she could respond.

Both heads swiveled to look at him, as though they had forgotten his presence. The redness abruptly faded from her face, leaving behind a small welt of color along one cheek. She swayed slightly and J.D. reached for her, but she stepped back quickly.

"My ex-husband, Larry Zalewoski. I have a restraining order."

Thompkins stiffened. "May I see it?"

Jackie hesitated, then led the way back to her bedroom. From the top shelf of her closet, she pulled down a small box and rifled the contents for a moment before coming up with a paper she handed Thompkins.

The second policeman stuck his head in the bedroom door. J.D. had forgotten about him, but apparently he'd been outside. His hat and shoulders were covered in snow, which was starting to melt against the material.

"I've got another call," he said, "but I had a look around outside. The garage is clean. No sign of an intruder."

"Thanks, Ted. Go ahead and take the call—I'll finish up here."

"Right."

The man disappeared as Thompkins opened the document and began to read. "This is from Indiana."

"That's where we lived," she explained.

"Six years ago?"

Her chin came up a notch. "He tried to kill me one night. Fortunately, I was expecting company. They arrived before he did any major damage."

J.D. forced himself to relax, but Jackie's stark words called up a surge of protective instincts.

"He do any time?" Thompkins wanted to know.

"No." Her voice dropped to a whisper.

"Could he have been the elf on your bed?"

Jackie shook her head, biting down on her lower lip. "No. But…I think…I have reason to believe Larry found me again."

"What reason is that?"

"Someone tied a teddy bear to the door of my store yesterday morning."

Thompkins never took his eyes from her. "A teddy bear."

Color flooded her face again. "A garish yellow teddy bear. Larry won one just like it at a carnival when we first started dating. This might have been the same bear. Except the eyes had been pulled off this one."

Tension vibrated through the room.

"Where is this bear now?" Thompkins asked.

"I don't know. I can't find it."

A trace of impatience entered his voice. "You lost it?"

"No! It must be in the store somewhere. Angel probably moved it. I was keeping it in case some child came in to claim it."

"I thought you said it was the one your husband won for you."

"I said it looked like that one." Her eyes glittered. "Yellow teddy bears aren't all that common. It reminded me of the one from the carnival. The way the eyes had been pulled off…I thought Larry might have done that to terrify me, so I hid it in a drawer in my office. It wasn't there when I went to look for it today." She blinked back moisture.

"You think he broke in your store and took the bear?"

Defiant, she lifted her chin. "Anything's possible. Someone has been watching my shop."

Thompkins shifted but gave no other sign as to what he was thinking. "Who?"

"I don't know. My partner and I own the ice-cream place at the shopping center." She turned toward J.D. "Right before you arrived tonight, I saw someone standing by the trees at the end of the parking lot. The same person has been there the past four nights right around dusk."

"Might have been waiting for a bus," Thompkins suggested.

"That's what I told myself the first two times—before the teddy bear."

Thompkins "looked" the question at him, but J.D. had to shake his head. Acid churned his stomach. His children had been in her store, in possible danger if what she said was true. "I didn't notice anyone. But I went looking for my kids. I wasn't paying attention to anyone outside."

Thompkins looked as though he expected nothing else. He handed her back her paper. "The items in that back bedroom. They belong to your ex?"

Jackie shook her head. "All of that stuff belonged to my partner's son. He was killed in a car accident last week. I was in the process of buying this house from Bessie before it happened. Since my apartment lease was up, and she didn't want the house standing empty after his death, she asked me to move in here until we can go to settlement. I've been collecting Donnie's personal belongings for her and storing them in there until Bessie is up to going through them."

"Bessie what?"

"Starnes, but her son's last name is—was Lieberman. Donnie Lieberman."

Thompkins scratched his chin. "The car crash out on Interstate 70?"

"Yes. Apparently, he was drunk when he went off the road and rolled down the embankment. The car caught fire and he burned to death."

The radio at Thompkin's waist crackled to life. He listened a moment and spoke briefly into it. "I have to go. I'll file a report, but there isn't much more I can do here tonight. I'll run a check on your ex-husband, Ms. Neeley, but if you believe he's dangerous, I'd advise you not to stay here alone."

The lights suddenly blinked for punctuation.

"Why don't you change into something dry?" J.D. suggested. "I'll see Thompkins out and wait for you downstairs."

Jackie didn't say a word. She simply watched them leave, her hand clutching the restraining order.

"I DON'T THINK SHE'S crazy," J.D. told Thompkins. "When I found her running down the street she was terrified."

"Uh-huh, but there's no evidence to back up her story. Bodies don't get up and walk away. Even if they did, they wouldn't smooth out the bedspread first." He shook his head. "And a stuffed teddy bear that disappeared, too? I don't think so, J.D. How well do you know this woman?"

"I just met her tonight."

"Uh-huh."

J.D. had to agree the situation was bizarre, to say the least.

"Well, I'll file a report," Thompkins promised, "in case any dead elves turn up matching her description. But we've got our hands full with all these damn burglaries lately. The thieves have been hitting some pretty significant residences around here and that puts all kinds of pressure on a small force like ours." As his radio crackled again, he shrugged and lifted the instrument, speaking quickly into it. "Car crash. Gotta run," he explained. "Watch yourself."

"Yeah. You, too."

J.D. closed the door behind him, noting the old lock. Even Todd could probably break in. Jackie should have dead bolts.

He headed for the back of the house—toward what he assumed was a kitchen and a telephone. As he listened to his aunt assure him that power had been restored at their house, as well, and the children were eating soup and sandwiches, he twiddled with a pair of glasses sitting on the counter. That was why her face had such an unprotected look tonight, he realized. Jackie had been wearing the glasses earlier. He held them up to the light and saw that the lenses were made of clear plastic. Now why would a woman deliberately wear a pair of ugly glasses that she didn't need?

Heather got on the line and J.D. set the glasses down to concentrate on what his daughter was telling him.

When he finally hung up, he stood for a moment staring vacantly out the kitchen window while his thoughts returned to the immediate situation. Like Thompkins, he wasn't at all sure what to believe. Jackie had seen something here tonight, but he tended to think Thompkins was right. Someone was out to scare her—or maybe play a practical joke. The elf had probably been nothing more than a mannequin.

He was contemplating that when a noise behind him sent him spinning around. Jackie stood framed in the doorway, a white towel wrapped around her hair. She'd changed from one set of baggy sweats to another. They were not an improvement.

"Why are you still here?" she greeted without warmth.

Good question. "You shouldn't stay here alone tonight," he told her quietly. "I don't think it's safe. Is there someone you can call?"

Her chin lifted. "You don't have to worry. I'm not crazy."

"Good, I'm relieved to hear it."

Once again, the lights flickered. He saw the flash of raw fear that exposed her vulnerability.

"Rain, sleet and snow are a bad combination," he told her. "We could easily lose power for the night."

Apprehension haunted her eyes. He crossed the room and touched her arm. Her delicate features weren't classically beautiful, but she was a pretty woman—or she would be if she skipped the phony glasses, did something with her hair and wore something besides the baggy clothing he'd seen her in to date.

She quivered beneath his fingertips. He knew then, he couldn't just walk out the door and leave her here alone.

"Jackie, I think you should come home with me."

She drew in a short, sharp breath. "No."

"You'd rather sit here in the dark by yourself?"

A shiver spasmed along her length. Her "no" was nearly inaudible. He checked an urge to draw her into the protection of his arms.

"Come on," he said gently. "I saw your purse on the hall table. We'll grab it on the way out. If you don't want to stay with me, you can tell me where to drop you off."

Seconds passed while she made up her mind.

"You're right, of course. I wasn't planning to stay here tonight. I just…I can't seem to think clearly right now. Let me get a few things." She turned, the limp more pronounced as she started back down the hall.

Shock, he suspected. Whatever had happened here tonight had left her in a mild state of shock.

"What did you do to your leg?" It wasn't any of his business. None of this was his business. She'd made it clear she didn't want or need his help, and frankly if she was in some sort of trouble, he should go home. He had the children and Aunt Dottie to think of.

But he couldn't just walk away when she was hurt and scared. She'd been kind to his kids. He owed her for that much, at least.

She paused halfway up the steps. "I twisted my ankle when I jumped off my neighbor's porch. It's okay. Just a little sore. I'll be right back."

J.D. waited impatiently at the bottom of the stairs until she reappeared, a small bag in one hand.

"You don't need to drive me. Bessie doesn't live far from here. I can drive myself."

Reluctance mingled with relief. She appeared calmer now. More in control. Her shock was fading, he decided, watching her come down the steps favoring the sore ankle.

"You can drive with that foot?"

"My car's an automatic and it's my left foot. I'll be fine."

"Are you sure?"

She reached the bottom of the stairs and headed for the hall closet. "I'm sure, but thank you."

She put on her jacket before he could offer to help and they stepped outside. Snow buffeted them instantly. At least an inch now powdered the world and it was falling so fast visibility was nil. J.D. wasn't sure he could safely drive the five blocks to his place under these conditions.

"Maybe we'd better wait until this slows down," he suggested as she locked the door.

"I'll be fine," she assured him.

Headstrong, he decided as Jackie started for the steps. J.D. joined her, hunching slightly in his coat against the cold. They stepped down and instantly discovered the layer of treacherous ice hidden beneath the snow.

Jackie slipped, grabbing for the icy railing to prevent her fall. J.D. landed with a jolting thud on his rear end on the top step. Snow swirled in his face, blinding him.

"Are you okay?" she asked.

A hiss of pain was his answer. J.D. uttered a string of epithets under his breath as he stood and moved carefully back from the edge to offer her his hand. "The steps are solid ice."

"I noticed." She grimaced, using his arm and the railing to make it back onto the porch.

"How bad are you hurt?" he asked.

"Let's just say my ankle is good and sore now and leave it at that."

"Well, we aren't going anywhere for a while."

Her expression became stricken, clearly visible in the light reflecting off the snow. "We can't stay here! Once we reach the car we should be all right."

"Are you nuts?"

Fear pinched her face. She stared into the blinding snow as if expecting something horrible to pop out at them. "We have to go," she said on a shaky breath.

J.D. shook his head. "Look, Jackie, I know you're nervous and upset, but go where? We can't even see the damn cars from here. There's no way we can drive with an inch of ice underneath the snow. It's foolish." Wind swept the porch with icy snow to add emphasis to his words.

"Be reasonable. I had no idea conditions were deteriorating this fast. Let's go back inside and wait it out. As hard as it's blowing, this should die down in a couple of hours."

She looked from the dangling keys in his hand to his

face and back again. Then she turned without a word and fumbled with her house key. It promptly jammed in the lock.

"You need to replace this old relic," he told her as he nudged her hand to one side and forced the front door open again.

"I know."

He stared at her. This was a woman used to facing things alone, he realized. Her delicate features were nearly translucent in the eerie light reflecting off the snow— haunting and terribly fragile. Yet he'd witnessed the strength of her will tonight. He had the strangest impulse to lean over and taste her pale lips.

Whoa. What was he thinking? And he was standing much too close to her.

J.D. drew back and pushed open the front door with the flat of his hand, shaking off the sensation that had gripped him. Jackie hesitated a moment before preceding him inside.

"Mind if I use your phone again?" he asked quickly. "I want to call the kids and let them know I might not make it home tonight."

"Wait a minute. You can't stay here all night!"

Her chin tilted in that determined manner he was becoming familiar with. J.D. rocked back on his heels. "I don't know that we're going to have a choice in the matter."

"But you can't."

"Why not?"

Her gaze darted about the hall, landing on his left shoulder. "Because."

He crossed his arms over his chest. "Now there's a definitive answer."

She glared at him. "Don't be sarcastic."

He leaned back against the door frame. "Who, me? I'm just the schmuck who stopped to rescue you, remember? Now that I'm the one who's stranded, you want to toss me out into a freak winter storm."

"You said it would clear up in a couple of hours," she argued.

"And it might. If it does, I'll gladly leave your gracious hospitality and go home where I belong."

They both heard the sound of sleet pattering against the side of the house. At least he wouldn't have to worry about anyone playing more tricks on her tonight.

"This can't be happening," she muttered weakly. "I don't even know you."

"Well, this seems like the perfect time to get acquainted," he responded with exaggerated politeness.

She was understandably scared. Scared and prickly and defiantly independent.

"May I use your telephone?"

She nodded wordlessly. J.D. headed toward the kitchen, only pausing when he noticed a door that must lead to the basement.

Warning bells clanged in his head. He moved forward slowly, hand reaching for the knob. Locked. He stared at the anomaly for several seconds, deeply uneasy for reasons he couldn't define.

Maybe while they were getting to know one another, he could ask Jackie why she had such a flimsy lock on her front door, but an expensive dead bolt on the inside door leading to her basement.

Chapter Three

The weather showed no signs of improving. In fact, conditions deteriorated as the evening wore on and snow alternated with sleet. Though the pain in her ankle was atrocious, Jackie pulled together a simple meal while J.D. opened the living-room couch and made up the sofa bed.

"So explain something to me," he said finally, putting down his fork and pushing aside his plate. "Why do you have a dead-bolt lock on your basement door when the rest of your locks are so puny my kids could get past them?"

Jackie worried her lip and cast a look in that direction. She hadn't given the basement a thought tonight. Not surprising, really, since she'd only been down there once and that had been months ago when she first came to view the property. After Donnie's death, Bessie had been unable to find a key to that lock.

"I don't know. Donnie had it installed."

"I thought this house belonged to his mother."

Jackie pushed aside her own plate. "It does. Donnie rented it from Bessie. He helped her get it ready to sell."

"By putting a dead-bolt lock on an inside door? What's down there, the family jewels?"

Jackie shifted. "The usual stuff—washer, dryer, fur-

nace.'' Her cheeks warmed as her uneasiness grew. ''I
haven't been down there since I moved in.'' She explained about Bessie's missing key. ''All of Donnie's
keys were destroyed in the fire. I meant to call a locksmith
yesterday, but I've been a little busy.''

His mouth dropped in astonishment. ''What do you
mean, you don't have a key?''

A sudden vision of the dead elf waiting to be found in
her basement accelerated her breathing. Was it possible?
The horrible suspicion grew to epic proportions.

''You think that's where the body is!''

''No,'' he said tersely, chopping off that idea with a
movement of his hand.

''But the police couldn't have searched the basement,
and the body wasn't anywhere else.''

''Of course they searched the basement. Thompkins
said they searched the entire house. The body's not in the
basement.''

Vehemently, she shook her head, feeling a new sense
of panic swell in her chest. ''That door has been closed
and locked since I moved in four days ago.''

They both stared at the offending object.

''No. It must have been open,'' J.D. insisted.

''I told you—''

''Yeah.'' He rubbed his jaw thoughtfully. ''But that
means the police did some awfully sloppy work, which
doesn't compute with what I know about Thompkins. The
other officer even looked in your garage, remember? Trust
me, they wouldn't overlook a locked door inside the
house.''

Jackie didn't bother pointing out that the two policemen
hadn't believed a word she'd said. How hard did he think
they had searched when the body wasn't where she

claimed? And now she couldn't stop thinking about that basement door.

She barely repressed a shudder. "He has to be down there, J.D. Someone put the body in my basement! I told you we shouldn't stay here tonight."

J.D. gripped her arm when she would have pushed back her chair and jumped to her feet. "Don't go working yourself into a panic."

His calm voice steadied her racing heart. She looked at his large hand resting on her sweatshirt sleeve. There was something soothing about his touch.

"I never panic," she told him.

He grinned, displaying those surprising dimples. "Right. I forgot."

Jackie lifted her chin and met his dark gray eyes. "But what if someone *is* down there?" she asked quietly.

The grin disappeared. J.D. turned his gaze to the door. Without a word, he stood and walked over to the telephone on the wall.

"Who are you calling?"

He lifted the instrument, pressed the disconnect button, listened again and glared at the object before setting it back down. "Apparently, no one. The phones are out."

Jackie shoved back her chair. Standing brought a cry of pain as soon as she put weight on her bad ankle. She collapsed back onto the chair.

"Hey, take it easy. I should look at that leg."

"We have to get out of here!"

J.D. laid a hand on her shoulder. "Jackie, there's no reason to panic."

"But the phone doesn't work." Couldn't he see the danger? Larry had cut the phone lines.

"The phone doesn't work for the same reason we can't go anywhere," he said calmly. "There's an ice storm outside, remember? The ice probably brought some lines down. They'll have it repaired by morning.''

That rationale brought little comfort to a mind clenched in fear. J.D. crouched in front of Jackie's chair, stroking her arm in a soothing gesture. "It's okay. I promise. There's nobody in the basement and no body, either. If you want, I'll break down the door and go look.''

"No!''

"Thompkins is not a sloppy cop, Jackie. I know him. Somehow, they looked in that basement. If they hadn't, you can be sure they would have asked you about the lock.''

"But they didn't believe me.''

He shook his head. "That doesn't matter. They would have done their job. I promise.''

She wanted to believe him, but she knew that door hadn't been unlocked. Jackie took a deep breath and exhaled slowly. Panic wouldn't solve a thing.

"You still don't get it, do you, J.D.? I'm all for the idea of an empty basement. But how did the police check it out if no one has a key to unlock the door in the first place?''

J.D.'s eyes darkened thoughtfully.

"I don't know what happened here tonight, but we'll get some answers as soon as the phone lines are working again.'' He rose, grabbed the back of one of the kitchen chairs and propped it under the doorknob on the basement door.

"I'm a light sleeper, Jackie. I'll be down the hall in the living room. No one's going to touch that door tonight without me hearing them. In the morning, we'll call the police and a locksmith.''

"Assuming I have a phone.''

"We'll have phones,'' he promised. "Trust me.''

"Right." But oddly enough she did.

Adrenaline still coursed through her system, but she had the fear under control. Jackie knew she wouldn't sleep a wink after all that had happened. And she couldn't possibly face the night in her bedroom. No matter what anyone else believed, a dead man had lain across the end of her bed.

She spent the restless night on the small bed in the upstairs office with the light on—ostensibly so she could read. In truth, fear had sunk its talons so deep she couldn't even lift a book, let alone face the darkness of the house.

A knot of dread lay in the pit of her stomach, unraveling a bit at every strange sound. And there were plenty of those as the ice built on the eaves and the branches of nearby trees. Having J.D. in the house was both a curse and a blessing. While she felt safer on one level, having him in her living room wasn't conducive to sleep, either.

She liked J.D., but she was unprepared to deal with the sudden glimmer of interest he'd shown in her outside. Men didn't come on to her any more. That was the way she wanted things. But she felt the pull of attraction all the same. She stared at the ceiling, wondering how he would taste and how he would feel against her body. And that was the worst part of all. Her reaction, not his.

The last thing she needed was another man in her life. She wasn't sure she'd gotten rid of the first one. That terrifying thought only added to her sleepless night.

What if Larry *had* found her again? A shudder made her tighten her hold on the blanket.

He hadn't.

She must believe that he hadn't. Even Larry wouldn't murder someone just to place a corpse on her bed. Now the teddy bear and the menu...she could see him doing things like that, but not killing someone just to frighten her.

So who was the elf? What had he been doing in her bedroom? Was he part of the gang of burglars plaguing the area lately?

Right. The burglars were hitting expensive places, not houses in the midst of a modest neighborhood. But then, who was he? And where was he now?

The police hadn't taken her seriously. In a way, she could understand. What proof did she have to offer them? If only she hadn't thrown away that menu...or could find the teddy bear.

What did J.D. believe? She didn't want him to think she was a crackpot—even if his opinion didn't really matter. Tomorrow she'd turn the store inside out until she found that bear.

Morning brought relief from her chaotic thoughts, but no telephone. She heard J.D. use the bathroom downstairs and then go outside. A frivolous stab of disappointment lanced through her when she thought he was leaving. Then, she heard the scraping noise and realized he'd only gone out to shovel the steps and the walk.

Motion, she quickly discovered, equaled agony. She couldn't put any weight on her ankle. She managed to dress, but getting downstairs proved an exercise in pain. J.D. found her sitting on the bottom step, tears in her eyes as she contemplated the impossibility of walking to the kitchen.

"Hey, what happened? Did you fall?" J.D. strode across the floor, reaching for her. His coat and gloved hands were cold against her skin and his cheeks were ruddy from his exertions outside.

She shook her head.

Dark gray eyes studied her in concern. "Let me see your ankle."

"Unless you number a medical degree among your accomplishments, I don't think there's much you can do." She tried for a light tone, when what she wanted to do was howl in agony.

He pulled off his gloves and knelt in front of her before she realized his intention. Icy fingers skimmed up the leg of her sweatpants, giving her no chance to pull away.

"Looks great," he told her, mock serious. "Just like the *Hindenburg* right before it blew."

"How reassuring." She tried to wiggle free, more disturbed by his touch than the pain in her leg. She didn't need him to tell her the ankle was badly swollen.

"What do you say to a quick trip to the hospital?" he offered.

"There's no such animal."

He grinned and she was startled anew by the sight of his dimples. They dissolved the harsh planes of his face, giving him a youthful, carefree appearance that only added to his disturbingly sexy charms.

He dropped her pant leg and stood. "That needs to be looked at."

"You just did. It's sprained."

"Do you have a medical degree?"

Jackie nodded. "I hang it in the bathroom at Sundae Delights," she told him sweetly, and was rewarded by his low, throaty chuckle.

"Come on. I'll carry you out to the car."

Her heart quickened at the thought of being held in his arms. With a day's growth of beard shadowing his jaw, his hair and clothing slightly rumpled, he looked more dangerously masculine than ever.

"I don't think so."

"The plows have been through," he cajoled. "The roads are sanded and everything."

There was no point in being stupid, she realized. The leg needed an X ray. "Okay, but you aren't going to carry me. If I hold on to your arm I can limp out to the car on my own."

"Suit yourself."

She didn't dare.

SHE'D BEEN RIGHT about two things. She had a severe sprain and it took half the morning for the diagnosis to become official.

J.D. had promised to find a working telephone and ask Angel to come in early and open the store for her. Jackie was both grateful and slightly nervous to find J.D. still waiting for her more than three hours later. She clutched a prescription for pain medication in her left hand, while using the crutches awkwardly.

"So it was broken, after all," he said, eyeing the cast as they made their way outside. Melting ice gave the world a fraying wonderland appearance.

"Sprained. This is a temporary cast held together with Velcro. I'm sorry you waited all that time. I told you it wasn't necessary."

"You were planning to walk home?"

"I was going to call a cab. I'm not going home, at all. I have to stop by the mortgage company to sign papers this morning."

"Under the circumstances, couldn't that wait?" J.D. set the crutches on the back seat before helping her inside the car. Each movement was sheer torture.

"No," she told him. "Bessie insists we go through with the sale as planned. Frank told her to put it off, but she's so distraught over Donnie's death there's no reasoning with her. She wants the sale of the house over with as quick as she can. Since the loan officer is a friend of theirs, he agreed to rush the paperwork."

"Who's Frank?" J.D. asked as he started the engine.

"Bessie's husband. They married six months ago. She's been liquidating her assets so they can retire to Florida. By this time next year, I'll own both shops and her former home." She couldn't help the trace of pride that crept into her voice.

J.D. frowned. "Where's this mortgage company located?"

"On Main Street, but you don't have to drive me. I know you need to get to work."

"No, I already called my office. My assistant can handle things this morning. In fact, sometimes I get the impression Carol is better at my job than I am. Guess it's a good thing I own the company." His smile told her he was amused rather than resentful. "And I called your friend Angel. She was happy to get some extra hours, so your store is open and running."

"That's fine, but—"

J.D. simply shook his head and demanded directions. "I've been thinking about last night," he began.

"I know, and I'm sorry you had to be involved," she hastened to interrupt. "I never even thanked you for your help."

"You're welcome, but I was thinking about the elf."

She stilled, watching his profile as he concentrated on his driving. She didn't want to think about the elf right now.

"Are you sure the body was real? Now, wait, before you get your dander up, could it have been a mannequin instead of a real person?"

Jackie fought past the anger and disappointment. She

told herself he wasn't trying to placate her. He was looking for other possibilities, that was all.

"You know, in the dark, maybe—"

"He was real, J.D. As real as you are right now. I know
what I saw."

"Okay. Sorry. It was just a thought." They left the
hospital in Frederick and drove the next fifteen minutes
in silence until they reached their exit. Kylerston, just a
tiny town between Hagerstown and Frederick, wasn't
even on most maps.

Sun had already melted away most of the ice from the
night before. The weather changes lately had been as rapid
as they were bizarre.

J.D. turned onto Main Street and waited for a Volvo to
pull out, then angled his car into the newly vacated parking space in front of a small building. "Here we are."

"Thanks." Jackie reached for the door handle, but had
to wait for J.D. to get her crutches from the back seat.
When they stepped inside the overly warm building and
she realized the receptionist was at lunch, Jackie was more
than grateful for J.D.'s continued presence at her side.
Seth Bislow scuttled forward to greet them. Behind his
thick-rimmed glasses, blue eyes watched her progress
with disturbing intensity.

"Were you in an accident, Jackie?"

"I slipped on the ice last night."

"Oh, that's too bad. Is your leg broken?"

"Sprained," J.D. replied for her.

Bislow regarded J.D., proffering his hand in a limp
fashion when introduced. "Sit down, sit down. This won't
take long. Frank tells me you've already moved into the
house," he said.

"Yes. Bessie insisted."

Bislow *tsked*. "Terrible thing about her boy. Are you getting settled okay?"

"Pretty much," she agreed hastily. "What do I need to sign?"

Bislow's mouth turned down in a disapproving frown. "I have the paperwork all ready for you. I need your signature here and here. What day are you going to settlement?"

"Thursday afternoon," she told him, picking up the documents and leaning back to read.

"Did you get contact lenses?" Bislow asked abruptly.

She lifted her head in surprise, then realized she'd forgotten all about her eyeglasses. J.D.'s amused expression was knowing. He must have found them in the kitchen and realized her deception.

"I've been thinking about getting them," Seth added, pulling at his thick black frames to settle them more firmly on his face. "What do you think?"

"Depends on how sensitive your eyes are," J.D. interjected smoothly. "Some people have trouble wearing contacts."

Jackie bestowed him with a grateful look. Seth Bislow was such an oily little man, but he and Frank were close friends, so she couldn't avoid him entirely. She went back to reading the papers. Satisfied they were in order, she signed her name quickly, wanting nothing more than to get outside again and away from this dreary, little office with its ominously loud clock.

Bislow slicked back his receding hair and shifted in his chair. "Bessie's taking her son's death pretty hard. Frank always said Donnie was a wild one, but what a horrible way to die."

Superimposed on a mental image of the demolished car

came a vision of the twisted face of the dead elf on her bed. Jackie shuddered in revulsion.

"I saw you at the funeral," Bislow continued, "but when I came over to say hello, you were talking to the minister."

Mainly because she'd seen him coming over to say hello. She reached for her crutches, desperate to get outside.

"His three friends were certainly distraught. What were their names again? One boy had an unusual first name, as I recall."

An image of three gangly young men huddled awkwardly at the graveside made Jackie stand quickly, sending a jolt of pain through her ankle. J.D. stood and cupped her elbow.

"I'm afraid we need to get going," he said smoothly. "Jackie has to get back to the shop and I have a two o'clock meeting."

"Yes, of course." Bislow pushed back his chair and stood, his limp hand reaching for hers before she could avoid the contact. Jackie pasted on a smile and clasped his moist fingers lightly, letting go quickly.

"Give my best to Bessie, and let me know if I may be of any further assistance to you."

"Thank you, Mr. Bislow."

"There's no need for formality, Jackie. Even here in the office I'm still Seth."

She nodded, once more grateful for the comforting presence of J.D. at her side.

Outside, she took a deep breath of the crisp air, noting the snow and ice were nearly gone as the sun beamed down benevolently.

"You okay?" J.D. asked.

"Fine." In truth, she felt like a football after a rough

game. Her leg hurt worse now than it had when she injured it.

"Let's stop and get that prescription filled, then I'll take
you to my house and we'll let Aunt Dottie fuss—"

"No!"

He cocked his head to one side and looked at her.
"Something wrong?"

"It's kind of you to offer, but I can't go to your house.
I need to go home."

J.D. opened the car door. "I don't think that's a good
idea, Jackie."

"I can't say I'm crazy about the idea myself, but it's
what I need to do. I have to get a locksmith out to change
the locks. And I'm not going to rest until I know there is
nothing in that basement." He started to interrupt, but
Jackie shook her head. "It's broad daylight, J.D. I'll be
fine. I'll just spend the afternoon on the living-room
couch."

He studied her expression, shut the door and came
around the car to slide in behind the wheel.

"What about a hotel?"

"J.D., I do have friends. If I need help, there are people
I can call, but I wouldn't be comfortable going to your
house. I promise I'll stay on that awful couch. I need to
go home."

She added the last with quiet emphasis.

J.D. contemplated her with a slight frown. "Awful,
huh?"

She smiled. "I guess I've no right to complain since
the couch came with the house."

"You should do that more often," he told her. His eyes
held a smoky sensual appraisal that choked all thoughts
from her mind.

"What?"

He touched the tip of her nose with his finger. "Smile. You have a lovely smile." Then he drew back and started the engine. "How come the couch came with the house?"

Flustered, she responded automatically. "All the furniture did except for my bedroom set. After her son died, Bessie wanted the contents of the house added to the contract. That's why I had to amend the purchase agreement." It was her turn to regard him with amusement. "You thought that stuff was my taste?"

He shrugged diplomatically. "Tell me about Bessie's son."

Jackie rubbed at her forearms. "I didn't really know him. He seemed nice enough the few times we met. He liked to party and I know that worried Bessie, but he was young and single and had a lot of friends."

"How old was he?"

"Only twenty-four," Jackie said sadly. "Bessie's still in shock. Thank God for Frank. He's a bit pompous, but he dotes on her."

Jackie realized they were on her street and took a moment to study the frame house as they pulled into her driveway. All her uneasiness returned full force. She didn't want to go back inside. For a nickel, she'd go with J.D. to meet Aunt Dottie. But if she did that, she might never be able to face her demons again.

Getting inside proved a painfully slow process. The muscles in her leg were in spasm. She was in agony long before they made it to the couch.

"Let me get your prescription filled," J.D. coaxed as he shifted furniture to make up the bed once more. Too exhausted to protest, she handed J.D. the paper. He didn't wait for her to change her mind. "I'll be right back," he promised.

"Why are you being so nice to me?"

Her muttered question brought him to a halt halfway through the doorway. It surprised her, as well. She hadn't planned to voice that aloud.

"Why shouldn't I be nice to you?"

Jackie squirmed, wishing she could recall her words. "You don't even know me. And I haven't exactly been Miss Congeniality."

He rubbed at the stubble on his chin, looking tempted to smile. "You haven't been that bad."

"But you don't even believe my story about what happened last night."

The amusement faded. He shifted, watching her closely. "You've been nice to my children," he countered. "Why shouldn't I be nice to you?"

She sat back feeling oddly deflated. He was being nice to her because of his children. "Oh. I see."

"What do you see?"

He crossed the room to stand directly in front of her.

"Never mind."

"But I do mind. Yes, you've been nice to my kids," he said softly. "Yes, I feel bad about whatever happened to you last night." She watched in mild alarm as he reached out to tip her face toward his. "But you must really need those fake glasses because without them I don't think you see things clearly, at all."

Before she could protest, he covered her startled lips with his own.

Tentatively, she responded. He cupped her face between his hands, stroking her scalp with his thumbs while letting his tongue glide over her bottom lip.

She shivered and parted her teeth, allowing his tongue entrance to her mouth. Her hands clutched at his upper arms, her body becoming pliant beneath his tender assault. Experimentally, she touched his tongue with hers, and a shaft of pure pleasure jolted through her. J.D. made a sound of satisfaction deep in his throat, then abruptly let her go.

"You don't see anything clearly," he told her, his gravelly voice husky, matching the passion in his eyes. He kissed the tip of her nose and straightened to his full height. "Including the fact that I like you, Jackie."

She touched her lips with two shaky fingers.

"Don't forget to elevate that leg," he admonished as he went out the door.

He'd kissed her. And she'd kissed him back. The knowledge stunned and alarmed her. She couldn't afford to want him or any man. She should never have allowed him to get so close.

Ha. As if she could have stopped him.

As if she hadn't wanted to taste him and feel those strong arms around her. As if she hadn't wanted that kiss to go on and on.

"Oh no, you don't," she admonished herself sternly.

Something in the way he touched her undermined all her well-built defenses. She had to remember that J.D. Frost was one of the sexiest men she'd ever seen and she wasn't his type. She wasn't any man's type and she wanted to keep it that way.

The house immediately took on a quiet, brooding feeling. Jackie headed for the telephone in the kitchen, pausing at the basement door which remained securely locked, the chair still tucked beneath the doorknob. Good.

The telephone worked, so she called the store. Angel insisted she had everything under control and was glad to work the extra hours. She'd already talked to the other part-time woman who would come in this evening to help.

Satisfied that at least her store was under control, Jackie hunted for the local telephone book. Amazingly, the small town boasted two locksmiths. At the first number she got an answering machine. A pleasant woman answered at the second number and explained she had no one available for nonemergencies until sometime the following week.

"All those burglaries we've had lately, you know," the woman confided. "Why, we're even getting calls from Boonsboro. We can't keep up with the demand for dead bolts and security systems." Jackie left her name and number and hung up. Glowering at the basement door wouldn't accomplish a thing, but it was a cinch she wouldn't sleep a wink until someone checked the contents beyond it.

Suddenly exhausted to the point of trembling, she entered the living room, removed the cast and her sweatshirt, so she could sleep in the T-shirt underneath, and collapsed on the miserable excuse for a mattress. The ceiling overhead offered no solutions to her dilemma. She couldn't stay and she couldn't leave. Her eyes drifted shut.

She roused groggily a short time later to find J.D. standing over her. There was no mistaking the masculine interest in his eyes. Though startled, she wasn't frightened or defensive—almost as if she'd known he stood there even before she woke.

Jackie followed his stare and realized her nipples had pebbled against the material of her T-shirt. She accepted the pill he held out then ducked her head, avoiding eye contact.

"You were sleeping so soundly I hated to wake you. Should I call Angel to check on your store?"

"I already did," Jackie mumbled. A yawn caught her unprepared. It was such an effort to keep her eyes open that she closed them.

"You rest. I'll come back with dinner later on," he promised. She attempted to protest, but the words got trapped around another yawn and her eyelids became too heavy to lift.

She thought she felt his lips brush her forehead. Then she stopped fighting and let sleep envelop her.

JACKIE NEXT AWOKE TO the memory of the most erotic dream she had ever experienced. She'd been so close to something wonderful. J.D.'s face smiled at her. A warm, sexy, knowing smile that created tingles of pleasure everywhere.

Then she opened her eyes.

Pain lanced her leg as she shifted, bringing recent events blazing back.

Muzzy from the medication, she reached for the glass of water J.D. had left sitting on the end table and gulped the tepid fluid gratefully. Her mouth tasted like the inside of a dirty sock.

Overhead, a low rumble that could only be thunder spread across the heavens. She jerked, knocking over the pill container as she set the glass back down.

Please, not another storm.

Had she slept the afternoon away? Darkness covered the house like a shroud and the air had grown much cooler. She fumbled for the switch at the base of the lamp, feeling more at ease once she had some light.

She debated the merits of getting up to go to the bathroom. The thought of what would happen when she tried to move her leg was offset only by the thought of what would happen if she didn't.

Struggling into a sitting position, she cautiously shifted. Movement hurt every bit as badly as she had thought it might. Breath hissed past her lips, but she reached for the crutches and maneuvered herself upward, trying to avoid the scattered pills that littered the carpeting.

The feeling of helplessness brought a surge of the old anger. She had spent years learning to become self-sufficient, years learning to trust her own judgment again. No one and nothing would take those accomplishments away from her. Not J.D., not a sprained ankle, not a lousy thunderstorm and not some disappearing elf.

From upstairs came a noise that froze her determination along with the blood in her veins. Jackie stopped moving and strained to listen. Minutes passed, but she heard nothing beyond the climbing howl of the wind outside.

All houses made noise. Hers more than most. There was no reason to be so jumpy. She would not become paranoid. According to the clock, she had indeed slept most of the afternoon away. Her grogginess probably had come from taking that blasted pain pill. She should call Bessie to let her know what had happened. She should also check on the store and be sure Angel wasn't having any problems.

Slowly, painfully, she made her way into the hall, pausing to listen intently while her gaze strayed to the brooding darkness that enveloped the stairs.

With a shiver, she hobbled to the tiny bathroom set beneath them. Cursing her irrational fears, she closed the door and turned on the light, blinking in the sudden glare. Every jolt sent pain coursing through her foot. She'd forgotten to put the cast back on.

Minutes later, as she maneuvered herself into a standing position, the bathroom light flickered. Jackie jerked. One of the crutches fell with a loud clatter. She held her breath, feeling foolish. The next flicker was almost reassuring. Wearily, she leaned over to pick up the crutch and paused.

Had she just heard someone on the stairs?

Listening with every fiber of her being, she waited until

the steady throb of pain from her ankle became unbearable. She couldn't cower in the bathroom all night.

"You're turning into a wimp. A basic coward. There is no one in the house but you." The sound of her own voice helped to calm her, but her nerves felt raw.

She fumbled for the doorknob. In the kitchen, the telephone began to ring.

"Hang on," she muttered. "I'm coming."

The lights dimmed, even as she reached for the wall switch in the hall.

"Don't you dare go off," she warned them. "My nerves can't take any more."

The kitchen light snapped on with a reassuring glow. She reached for the telephone only to hear a click as the caller hung up.

"I hurried as fast as I could," she told the infernal dial tone. The lights dimmed further.

Jackie started for the drawer with the flashlight and stopped. She remembered exactly where that flashlight was—and why. Her body tensed.

"I will not be left in the dark again."

The distinctive creak of the stairs came again.

"Obviously, the stairs are haunted," she whispered. But she picked up a paring knife, feeling foolish, and waited. Nothing happened other than another warning rumble of thunder.

No! This was too bizarre. Didn't Mother Nature know it was December? Thunderstorms were for spring and summer.

The silly thought calmed her. Was she going to allow herself to be spooked by every single noise? She set down the knife, aimed her crutches in the direction of the pantry, and wished she had taken time to put her cast back on. God, her foot ached.

Matches were on the top shelf and there were two yellow candles next to them. She found the holders after only a few tries and felt much better once they were on the table and glowing softly. Now, even if the power went out, she wouldn't be without light of some kind.

There were four candles in the poinsettia arrangement on the dining-room table, she remembered, and a squat black-and-silver candle on the living-room coffee table. She would light all of them, then there would be no dark rooms if the power went out again.

As she lit the last candle in the dining-room centerpiece, a resounding crash of thunder severed the heavens and the lights went out as though programmed. Jackie dropped the book of matches.

Heart pounding, she gripped the crutches like a lifeline. She hated thunderstorms. Hated them!

Her hand trembled so badly as she bent for the matches that she nearly dropped a crutch again. Frustrated, angry and on edge, she tried not to think about the way her foot was giving her absolute hell or the thumping noise she thought she had just heard from somewhere inside the house.

Fear clogged her mind. She couldn't swallow, couldn't breathe. For just a second, she thought she might pass out.

Imagination was a terrible burden.

And that's what it was. Imagination. Angrily, she gripped the crutches and began to cross the dark hall into the cavernous blackness of the living room. She did not look up those stairs.

Jackie concentrated on remembering where J.D. had put the coffee table. Over by the windows, sandwiched between the television console and the other end table. She moved forward carefully and bent to light the candle.

A tiny noise caused her to look over her shoulder.

She saw him clearly. The elf's lifeless face still twisted in its silent grimace. He lay sprawled unnaturally on the black chair as though dumped there hastily.

From beside the sofa bed, a figure rose.

Without thought, Jackie raised the crutch defensively. Ice-cold nerveless fingers slashed the crutch toward that dark menace. Her weight came down on her bad ankle and her leg twisted under the misstep. Her temple caught the edge of the coffee table as she fell.

Chapter Four

Something was wrong.

J.D. replaced the receiver and stared at the piles of papers crowding his In tray. Even on crutches, Jackie should have answered the phone by now. Unless the pain pills had knocked her out.

A glance toward his office window showed a dark bank of clouds working their way across the sky. Thunder grumbled in the distance. A strange sense of unease built in his chest. Why hadn't Jackie answered her telephone?

He was here...right there on the end of the bed.... You believe me, J.D. Don't you?

No, he hadn't believed her. But what if she had been telling the truth? He'd left her there all alone in the house.

J.D. reached for his coat.

"Something wrong?" Carol looked up from her computer in surprise as J.D. strode into the outer office.

He hoped not. God, how he hoped not.

"Close up for me, will you? There's something I have to take care of right now."

She nodded, staring at him in confusion. "Are the children all right?"

He paused, hesitating only a second. They wouldn't go to Jackie's shop today. Not after his stern lecture yesterday. "I'm sure they're fine. This is something else. I'll see you tomorrow." He didn't wait for a response. He crossed the room, reaching for the doorknob.

Maybe Jackie was asleep.

The bottle said the medication could make her drowsy. But what if she wasn't asleep? She was vulnerable. On crutches. She could have fallen. Maybe she became disoriented from the pain medication. J.D. raced across the parking lot, unmindful of the blowing rain. He jammed the key into the ignition and slammed his car into reverse.

Maybe she wasn't answering the phone because she couldn't.

He pulled into traffic abruptly, ignoring the horns protesting such a brash move on the rain-slicked pavement. Visions danced through his mind. Ugly visions.

Something was wrong and he knew it.

The light changed. J.D. gunned the engine and raced through the intersection.

Damn! Couldn't those cars move any faster?

He depressed the accelerator, weaving past the traffic. His breathing came faster, more shallow. The sense of urgency increased. He clenched the steering wheel as lightning forked the troubled sky. Thunder bellowed in its wake. Out of nowhere came an image of his son clinging to Jackie's baggy sweatpants. She hated thunderstorms.

A garish yellow teddy bear...the eyes had been pulled off this one.

He didn't relax even when he took the turnoff to Kylerston. Main Street. A few more blocks to go.

Jackie had such compelling eyes. Troubled. Vulnerable. Her fear was real. Would anyone really make up such a bizarre tale?

Traffic lights suddenly winked out, leaving drivers to stare up at their deadened eyes. He'd never get through the snarled intersection now, and he was only a street away. He glanced around.

The lights were out.

The thought seared his mind. All the lights were out up and down the street.

And Jackie was alone in that dark house with a locked basement door.

You believe me, J.D. Don't you?

Two vehicles collided gently. A third one missed the tangle but stopped, blocking the lane ahead. J.D. yanked his car to the side of the road, threw it into park and was out and running, dodging patches of ice.

He tried to kill me one night. Fortunately, I was expecting company.

Her side street was dark. No headlights here, and no lights in any of the houses that he passed. J.D. pushed himself harder as the rain and snow sleeted against his eyes. A large maple tree hunkered in Jackie's front yard like an evil guardian. As he drew closer he saw a flicker of light near her front window.

Candlelight?

Suddenly, it flamed, starkly orange against the dark window.

J.D. sprinted up the slippery porch steps two at a time, his hand clawing for the house key he had taken from the hall table next to her purse. As he inserted it in the door and pushed his way inside, the lights snapped on. All the lights. Her downstairs was an explosion of lights, just like the previous night.

"Jackie?"

And then he smelled the smoke.

J.D. turned to his right. His eyes automatically absorbed the scene, even as he leaped forward. Jackie lay on the carpeting like a discarded rag doll. Flames inched their way across the rug, advancing on her baggy sweatpants.

"Jackie!"

As he scooped her into his arms, the bottom of the drapes suddenly writhed into horrible life. J.D. raced outside and set her on the porch swing. He whirled and went back inside, reaching for the heavy white satin material. Flames licked its length, devouring the fabric in a terrifyingly greedy display. In minutes the room would be engulfed.

One hard pull yanked the material from the wall. Frantically, J.D. dragged the burning mass outside, tossing it to the sidewalk in a hail of hissing sparks.

Heart pounding, he went back inside. Flames crept across the carpeting in search of prey. He grabbed Jackie's water glass and tossed its remains, dousing the burning candle where it lay on the floor, feeding the flames. Smoke filled the room in a bilious cloud.

In the bathroom, he refilled the glass, wet down a towel and returned to do battle with the rest of the flames. Heart-pounding fear made him stamp and grind his leather-soled shoes into the charred wreckage even after the fire was out.

Jackie.

Coughing, he rushed back outside to see her eyelids flutter open. An unborn scream parted her lips.

"Jackie!" The scream yielded to a cry of pain as he jerked her into his arms. Belatedly, he remembered her ankle. He cradled her against his chest. If he'd been two minutes later, he would have been too late. The thought made him ill. Another cough wrenched smoke from his lungs.

"It's okay," he murmured. "Easy, now. You're safe." Meaningless words rolled from his lips.

A sudden noise at his back brought him spinning around. J.D. found himself facing the business end of a revolver.

"Police. Hold it right there."

FOR THE SECOND TIME that day, J.D. sat in the hospital waiting room. He was relieved when Ben Thompkins finally strode from behind the No Admittance sign. The rangy policeman surveyed the waiting area, spotted J.D. and sauntered over, claiming the empty seat beside him.

"Met her yesterday, huh?" Thompkins opened.

J.D. glared at him. "How is she?"

Ben shrugged. "Mad as hell. You okay? You look worse than she does."

"I'm fine. Did she say what happened?"

"The dead elf reappeared in her living room."

Thompkins kept his tone neutral, his expression blank. J.D. muttered a fervent curse. "I take it you didn't find anyone else inside the house?"

"Good guess."

"What about the basement?"

Thompkins frowned. "What about the basement?"

"Did you check down there?"

"Of course. We checked the house from top to bottom, J.D. Just like last night."

"How did you get through the locked door?"

"What locked door?"

J.D. swallowed his exasperation. "The one leading to the basement."

Thompkins frowned. "The basement door was standing open, just like last night."

"No. It was closed and locked last night. At least it was after you guys left."

Obviously puzzled, Thompkins scratched his jaw. "Ted

might have closed it when we came back upstairs. What's your point?''

"Jackie says she doesn't have a key to that door."

Thompkins lifted his brows in disbelief while J.D. tried not to wonder if he'd been played for a sucker.

"Is that what your call to the station house this morning was all about? I didn't get the message until a short time ago."

J.D. nodded. "Jackie says she hasn't been down there since she moved into the house. Her friend misplaced the key."

Pity flared to life on Thompkins's harsh countenance. He studied J.D. and shook his head. "She also claims there was a dead elf in her bedroom, who conveniently disappeared before we arrived. Now, she claims he reappeared. Only, you'll notice he was gone again when you got there? I can't figure out what sort of a game she's playing, but the basement door was open, J.D. Both last night and today. I went down there myself. It's a basement. A large, open, empty basement."

J.D. muttered a profanity. "Why would she lie to me? That's crazy."

His shrug was eloquent. "She *says* the elf was sitting in the chair in the corner. She *says* someone else came at her from beside the bed. She *says* she tried to hit the other guy with a crutch and fell."

"And you don't believe her."

"I'm a cop. I look at evidence, J.D. There isn't a lick of proof to support the word of an obviously stressed-out woman on medication. She can't even give me a decent description of the man she claims attacked her. All she remembers is he had blue eyes."

J.D. grimaced. "What about the fire?"

"She admits to lighting candles because she was afraid

of the storm," Thompkins said patiently. "They were burning in almost all the downstairs rooms. She's on crutches and she's been taking medicine that could have made her drowsy. At a guess, she lost her balance, fell, knocked the candle over and the flame set fire to the carpet and the drapes. Nothing indicates anything else."

"But there could have been someone in her house?" J.D. persisted.

Thompkins groaned, his expression pained. "And I thought the rash of burglaries was gonna drive me nuts. Sure. Santa himself might have been there looking for his missing elf. The back door was unlocked," he added grudgingly, "but that doesn't mean a thing. You didn't see anyone, did you?"

"Just Jackie and the fire." The memory tightened his gut.

"That was a damn fool thing to do, too," Thompkins scolded. "Once you got her out you should have waited for the fire department."

"The entire house would have gone up in a matter of minutes."

"And you could have died if you hadn't been fast and lucky with those drapes."

J.D. didn't want to think about that. His reactions had been instinctive. "Jackie isn't the sort to leave a door unlocked," he told Thompkins.

That netted him a glower as Thompkins drummed his fingers against the armrest. "Look at this logically, J.D. She couldn't have been unconscious for more than a few minutes or that fire would have spread a lot farther."

Thinking how close it had come to reaching Jackie's clothing made him want to shudder.

Thompkins warmed to his objections. "Do you have any idea what a dead body weighs? You don't just tote one around like a houseplant. Think about it, J.D. How the hell would anyone get a body inside the house without being seen? It was late afternoon—dinnertime. Someone would have noticed a body being carried in or out of her house."

J.D. forced his fingers to uncurl. He didn't want those words to make sense, but they did. "What about her ex-husband?"

Thompkins sighed. "We're still checking. I don't have much info yet, but I do know her restraining order is legit."

So she did have a reason to be afraid.

"What's your stake in this, anyhow?" Ben demanded. "I thought you didn't even know the woman."

"I don't. But my kids like her." J.D. fidgeted uncomfortably. So did he, damn it. He recalled the amazing softness of her lips, her skin flushed with the delicate heat of passion. J.D. shifted in the plastic chair.

"So the official police stand is that she was dopey from medication and fell because of the crutches?" he asked. "And let's not forget that she's hallucinating because she's high-strung, on medication and afraid of storms?"

Thompkins heaved another sigh. "Rather crudely put, but yeah, at the moment that's it in a nutshell."

J.D. scowled. "Not funny."

"I wasn't trying to be funny. Look, J.D., I don't know what to think. Her story is far-fetched, you have to admit that."

Thompkins was right. J.D. didn't really know anything about Jackie. They hadn't talked much last night because she'd been too nervous. Justifiably so. Any intelligent woman would have been on edge with a complete stranger spending the night in her house...elf or no elf.

"She didn't seem crazy," he muttered.

Thompkins rose to his feet. "Just be careful, J.D."

JACKIE WASN'T HAPPY to see him. Her hair was doing its best to escape the confines of the pins she had used to trap it on top of her head. She swiped futilely at several tendrils, scowling after a departing nurse. Her eyes were sunken hollows, the only color on her pale face coming from the darkening bruise near her temple. Yet she lifted her chin, proudly defiant, her doe eyes so vulnerable they stabbed at his heart.

Before he could think about it, J.D. walked over and kissed her. Her lips were as soft and sweet as he remembered. Jackie's mouth was a round O of surprise as he stepped back.

"What did you do that for?" she whispered.

"The kids always say a kiss makes the hurt better. I figured if it worked for them—"

She shook her head. "He was real, J.D. I'm not crazy. I'm not!" Tears of angry frustration pooled in her eyes. He controlled an urge to gather her tightly against his chest.

"No one said you were crazy."

She wiped at the moisture that spilled from her eyes. "No, your friend didn't say the word, did he? But his thoughts came through loud and clear. He doesn't believe me."

J.D. couldn't argue.

"And you don't believe me, either."

He refused to be drawn into battle. "Jackie, the police need proof. They're checking out your story. My question is, what do you want to do now? Do you want to spend the night with two magpies and Aunt Dottie, or do we go back to your house?"

Her body tensed. "We?"

"You shouldn't stay there alone tonight."

"You can't spend another night with me," she protested.

From out of nowhere, J.D. had to struggle with an image of Jackie without those baggy sweats, her hair unbound, lips parted, arms reaching out in welcome. The wash of pink that stole over her cheeks told him she was thinking along similar lines.

"I am the perfect houseguest."

She shook her head.

"I'm not the perfect houseguest?"

"I don't even know you," she protested.

"But you want to."

Her breathing quickened. Oh, yeah. She was attracted, all right. She looked away, then raised her head. As glares went, the one she attempted was really wimpy.

"You're arrogant."

"And you're beautiful. Stop pushing at that hair." Before she could move, he leaned down and fumbled in her hair for the pins that held the heavy mass in place.

"Stop that. What are you doing?" She batted his hands away, but not before her hair tumbled around her shoulders like a curtain of silk.

"I was helping you take it down."

"I didn't want it down." But she stopped fussing to chew on her lower lip—while conflicting emotions warred on her features.

J.D. squeezed her shoulder and smiled. "Then, I'm sorry. Do you want me to help you put it back up?"

She lifted her head, alert, wary, watchful. Once again, her vulnerability clutched at his soul. And damn it, he just couldn't believe she was crazy. Or a liar. She'd seen something in that house.

"No." She tucked a strand of hair behind her ear.

His smile widened. "Good. You really are quite lovely."

She went back to chewing on her bottom lip.

"Don't do that," he requested quietly. "It makes me want to taste that mouth all over again."

Jackie gasped, but his teasing had the desired effect. Vulnerability vanished beneath a sea of indignation.

"Try it," she suggested. "You'll sing soprano for a year." She reached for her crutches.

J.D. grinned, relieved to see her defiance. "I make a better baritone," he teased. "What's it going to be? My place or yours?"

"Neither one. I don't like the idea of someone chasing me out of my house."

"I admire your grit, if not your common sense."

She glared at him. "Good," she said tartly. "Then after we stop at the house to pick up my overnight bag, will you please drive me over to Bessie's?"

He raised his eyebrows.

"I'm not stupid, either."

BESSIE AND FRANK STARNES already had company. Jackie tensed as soon as she spotted Seth Bislow sitting in a chair drinking a beer. She caught his lustful expression and wished J.D. hadn't taken her hair down, or that she had put it back up before they entered the building.

Even Bessie and Frank seemed startled by her appearance. Or maybe it was the sight of J.D.'s possessive arm on her shoulders.

Jackie had felt jittery since the moment they left the hospital. She put her unease down to the horror of what had happened, but as soon as she stepped into the parking lot, she couldn't shake the sensation that she was being watched. Darting looks around had revealed nothing to alarm her, yet the sensation wouldn't go away. It grew stronger when she stepped from the car outside Bessie's building.

She loved Bessie and was glad Frank made her happy, but secretly Jackie had never figured out what her friend saw in the man. Seth Bislow, on the other hand, flat out gave her the creeps. Now she tried to relax as Bessie fluttered about, smothering her with motherly hugs and *tsk*s of sympathy over her injuries. The strain of her son's death showed clearly in the sadness of her eyes. She shouldn't have brought her troubles here, Jackie realized. Bessie had enough on her mind.

"Come in and sit down. You poor dear. You need to get off that foot. Seth was just telling us how you'd injured yourself. You should have called me. You'll spend the night, of course. The rain is supposed to change to snow again after midnight."

Frank's thick lips thinned in annoyance, but he quickly pasted a smile on his face when he caught her watching. "Bessie's right," he said jovially. "We can't have you running around on crutches by yourself."

"She isn't by herself," J.D. said quietly.

Everyone stared.

"Of course she isn't," Bessie said uncertainly. "You're welcome to stay, as well. We'll just put her in the spare room tonight and Seth can take the couch and we can put a sleeping bag on the floor—"

"That won't be necessary," J.D. said.

Bessie blinked rapidly. "Oh, it's no trouble. The men will be gone before sunrise, if you can imagine."

"We need to get an early start if we want to spend the day on the slopes," Frank explained.

"You're going skiing?" Jackie asked in surprise. Frank looked slightly guilty, but Bessie nodded. "They've had this trip planned for some time. I told Frank they should go ahead.'' She gave her husband a subdued smile. ''Nothing we do will bring Donnie back.''

Jackie hugged her, wishing she could do something to ease the other woman's pain.

''Yeah, well, you might as well stay, Jackie,'' Frank said gruffly into the silence.

''Jackie will be staying with me tonight,'' J.D. stated quietly.

J.D. captured everyone's attention with that gritty declaration. Jackie's mouth opened in surprise. She quickly shut it at J.D.'s warning look, but knew her shock showed when he drew her carefully against his side. Tension radiated from him. Jackie wondered why.

''J.D., could I speak to you for a moment?'' she asked.

He glanced down and smiled, but it wasn't a true smile. His eyes silently demanded her trust. ''Sorry, sweetheart, I know you wanted to ask Bessie about the key.''

She did?

Sweetheart?

He turned to Bessie. ''Have you found the key to the basement yet? We need to do some laundry.''

''Oh, dear.'' Bessie twisted her hands together. ''No, I'm sorry, Jackie, I haven't even looked for it. Frank, do you know where the basement key to the house is?''

Her husband shook his shaggy head. ''Nope. Didn't know it was missing.''

''Oh, Frank. I told you I couldn't find that set of keys after...after Donnie...'' Her voice cracked. Jackie pulled free of J.D.'s embrace and moved to hug her friend again.

''Don't worry. It's not that important.''

''Well, of course it's important, girl,'' Frank said impatiently. ''Your boyfriend here just said you needed to get down there.''

Frank's easy pairing of her and J.D. tripped her heart rate. She didn't glance at him to see how J.D. accepted the comment. "Don't worry," she told Bessie again. "A locksmith can make me another key."

"Might have trouble getting one to come out if the weather turns bad," Seth Bislow offered.

They all turned and glanced at the large window near the end of the room. J.D.'s arm suddenly spanned her waist again.

Bessie appeared stunned. Jackie felt a little stunned herself. She also felt oddly protected, and the dichotomy kept her silent. Why was J.D. acting like this? Probably because he knew how uncomfortable she was around Seth, she decided. She should pull away, but, with his strong body pressed securely against hers, it was hard to remember why his taking charge was such a bad thing.

"Going back to your house?" Seth asked Jackie. He shoved his thick glasses against the bridge of his nose.

"Yes," J.D. answered. He held out his hand to Bessie, and Jackie saw genuine compassion in his expression. "I'm sorry we have to meet and run, but we need to go before the weather changes again."

"I understand." But it was clear Bessie didn't understand, at all. She looked to Jackie, questions momentarily replacing the grief that normally lined her face.

J.D. hustled Jackie to the door and out, before she could protest or explain.

Alone in the elevator, Jackie faced him. "You want to tell me what that was all about in there?" she demanded.

"No."

"You can't tell me no. Those are my friends!"

"I thought you didn't like Bislow."

"I don't."

"Me, either. He leers."

"He does not." But he did. "That's not the point. Did it ever cross your arrogant masculine mind that I might be able to speak for myself?"

J.D. ignored her question in favor of his own. "Don't you think that apartment would have been a little crowded with the four of you sleeping there tonight? There's more room at my place."

"I thought we were going back to my house."

They moved outside into the crisp night air. A prickle of unease slid right back up her spine.

They were being watched.

Jackie sent a fearful glance in all directions.

"What's wrong?"

"Nothing." How could she explain her sudden anxiety without sounding foolish? J.D. helped her inside the car, but the sense of being watched wouldn't dissipate.

"Do you really want to go back to your house tonight?" he asked.

The mere thought made her shudder.

"I'll take that as a no." He walked around the car and got in behind the wheel. "It's just as well. I need to get home to the kids."

"I can't go home with you," she protested automatically. She scanned the sidewalks, expecting to see the watcher nearby.

J.D. steered the car out into traffic. "I can't protect you at your house, Jackie. Those locks are too old. You'll be safer at my place."

Memory of what he'd already risked for her tonight buried her unease. "I didn't even thank you. For rescuing me, I mean."

Light glinted off his teeth as he smiled. "You were too busy scolding me."

"I'm sorry. I really am grateful."

"Then you'll come to the house?"

More fear drained away, though the uneasiness remained. "Are you trying to blackmail me?"

"Whatever works. Besides, the kids will be thrilled. They like you."

"I like them, too, but I don't think I should spend the night with you."

His dimples showed in the light reflected off the dash. "Don't worry, for that sort of activity, we would have to go to your place. There's almost no privacy at my house."

He was teasing her. Of course he was teasing her. So why did his words make her breath catch in her throat? Why did images of the two of them together keep skirting the edges of her thoughts? J.D. wasn't really interested in her, despite the fact that he'd kissed her.

Twice.

His dimples deepened as if he could read her thoughts. "I gather you know a lot about computers."

If his goal was to keep her off balance, he was succeeding admirably. She'd been living in a state of fear for so long, she wasn't sure she could remember how to relax.

"Why would you think that?"

"You have two in your spare bedroom. I noticed them the other night."

"Oh, those aren't mine. They belonged to Donnie. He had all sorts of equipment. Bessie and Frank aren't into computers, so Bessie insists they come under the heading of household furnishings," she explained.

J.D. arched his brows in surprise. "Nice furnishings. I'm thinking of buying one for the kids for Christmas. They won't stay off mine at home."

"Better them than me. I know where the On and Off switch is, and that's about it. Though, I admit, I was thinking of taking some sort of class."

"The kids could teach you."

He was probably right, but she didn't want to talk about computers right now. "Why did you rush us out of there tonight?"

His glance was unreadable in the dark car. "Your friend already had enough to deal with. Don't you find it a bit odd that her husband and his friend are going off on a skiing trip, when her son's been dead less than a week?"

Jackie wasn't sure how to respond because she did find it odd. But Bessie didn't seem unduly upset.

"Could we swing past the shop for a minute? I'd really like to check and be sure everything is all right."

"No problem."

Angel was just getting ready to close. There were no customers inside, so she came to the curb and reassured Jackie that the evening had gone well, though there hadn't been much business. Angel promised to open again in the morning.

"Feel better?" J.D. asked as they drove away.

"Yes." But she cast a nervous glance at the tree line near the edge of the parking lot. There was no sign of the watcher or anyone else.

Heather and Todd burbled with excitement when Jackie entered the house a few minutes later. Aunt Dottie welcomed the unexpected houseguest with unruffled calm. Jackie had thought she wouldn't care for the woman, but J.D.'s aunt turned out to be a kindly lady who reminded her of her grandmother. Aunt Dottie simply had an affinity for television shows and a lot of trouble keeping up with two active children.

Though everyone made her feel welcome, Jackie couldn't rid herself of a growing disquiet. She spent much of the evening watching the children play on J.D.'s computer while he readied the spare room for company.

When J.D. supervised their bedtime a short while later, Jackie returned to the family room to watch television with his aunt.

"Dear, would you mind very much if I excuse myself?" Dottie asked hesitantly. "I'm afraid I've gotten in the habit of getting ready for bed myself about this time."

"Of course, please don't let me keep you. I'll be fine."

"I know you will, dear."

Dottie smiled and two dimples flashed, clear evidence of her relationship to J.D.

Left on her own, Jackie found her mind straying from the television program. Her gaze kept drifting to the windows, until she finally rose and hobbled over to stare out at J.D.'s silent neighborhood.

Was that a movement by the base of the tall maple tree? She stared until her eyes hurt, unable to decide if someone stood beside the tree or not. The tree was five houses away and across the street. Even if someone lurked there, she had no reason to believe it was the watcher. No reason, at all, except the anxious fear tightening her chest.

"Looking for Santa Claus?" J.D. asked.

She turned to find him watching her from across the room. He had changed clothing, and the dark jeans he now wore molded his frame, displaying hard, muscular thighs and a trim physique—proof that he did something besides sit behind a desk all day.

Well, he'd told her last night he played a lot of sports. Studying him, she could easily picture him running from base to base or spiking a volleyball over a net. In his navy blue sweater with his white shirt collar peeking over the top, he was as sexy as any man she had ever seen.

"Just checking to see if it was snowing yet," she lied.

"Uh-huh. Come join me." He indicated the couch and she moved slowly away from the window. He sat beside her, close enough that she could see he had shaved. She could even smell the light scent of his cologne.

She didn't want to be attracted to this man. Men were dangerous, unpredictable creatures. Strange, then, that his warmth made her want to curl against his side.

She was so distracted by his presence, she never heard the start of the newscast. It wasn't until a vaguely familiar face flashed on the screen that she suddenly sat forward, her attention completely riveted.

"Police have no apparent motive in the shooting death of Ogden Korbel, Jr., earlier tonight outside this popular local hangout."

Her indrawn hiss drew J.D.'s attention. "Jackie? What is it? What's wrong?"

She heard her voice, as if from a great distance. "That's Oggie," she whispered.

His hands were warm and protective as he cradled her face, forcing her eyes to meet his. If only she could absorb some of that strength and warmth. She was so cold.

"Who's Oggie?" he asked.

Her fear was unreasonable. Oggie's death had nothing to do with her. How could it? She didn't even know the young man.

"Jackie?"

"Oggie Korbel was one of Donnie's best friends."

Chapter Five

When the lights failed, so did her courage. She jumped at a loud clap of thunder. Lightning illuminated the tumultuous spring sky outside her grandmother's living-room window. The brewing storm had turned the twilight into a dark winter's night, allowing the cozy rambler to take on menacing dimensions. She made her way to the bedroom, wishing her friends Bill and Donna would hurry.

The open-handed slap whistled out of the blackness, catching her across the face and ear. She reeled against the bedroom dresser. A stream of profanity poured from her husband's mouth, sending terror through every fiber of her being. She screamed as his calloused hands reached for her.

JACKIE JERKED AWAKE, bolting upright on the bed. Tremors shook her body while her breathing came in short, choppy gasps. At least, she thought shakily, she hadn't screamed out loud this time.

She replaced the cast on her ankle, reached for her crutches and swung from the bed. If only she didn't have to face an entire household full of people right away.

Schools were delayed two hours due to road conditions, so the children claimed her attention even before her first cup of coffee. If her pounding headache showed or anyone noticed the fine tremor in her hands, no one commented.

Remnants of the dream left her shaky. She couldn't force food past the fear that continued to jam the back of her throat. Oggie's death had acted as a catalyst for the return of her nightmares, even though she'd only met the young man once at Donnie's funeral.

"Come on, Jackie, we'll show you how to use the CD-ROM," Todd coaxed.

Jackie followed the children into J.D.'s den, grateful to be away from his discerning gaze.

Todd had an intuitive understanding of computer programs. He was patient and endearing as he and Heather tried to teach her some basics.

"Bus in ten minutes," J.D. warned a short time later. "They haven't driven you crazy yet?" he asked Jackie as the children scampered off to collect their schoolbooks.

"Not at all. They're so smart it's scary."

"Tell me about it."

He stood much too close to her again, but she couldn't bring herself to move away. She inhaled the light, spicy scent of him, aware of the broad wall of his chest. If she reached out she could touch his freshly shaven cheek— not that she would, of course, but...

"I called a locksmith for you," J.D. said. "He's going to meet us at your house around one. He's also going to bring some information on a security system I think you should take a look at."

Jackie tensed, immediately annoyed by his presumptuousness. "I can pick up a telephone myself, J.D. And I can't afford a security system."

"Ben says there've been a lot of robberies in the past few months."

"Ben?"

"Thompkins. The police officer—"

She nodded, cutting him off with a wave of her hand that brushed against his impeccably tailored suit. "Doubting Thompkins. I know who you mean."

That elicited a reluctant chuckle. "He's a good cop, Jackie. He's just doing his job."

"And what is it you're doing, J.D.?"

Irritation flashed in his eyes. "At least look at the security system with an open mind."

Her headache pounded with renewed energy. "My mind is always open. It's my pocketbook that's closed."

He grew larger and more intimidating, somehow, as he leaned toward her. "I can lend you—"

"Absolutely not."

"Will you stop being so obstinate?"

"As soon as you stop being so pushy."

"Pushy?" His outraged expression was almost comical. Heather called out before he could say another word.

"Daddy! I can't find my gloves!"

Jackie wasn't cowed by his glare. Unlike her former husband, J.D. knew how to control his temper.

"I'll be right there, Heather," he called, calmly.

He started to reach for her again, but she turned away. "Go, before they miss the bus."

"This conversation isn't over, Jackie."

HE WAS WRONG. The telephone rang as the children went out the door and J.D. found himself dealing with work he couldn't push aside. It wasn't until Aunt Dottie called him for an early lunch that he even saw Jackie again. Dottie's bridge group was meeting across the street, so she left the two of them with a cheery wave. Jackie didn't appear thrilled to be alone with him.

"I have to go to the office," he told her without preamble. "I have a meeting I can't get out of."

"Fine. If you'll just drop me at the house—"

He cut her off. "I want to be there when you talk to the locksmith."

"Excuse me, but who put you in charge of my life?"

J.D. paused, a soupspoon halfway to his mouth.

"I believe the locksmith is coming to my house to view my locks and discuss my security problems."

He swallowed the soup to keep his twitching lips from breaking into a smile. The lady had spunk. "You're going to be difficult, aren't you?"

"If you mean I'm not going to let some arrogant male I barely know treat me like one of his children, then, yes...I plan to be very difficult, indeed."

"Jackie, I wasn't trying to—"

"Control my life?" she interrupted sweetly. "That's probably because you aren't looking at this from my perspective." She blotted her lips and set down her napkin.

J.D. swallowed his annoyance along with the soup. She had a valid point. He was pushing the bounds of their tenuous friendship.

"Tell me something, do you have any family here in Maryland?"

Instantly, her body stiffened. "No."

Innocuous family questions were off-limits, too? Why? "What about in Indiana?"

"My grandmother is dead." The terse answer held a wealth of pain.

He laid a sympathetic hand over hers. "What about your parents? No brothers or sisters?"

Jackie pulled her hand free. Anxiety showed clearly in her rigid posture. She didn't want to answer these questions, but grudgingly, she did.

"I have two older brothers," she replied, her words only slightly less clipped. "One lives in Germany and the other in New Mexico. They were already grown and out of the house when my parents found themselves expecting me."

She toyed with the edge of the place mat and her discomfort made his heart ache.

"What happened?"

Jackie glared. "They went out to the cabbage patch one morning and there I was."

He shook his head, but added resiliency to her spunk. "I imagine it's hard on your parents with you living all these miles away from them, too."

"They prefer it that way," she answered grimly.

"Why?" he asked.

Her brown eyes flashed. "None of your business."

He pushed aside his dishes along with all pretense of eating. "Probably not, but I've a feeling this is important."

"To whom? My family has nothing to do with me. Nothing, at all."

Cautiously, he probed the wound he'd uncovered. "Because you moved here?"

"Because I was a big disappointment to them, all right?" Words tumbled from her lips as if the layers of buried emotions churning inside her had suddenly burst free. "Because Larry was their handpicked choice and I walked out. Worse, I filed charges. A good wife, a dutiful wife would have remained—a devoted doormat."

He frowned and rested his fingers on her forearm. "What about your brothers?"

Jackie tried to pull her arm free, but J.D. wouldn't release her.

"My brothers are strangers. I barely saw either of them growing up."

"But you had your grandmother," he said softly.

Her expression gradually calmed. "Yes. I always had Grandma. She used to say my mother had been born without a backbone. That's why my father suited her so perfectly."

And that explained Jackie's fierce independence. Her formative years must have been a battleground. "I'll bet Grandma didn't like Larry, either."

He released his grip. Jackie slowly relaxed. "No. I've often wished I'd listened to her, but I was so flattered when this older man from next door started paying me attention."

"He lived next door?"

"He rented the house when I was in high school. He was always doing things for my parents—carrying in groceries, helping Dad work on the car. Everybody loved Larry."

Jackie's eyes closed and her voice dropped to a husky pitch. "The first time he hit me I was so shocked." She opened her eyes and her voice deepened with contempt. "His tearful apology came with a necklace. Diamond and ruby chips in the shape of a heart."

J.D. fought growing anger on her behalf. He wondered if she'd ever told anyone beside her grandmother the painful truth behind her marriage.

"The next time he hit me I went to my parents. My father looked at my bruised face and said I should apologize to Larry."

J.D. couldn't prevent a low rumble of anger.

Jackie lifted her chin. "Grandma gave me refuge and helped me deal with the authorities, but we lived in constant fear."

Not normally a violent person, J.D. wished for five un-interrupted minutes with her ex-husband. He couldn't do a thing about her parents, but if he ever got his hands on Zalewoski...

"I'm sorry," he offered.

"I'm not looking for pity."

J.D. nodded. "I know."

"The past is over."

"Unless he's found you again."

The fear that never lurked far from her eyes flashed to life once more.

The telephone rang.

J.D. pushed back his chair and snapped a greeting at the person on the other end. Carol's voice filled his ear with the newest work problem as Jackie quickly began stacking plates, a fine tremor in her slim fingers.

JACKIE WISHED SHE hadn't exposed so much of her past. Until now, only Bessie had known her history. She worried that J.D. would continue his interrogation, but he remained silent during the short ride to her place. His business problems must be distracting him, she decided.

Dread filled her as soon as they turned down her street. Malevolent windows seemed to watch J.D.'s car pull in behind her battered coupe in the driveway. Jackie shivered.

The house was not alive and it was not evil, she told herself as she climbed from the car. No one watched them from within.

Yet the crawly feeling wouldn't go away. She scanned the street, looking for another source.

J.D.'s phone call had made them late. The lanky lock-smith stepped from his van at the curb and started forward with a rolling gait. Had it been his stare she felt?

But the stranger only eyed her curiously and greeted J.D. like an old friend. He shook his head over her front-door lock and followed them into the dining room, where he wasted no time launching into his security spiel. Jackie listened, toying with the mail J.D. had plucked from her mailbox. She cringed when the locksmith reached the bottom line.

"Security systems aren't cheap," she muttered.

The man called Luke chuckled, displaying a gap between his upper front teeth. "Nope. But we're doing a booming business with all these robberies lately. People don't want to take a chance on surprising a burglar in their house."

How right he was. A burglar or an ex-husband.

"Think about it," J.D. said softly. "My offer of a loan stands."

"Don't you have to get to work?" she demanded.

He glanced at his watch and grimaced. "Yeah. Luke, thanks for the favor. I appreciate you coming out on such short notice. I've gotta run, but I should be back before you leave."

"Why?" she asked.

J.D. gave her a droll look.

Luke glanced from one face to another, then scratched his chin. "No problem, J.D. Anything for a teammate."

"Don't tell me you play sports, too?" she asked.

"Softball. Right field," Luke acknowledged.

"I should have known." Privately, she was glad. Their friendship made J.D.'s call to him less insulting, and explained the priority her house had been given.

J.D. stood. Before she realized his intent he took her face between his hands and kissed her full on the mouth. "Behave yourself."

He left before the protest could pass her lips. Luke

grinned. "Let me think about the security system," she told him crisply. "In the meantime, you can start by replacing the locks on the doors."

As he set to work, she started sorting through her mail. There was a forwarded letter from Brenda, the only friend in Indiana she still kept in touch with. She'd have to write and give Brenda her new address. Jackie started to open the envelope when she spotted what appeared to be a Christmas card bearing yesterday's postmark.

Odd. The card hadn't been forwarded. In fact, it had been mailed from the Main Street post office. Bessie, of course. She was the only one who had this address. Jackie set aside the letter and reached for the card. From overhead came a creak followed by a soft thump.

Jackie froze. Chills raced up and down her arms as she lifted her head to stare at the ceiling. No wind to speak of, no ice to crackle and creak. What had made that sound?

Her eyes flew to the hall. Luke whistled a country-western tune off-key as he worked on her front door. The noise hadn't come from there. It had come from overhead. She waited, heart pounding, for any further sound.

"Here you go, ma'am. I'll get the back door next, okay?"

Jackie tried to smile, but her lips felt stiff as she took the shiny new keys from his hand.

"Uh, Luke, did you hear that noise a second ago?"

"What noise?"

Her heart beat a rapid tattoo against her chest. "Like something fell. Upstairs."

He cocked his head at the ceiling and frowned. "You sure you didn't just hear me changing the lock?"

"I'm sure. It's probably nothing," she hastened to assure him, not wanting to look like a paranoid fool.

"I'll go up and check around if you'd like," he offered.

Oh, yes. She'd like very much. But there was already a dead elf to account for, she didn't need a dead locksmith, as well. "I have to go up there, anyway," she lied. "The noise just…startled me."

"Why don't I go up with you and have a look around?"

She knew he saw her obvious relief. "Thank you."

As they stepped into the hall, he nodded in the direction of the living room. "I see you had a fire."

Jackie shuddered. She'd avoided looking at that room until now. The missing drape, smoke-stained walls and charred carpeting were hard to miss.

"Yes," she agreed without explaining further. "The noise came from the spare room on the left," she told him at the top of the stairs. Luke obediently turned to the room across from the master bedroom.

"Here's the culprit," he said immediately. He retrieved something from the floor and turned, holding a small print in his hand.

Jackie took the picture, sick with apprehension. "Pictures don't just fall off the walls."

His eyebrows beetled in concern. "They do when the tape lets go. See? Someone hung this using one of those stick-on tape hangers."

He handed her the tape in question. The once gummy backing was old and brittle.

"These things are worthless. The glue always gives out eventually and then the pictures fall. You're better off poking a few tiny holes in the wall. Pictures tend to stay up when they're nailed in place."

Jackie couldn't return his smile. She stared at the tape thinking he was probably right, but her adrenaline kept sending her impulses to fight or run. The sense of wrongness wouldn't go away.

Feeling only slightly foolish with Luke watching, she stepped farther into the room and opened the closet. Empty. Of course it was empty. The picture near the door had simply fallen. No one had brushed against it, jarring it loose. Luke looked puzzled.

"I'm a little jumpy after the fire," she explained.

"Oh, sure, I understand. Don't blame you. My wife hates strange noises, too, but these old houses...they're full of 'em. If I were you, I'd invest in some nails and rehang all these pictures."

"I'll do that. Thanks."

She stood in the hall after he went back downstairs, trying to settle her racing heart. She couldn't do this, she realized. She couldn't live in this house. She'd never feel safe here again.

Jackie left the bedroom door open to add light to the hall. Maybe opening all the doors might alleviate the sinister feel to this level of the house. She opened her bedroom door and glanced inside. Empty. The picture had fallen as Luke explained. Still, she moved down the hall, opening doors and glancing inside each room, refusing to give in to her desire to check the closets and under the beds.

At the head of the stairs, she found Luke starting up toward her.

"Do you want a new lock on that basement door or do you just want me to rekey it?" he asked. If he found it peculiar that she had a dead bolt on her basement door, at least he didn't voice his opinion out loud.

Jackie started down the steps, maneuvering the crutches with care. "Whichever is cheaper."

With a nod, he trundled back down the hall toward the

kitchen. She decided to take advantage of Luke's presence to check out her mysterious basement. She'd feel better after confirming the elf didn't lay on the cement floor.

While Luke worked at the top of the stairs, she descended carefully. A stack of boxes boldly marked Christmas in black marker, reminded her that she needed to sort the contents for usable decorations. The metal shelves with their assorted odds and ends sat against the far wall opposite the washer and dryer. There was nothing else to see down here. No way in or out of the basement except the steps, unless someone broke through the heavy bubble-glass windows set high in the walls. Why, then, had Bessie's son put a lock on the door?

Jackie made her way up the open steps carefully, watching where she set each crutch. She smiled at Luke who had moved on to the kitchen lock, and started down the hall. The front door gaped open.

"Luke? Did you leave the front door open?"

He looked up in surprise. She heard his indrawn breath. "No."

He strode to the front door, flung it all the way open and peered outside. "There's no one out there. I must not have latched the door when I finished. The wind probably took it."

And maybe Larry had been hiding upstairs the entire time.

"That must be what happened," she agreed, desperately wanting to believe his explanation.

Her ankle throbbed. She entered the dining room and sat down. Her hand trembled as she absently reached for the unopened Christmas card.

Santa being run over by his reindeer and sleigh made her frown. Bessie liked sparkly, glittery cards. This couldn't be from her.

Jackie never read the preprinted greeting inside. A hand-printed message sucked all the air from her lungs. She fought against the blackness that threatened to envelop her.

Happy holidays, Jack. See you real soon.

The card was unsigned.

He didn't need to sign it. Only Larry ever called her Jack, usually in an insolent, insulting tone of voice.

Her fingers shook so hard she could barely turn over the envelope. Her address stared up at her. Not the apartment address. This address.

He knew where she lived. What if he *had* been upstairs only moments ago?

"Ms. Neeley? I'm gonna start on the windows now and…you okay?"

"No. Yes." She dropped the card to the table and shook her head, trying to keep the horror from her voice. His concern reassured her. She was safe. As long as someone else was around, she was safe.

"Luke, how soon can you have that security system installed?"

He scratched at his chin in surprise. "Well, I've got several orders ahead of yours—"

"I'll pay you double to put it in right away."

Concern wreathed his face. "I really might have left that door ajar."

She wanted to laugh, but if she gave vent to that urge she wouldn't be able to prevent the outbreak of hysterics that beat against her rib cage. If it weren't for Bessie, she would pack her meager possessions right now and leave town without a word to anyone.

But where could she run that he wouldn't find her again? She'd promised herself—promised!—that she'd never let anyone terrify her again. Oh, God, she was such a coward.

Footsteps on the front porch sent her head spinning toward the windows. Two small bodies, faces beaming with excitement, plunged up the steps and raced toward the front door. J.D. followed behind.

Jackie took several deep breaths, willing herself to face them calmly. After all, hadn't she known from the first moment she saw the watcher outside her shop that Larry had found her again?

She made her way to the front door and opened it.

"We came to rescue you," Heather announced, bursting inside. Her pink cheeks gleamed with childish pleasure.

"Yeah, Jackie," Todd added. "Dad says you can come with us instead of sitting around the house. We're going Christmas shopping."

Jackie lifted her face to J.D.

Instantly, he took a step forward. "What is it? Is something wrong?"

She shook her head and tried for a smile. "No. Nothing." Her gaze dropped to the children. "So you're going shopping, huh?" she asked with false heartiness.

"Yeah. Dad says we hafta go see Santa. But I'm not sitting on his lap," Todd announced.

J.D.'s frown remained in place as he touched her shoulder. It was crazy. A simple touch and all she could think of was that kiss.

"I wouldn't think Santa would want a big fellow like you sitting on his lap," she agreed.

"How's it going, Luke?" J.D. asked as Luke ambled forward. But he didn't drop his hand from her shoulder. Instead, his fingers began a gentle massage.

Luke forced a troubled smile. "Hi, kids. Almost finished, J.D. I'm ready to secure the downstairs windows and that's about all I can do for today. I'll need to go back to the shop to check on when I can install the security system she wants.''

J.D.'s fingers stopped moving as he turned to her in surprise. ''You're going ahead with one?''

''Yes.'' In a way, she was grateful the children were here. Otherwise, Jackie knew she would have made a complete fool of herself. J.D.'s touch had planted strange desires. She kept thinking how nice it would be to let those broad masculine hands hold her and offer comfort.

''Good,'' J.D. said. ''Anything you want to do before we leave?''

Leave? For a second, Jackie didn't know what he was talking about. She tried to think, but her thoughts kept getting lost in the dark intensity of his deep gray eyes.

He pushed back a tendril of her hair. The simple gesture made her quiver. His forehead furrowed, even as awareness flickered to life in his expression. ''Are you sure nothing's wrong?''

''No. Nothing. I'm just not in the mood for shopping tonight,'' she managed.

J.D. stepped even closer to her, making it difficult to draw a decent breath. The children erupted in a chorus of pleas that drowned out his whispered question.

''What *are* you in the mood for?''

Heat washed her face. A crazy shaft of excitement pierced her. Heather grabbed her hand, drawing her wayward thoughts back to reality.

''Please, Jackie,'' Heather begged. ''I want to show you that telescope I told you about.''

''And we're gonna get Mexican for dinner,'' Todd put in. ''It won't be fun if you don't come.''

J.D. smiled wryly.

"Yeah, Jackie. We can rent you a wheelchair and take turns pushing. It'll be fun."

Jackie shook her head, swallowing horror at the thought of being pushed around the mall in a wheelchair. Talk about a sitting duck.

"Heather, thanks anyhow, but—"

"Come with us, Jackie," J.D. added, his deep, gravelly voice washing over her like a caress. She drew in a deep breath, instantly regretting it as his sexy aftershave filtered past her nose to imbed itself in her awareness. Jackie tried to take a hasty step back. "I promise. We won't be out late and we can sit down whenever you get tired. I conned the kids into getting their pictures taken with Santa. They agreed to do it only if you came with us."

Jackie managed a weak smile. J.D. was seducing her without even trying, making her yearn for what she couldn't have. She wanted to go with them. Wanted for just a few minutes to grab this heady sensation of feeling attractive and see where it might lead.

"But I'm not gonna sit on his lap," Todd warned his father again, effectively breaking the strange spell J.D. had woven.

J.D.'s look was rueful, but then a smile etched those devastating dimples on either side of his mouth. "Go get ready," he urged.

She shouldn't. Larry was a threat they couldn't begin to comprehend. On the other hand, Larry had always played the conciliatory husband in front of witnesses. He'd wait to catch her alone before he came for her. She'd definitely be safer at the mall.

"You'll finish securing the windows?" she asked Luke as she grappled with her misgivings.

"Yes, ma'am," he assured her.

"Can I go see your computer?" Todd asked.

Jackie nodded absently. "It's upstairs. You and Heather can look at it while I run a comb through my hair." She found J.D. watching her closely. "I'll only be a minute. If you're sure?"

"Very sure," he promised.

The glitter in his eyes disturbed her senses all over again.

"Need some help?" he asked.

Before a fully formed image of the sort of help he had in mind could form, Heather piped up, "I can help. Me an' Jackie are friends, right, Jackie?"

Jackie tore her gaze from J.D. and placed it safely on his daughter's small face. "That's right, Heather, we're friends. I'll just be a minute."

She wasted a second worrying about what Luke might tell J.D., and then decided it didn't matter. She was nervous and she was scared, and now she had more than one reason to be both.

Upstairs, the children entered the den while Jackie hurried to examine the sparse contents of her closet. For the first time in years, she wished she had something to wear that wasn't dowdy or frumpy. Playing down her looks might have kept men from noticing her, but in the long run it hadn't done a thing to keep her safe. Larry had found her anyhow.

Shutting the closet, she settled for washing her face and braiding her hair. With deft, sure movements, she rolled the tight plait against the back of her head. The tiny pair of crystal earrings Bessie had given her last Christmas lay on the bathroom shelf. A silly, harmless bit of femininity, but Jackie slipped them into her ears with fingers that shook.

She took several deep breaths and faced her image in the mirror. The high color in her cheeks gave her a feverish appearance, but at least it drew a person's gaze from the tiny red welt on her cheek and the bruise at her temple. Her eyes had a wild, feral look.

Maybe some lipstick would help? She didn't have any other makeup. Heather knocked and Jackie gave up the search of the medicine chest.

"An' you could bring one of the computers to the store," Todd was explaining as they reached the foyer. "Then I could show you how to do neat stuff when we come after school."

They could not be allowed to come by the shop any more, she realized. Larry could strike at any time.

"All set?" J.D. growled.

Gone was the teasing behavior from before. J.D. looked upset. Luke must have said something to him about the way she'd been acting. Soon the entire town would be talking about the crazy lady who ran the ice-cream shop.

She lifted her chin and stared at him defiantly. "I'm ready."

"Good. Luke gave me the basement keys. Where do you want them?"

"The hall table is fine," she told him, pointing to the surface where she always dropped her keys and purse as soon as she came inside.

J.D.'s scowl deepened. "Not smart, Jackie. Anyone could walk out with your keys or your purse."

"Like you did?" she reminded him.

"Here." He thrust the entire collection of keys into her hand. "Luke will come back to finish the windows."

Jackie knew the windows didn't matter. Locks wouldn't stop Larry. But there was nothing to be gained by mentioning the fact.

"Fine." She stuffed the keys into her purse.

"I'll carry your purse, Jackie," Heather offered as they filed outside.

"When we get back, you and I are going to have a talk," J.D. said so softly no one else heard him. "I want to know exactly what happened after I left and what scared you about that Christmas card on the dining-room table."

THE MALL WAS CROWDED with harried shoppers and excited children. J.D.'s two were no exception, darting from place to place. Even if she hadn't been on crutches, Jackie knew she would have been hard-pressed to keep up with them.

"Are they wearing you out?" J.D. asked. He rested his hand on her shoulder and began to rub, an absent caress. Eating seemed to have restored his humor. She had to admit it had lightened her mood, as well. For the past few hours she'd almost felt like part of a family.

Except that she couldn't get away from her awareness of J.D. He sat a little too close to her at the small table. Close enough for her to feel his thigh pressing against her leg. Close enough to again smell the mild scent she'd come to associate with him.

Chatting with the children was the easy part. She did that every day and genuinely enjoyed hearing about the things that interested them. But she was distracted by J.D.'s small touches. Touches that sent an electric charge right through her. And time after time she caught J.D.'s eyes watching her, the way a man watches a woman he wants to make love with.

Impossible, of course. She'd done nothing to lure him. Yet she knew, if things had been different...

Jackie tried to bury that thought. She must keep reminding herself that the last time she'd felt like this she'd married the man—and nearly been murdered as a result.

They stood inside a large science store, letting the kids explore.

"Don't do that," she said.

His fingers stilled on her shoulder. "Do what?"

"Rub my shoulder like that."

His fingers changed the rhythm. Now they stroked her more boldly, sliding up her neck in a lover's soft caress.

Jackie drew in a sharp breath.

"Is that better?" he asked, eyes shimmering.

Infinitely better, but she'd die before she told him so. "No."

"Sorry. But I can't touch you any more intimately here or we'll be arrested."

His bold words stole her breath.

"You shouldn't be touching me, at all."

"Why not? I like touching you."

She liked it, too. Too much. "No."

"Sure I do." His hand dropped from her shoulder to slide up and down her spine. The coil of desire tightened low in her belly.

"Why are you doing this?"

His eyes bored into hers. "Do you find my touch offensive, Jackie?"

"No!" She should have said yes, but she couldn't lie. And it would have been a terrible lie. "You could have your pick of women. Why me?"

He frowned, staring at her as if trying to read her soul. "Why not you? You're a very attractive woman."

"No, I'm not."

"We're going to have to do something about your self-confidence," he told her. "If we were home alone right now, I'd release that prison you've made of your hair—"

his hand stroked the back of her head "—until it tumbled around your shoulders in a silky mass."

With a fingertip, he began tracing her lips, which parted in surprise. "Then I'd kiss you—thoroughly." He gently brushed her cheek, but it was the power of his stare that held her riveted, vibrating in anticipation.

"If I could lead you to a mirror right now, you'd see how truly beautiful you are."

"Dad! Dad! C'mere." Todd waved to them from across the store. "You gotta see this. It's awesome."

"Later, we'll finish this discussion," J.D. promised softly. "On my way, Todd."

Jackie stood where he left her, heart thudding madly against her chest. She couldn't move—couldn't take in a deep breath. She was barely aware of the people pushing past her on either side.

She hadn't been imagining the attraction. It wasn't just one-sided. J.D. wanted her, and the feeling was so mutual it scared her to death.

Heather and Todd didn't want to stand in line with the younger children to have their picture taken with Santa. While J.D. coaxed them, Jackie opted for a seat where she could watch the proceedings and maybe gain a measure of control.

The sensation of being watched built slowly. Jackie sat up straighter as her thoughts left J.D. and she became more aware of her surroundings.

She looked around, seeing nothing alarming. No one watched her except maybe J.D. She mustn't allow her imagination to take over because of the Christmas card.

But the feeling persisted.

Her breathing grew rapid. This was nuts. Larry couldn't know she was here...unless he'd followed them. The front door and the picture laying on the floor took hold of her imagination. Larry had been inside the house. She shook her head, but as the ugly warning prickle grew stronger, her eyes skimmed nearby faces. No one paid her more than fleeting attention. Yet her heart began to race as her unease worked itself into a full-blown case of fear.

Someone *was* watching her.

She forced her breathing to slow, fingers tightening on the crutches at her side. She sifted past each face more slowly.

J.D. and the children were close to the front of the line. Her gaze traveled beyond them, across the little boy sitting on Santa's lap, past a diminutive woman dressed in an elf costume, to collide with a pair of light blue eyes.

Jackie gasped. An older woman sitting near her turned with a curious expression. Jackie couldn't tear her gaze from the elf. His eyes widened in immediate recognition and he turned swiftly back to his camera.

A group of teenagers suddenly blocked her view. Jackie struggled to her feet. Awkwardly, she started through the crowd, cursing her clumsiness with the crutches.

J.D. She had to get to J.D.

Two little girls darted in front of her. She stumbled and nearly fell. A contrite father scooped a child into each arm, but Jackie barely heard his apology. She focused on J.D. He saw her approaching and murmured something to the kids before meeting her halfway.

"What's wrong?" he demanded.

"The elf!" Words jammed in her throat in a desperate bid to rush forth. "The one with the camera."

His head pivoted, but their view was now obstructed by a throng of people.

"He's the one who attacked me in the living room."

"Wait here."

J.D. shoved his way through the crowd. He ignored the

angry comments of parents and sidestepped the small children with reckless grace. When he reached the roped-off section, he stepped over the thick braided cord, intent on his goal.

"Sir, I'll have to ask you to—"

He ignored the Santa's helper who came forward.

"Sir! I'm going to summon security!"

He reached for the camera elf's shoulder and spun him around. Only, the cameraman turned out to be a camerawoman who stared at him with wide, frightened brown eyes.

Chapter Six

Jackie wanted to cry. J.D. wouldn't even look at her. He'd spun the woman behind the camera around like an avenging angel. The poor girl had been terrified.

How could she be the wrong elf?

Security arrived in the form of two determined young men who hustled J.D. away before Jackie could get close enough to explain. Heather and Todd huddled against her sides.

"Why did Daddy jump over the rope and grab Santa's helper?" Todd asked fearfully.

"Are they gonna arrest Daddy?" Heather asked in a small voice.

"No, sweetheart," Jackie assured her. "This was all my fault. It's just a misunderstanding. I'll straighten it out. I know where the security office is. Come on."

Her crutches made slow work of walking. Both children kept an anxious pace at her side.

At least, Jackie thought with black humor, she wouldn't have to worry about Larry any more. J.D. was going to kill her first.

Was she losing her mind?

No!

The elf who had stared at her had been a male with

blue eyes. He'd recognized her, she knew he had. The moment she saw his eyes she knew he was the man from her living room. Find him, and she'd find out about the dead elf. They wore the same costume, after all.

The elf had disappeared in the blink of an eye. Since she wasn't crazy, he must have changed places with someone while she made her way over to J.D.

That meant her elf was still back there.

The thought brought her to a standstill. If she hurried back to the center of the mall, she could probably catch him.

"Jackie, come on. I don't see Daddy any more," Heather urged.

Two small faces peered at her in distress. The elf would have to wait, she realized. First she needed to rescue J.D.

HE'D LOST HIS MIND. There wasn't any other explanation. He'd taken one look at Jackie's frightened face and simply reacted. Hadn't Thompkins tried to warn him? Jackie Neeley was a fruitcake.

And J.D. was an idiot.

If he'd taken a minute to think, he would have realized this was the first time Jackie had indicated the second person in her house was also an elf. Until now, only the so-called dead body had had that dubious distinction.

Obviously, Jackie had an elf fixation.

"Are you sure you don't want to press charges, Ms. Boreman?" the senior security man asked the young woman.

The girl pushed back her elf hat and shook her head. "No, it's okay. He didn't hurt me." She sent an edgy glance toward J.D., as if she wasn't sure she was making the right decision.

"I really am sorry," he told her. "I honestly thought you were someone else."

"That may be," the security man said, "but you had no business climbing past the barrier."

"I realize that." He kept his voice—and hopefully his expression—low and humble. "I can promise you, I won't make the same mistake again." The impassioned force of his words seemed to pacify everyone.

J.D. meant every syllable.

He would take Jackie Neeley home and forbid his children to go near the shopping center ever again. The woman was a menace. Those soft, pleading eyes could steal a man's soul—or at least his ability to think. How was it they gave no hint to the madness behind them?

He gave a mental shake. He'd learned his lesson. He had his children and his reputation to consider. The kids must be frightened to death. He could only imagine what they must be thinking. Thankfully, the security man finally dismissed him.

He threw open the door and nearly knocked Todd off his feet. The youngster released the door handle and backed into Jackie. She teetered. J.D. reached for her arm. Only his quick reflexes kept her from falling at his feet. He held her steady, all too aware of her fragility beneath that bulky sweatshirt. Quickly, he released his grip.

"Are you okay?" he asked gruffly.

"Yes, of course."

J.D. released her and turned to his children. "How about you guys? You okay?"

Heather nodded, her eyes too large in her small face. Todd immediately stared up at him. "Are they taking you to jail?"

"No. Of course not." Heat suffused his cheeks. "I

apologized to Ms. Boreman and told her I made a mistake. She very nicely—''

"I figured out what happened," Jackie interrupted. Her face was animated. Urgent. "The elf must have traded places with that woman before I reached you. If we hurry back there we can probably catch him."

"No!"

Everyone stared at him. J.D. took a deep breath, struggling to control his temper. "We are going to the car and we are going home."

"Good," Todd said. "Then I don't hafta sit on Santa's lap."

"But J.D.—"

"Not now," he warned Jackie. "You and I need to have a talk. Later."

Her stunned expression faltered, changing to one of hurt disbelief. J.D. hated that look—and the irrational urge that made him want to draw her into his arms and offer comfort. He had to remember the woman had nearly caused him to be arrested. She wasn't playing with a full deck and she was making him crazy, too. How could he still be feeling an attraction to her?

Jackie's slim fingers tightened around the crutches in her hand. She glanced at the children, and the protest so clearly evident on her face shuttered closed. Without a word, she pivoted and started back the way they had come.

They headed to his car in silence. Heather and Todd scooted ahead to walk with Jackie. Jackie refused to ride in the front seat, suggesting it was Todd's turn. Heather didn't even protest.

With the children watching so closely, J.D. felt it best not to object. His embarrassed anger was still too near the surface. Grimly, he helped Jackie into the vehicle. She stiffened at his touch, climbing in in prickly silence. The children slid in without a word.

Why was he feeling so guilty? He had nothing to feel guilty about. The woman was a menace.

Once he put the car in gear he realized he had another dilemma on his hands. Despite the rational side of him that wanted to take Jackie home and dump her on her front steps and never look back, he realized he couldn't do that. Whatever was going on inside her head, she'd already fallen once and nearly burned the house down around her shoulders. No telling what might happen if he left her alone tonight when she was all upset.

Besides, he needed to talk to her. He'd seen the unsigned Christmas card with its message. Luke said she'd become agitated right after opening the mail. Her elf hang-up might be crazy, but she did have that restraining order against her ex-husband. There might be a basis for her fears that would explain her irrational behavior. Maybe a connection between her ex and her fear of elves.

Or maybe she'd sent the Christmas card to herself.

J.D. groaned.

"You okay, Dad?" Heather asked.

"Peachy."

He regretted his pithy retort immediately. Heather gave him a reproachful look and snuggled closer to Jackie on the back seat. She draped a comforting arm around Heather's shoulders and squeezed gently. J.D. gnashed his teeth.

What a fiasco. The evening had been a disaster from start to finish. Next time he nearly ran over a woman with his car, he wouldn't stop to play good Samaritan.

"Let me off first," Jackie said quietly.

Was she reading his thoughts now? "No. You're going to have to spend the night again."

"Excuse me, but I don't have to do anything. I have new locks," Jackie told him decisively. "I'll be fine. Take me home."

With his juvenile audience listening, J.D. wasn't about to let her start an argument. "Look, let me drop you off with the children while I run to the store for Aunt Dottie like I promised. Then I'll come back and pick you up."

"That's stupid. I only live five blocks from your house. Just drop me off on your way past."

"We'll wait in the car while you get the milk, Dad," Heather offered.

"Yeah, Dad, we don't mind."

He clenched the steering wheel and scowled at Jackie in the rearview mirror. She glared right back.

"I don't mind—"

"I do." He said with quiet emphasis. "I'm driving, so we'll do this my way. Okay, everyone?"

"Daddy, are you mad at Jackie?" Heather asked.

He wanted to shout an emphatic yes, then he remembered it wasn't really her fault. Crazy people couldn't help being crazy. Could they? If only he wasn't so drawn to her.

"No, Heather. I'm just tired. It's been a long day."

J.D. wished he could close his eyes. Actually, he wished for a lot of things—most of them totally impractical. He ran a hand angrily through his hair.

Heather's concern worried him. Jackie's influence was much stronger than he'd realized. He would have to do something about that.

He'd dated any number of warm, wonderful women, but he'd never seen his children so animated with any of them. In fact, he'd never seen his kids respond to anyone the way they did to Jackie.

Hell. He'd never responded to anyone the way he had

to Jackie. And for the life of him, he couldn't figure out why. Maybe it was that guileless, untouched air about her. But she was hardly an innocent. She'd been married and divorced.

Yet, her almost chaste reaction to his teasing tonight had spurred him on, heating his blood. He could still taste that kiss they'd shared earlier.

He'd dated more beautiful women over the years. But none whose features had captivated him the way hers did.

He pulled onto his street in relief. They'd made it home without incident.

Or so he thought.

"I'd really rather you take me to my place," Jackie said quietly when he tried to help her from the car.

"Later," he told her, thrusting her crutches into her hands.

She climbed out and faced him. Anger added color to her cheeks, clearly visible in the moonlight. The children darted ahead to the front door.

"You are not my keeper," she whispered fiercely.

"Damn right, I'm not. Nor am I applying for the job."

"Then take me home. You'll never have to see me again."

He shook his head. "I couldn't live with the guilt. Yesterday you nearly set the place on fire. God knows what you would do tonight if I left you all by yourself."

She jabbed an index finger against his jacket. "Who do you think you are?"

"The man who nearly got arrested chasing after one of your phantom elves," he reminded her.

"Jackie, come on," Todd called out.

Color faded from her cheeks. He felt like he'd just kicked a puppy. How did he let her keep doing this to him? He was normally such a sane even-tempered sort of a person. Taking a firm grip on his anger, he nodded toward the house.

"Please go inside. I'll be right back and we'll talk."

She hesitated before limping past him without a word, head high, her carriage unnaturally stiff despite the crutches. J.D. watched her slow ascent up the steps and into the house. He felt rotten.

He drove to the shopping center and parked outside the convenience store. He stared at the lights inside and tried to remember why he was here.

No woman had ever gotten under his skin the way Jackie did. She had a way of peering up at him from under those silky long lashes with an innocence that stole his common sense. He wanted to shake her. He wanted to toss her in his bed and make love to her until neither of them could walk without help.

Aw, hell, she wasn't the crazy one around here. He was. J.D. got out of the car and went inside the store.

He was calm when he pulled into his driveway. He decided to talk to Jackie quietly and without acrimony. He'd use logic to explain why the children must stay away from her in the future. He would again offer her a loan if she needed one to pay for the security system. Then, he would let her spend the night. But, in the morning, he would take her home and wash his hands of her.

The children met him at the door.

"Jackie's gone," Heather announced without preamble.

Fear tightened his belly. "Gone where?"

"She called a cab and went to Bessie's. She said we can't come to the store ever again." His daughter's eyes welled with tears.

"Yeah, Daddy. How come she doesn't like us any more?"

Aunt Dottie joined them in the hallway. Even her features were accusing. J.D. looked from face to face, watching tears trickle down his daughter's cheeks. Without a word, he handed Dottie the groceries and turned to go back outside.

"Where are you going?" Dottie called after him.

"To bring her back," he growled.

Only, he couldn't bring her back. Jackie refused to even talk to him. And Bessie wouldn't let him inside the apartment.

"She went to bed," Bessie snapped. "I won't wake her, either. She's upset. Since Frank and Seth are out for the evening, I hope you won't mind if I don't invite you inside." Her cold voice told him it would be a long time before he got another invitation inside her home.

And he did mind, he realized. He minded a whole lot. He needed to talk to Jackie. When he realized he wasn't going to accomplish that tonight, he finally turned away.

At least she'd be safe staying with her friend.

The thought brought him little comfort.

JACKIE FACED THE MORNING with determination. Her eyes were gritty from lack of sleep, but she had formed a plan of sorts. She would have a long talk with the obnoxious Officer Thompkins. If she explained the situation calmly, surely he'd listen to what she said.

Bessie had offered to let her out of the purchase agreement the previous night. She'd even offered to lend Jackie money to disappear again.

Only Jackie had decided not to run. She was tired of being afraid. She would not cower or be chased from the life she had created here in the sleepy foothills of Maryland.

She used the bathroom, trying to be as quiet as possible.

Frank had come home quite late last night—intoxicated, from the sound of him. She had no desire to sit across from him at a breakfast table and make conversation. She couldn't understand his heartless behavior when Bessie was so obviously grieving over the loss of her only son. But since Bessie didn't seem to object, Jackie knew it wasn't her place to criticize. Still, she felt uncomfortable around Frank and his circle of friends.

Quietly, she made her way to the kitchen and the pad of paper Bessie kept by the phone. She left a short message and started to turn away when the small row of hooks beneath the corner cupboard caught her eye. Spare keys hung there, neatly marked. Her former house keys were on the outside hook, easily recognizable without reading the tag. It was the third key on that same chain, however, that started her breathing more quickly.

With trembling fingers, she lifted them. The odd key could fit any lock. Why was she so certain the tiny bit of metal had fit the dead-bolt lock on her basement door?

A tremor passed through her. She must be mistaken. Bessie wouldn't lie. Jackie was seeing bogeymen where they didn't exist. Maybe this key went with the garage behind the house.

Only she knew it was too new, too shiny to fit that rusted old lock. Besides, Bessie had told her there wasn't one for that door.

She closed her fingers over the cool metal and tried to control her breathing. There was an explanation. There had to be an explanation.

A toilet flushed somewhere in the apartment, making her jump. As quickly as she could manage, Jackie headed for the hall closet. Her stomach clenched alarmingly. She grabbed her coat and fumbled to release the front-door lock. The last thing she wanted was a confrontation with

Bessie or Frank right now. She needed time to think this through. She was almost positive she was overreacting, but the keys, still clutched in her hand, had taken on ominous proportions.

Despite her grief, it would have taken Bessie only a second to look at the spare-key rack. Why had her friend lied to her?

Using the phone in the main lobby, she called for a cab. The wait seemed forever. She moved out into the crisp morning air when, at last, the cab pulled in front of the building.

Her house sat dark and silent on the quiet street. She would never be able to think of this place as home. Her eyes constantly scanned the neighborhood as she hunted for the new keys to get inside. Such a quiet, innocuous neighborhood. Lights were on in several nearby houses as people got ready for another day. There was nothing sinister. No sense of danger.

She opened the door and stepped inside, willing her heart to stop fluttering. Setting her purse and keys on the small table alongside her old ones, she swept the silent rooms with a watchful gaze.

The downstairs appeared exactly as she had left it, even the living room. She would have to purchase drapes today and maybe some sort of floor rug to cover the fire damage.

"Right. Who's going to hang them, or carry a rug inside for me?" She wouldn't be asking J.D. for any more help, that was for sure. This sense of loss was ridiculous, but how she would miss the children.

The living room needed cleaning. Her pills still lay scattered on the floor. Her gaze strayed to the chair in the far corner.

Why hadn't they found any trace of the elf? How could a body just appear and disappear?

Forcing back painful thoughts, she went through the downstairs checking windows and doors. She double-checked the lock on the basement. The key she'd taken from Bessie's was the same brand as the lock. Why had Bessie lied?

Upstairs, she hurried from room to room to be certain no one lurked in a closet or hid in a spare room. Her leg throbbed, but the ache was definitely less severe today than yesterday.

She craved a bath. At the least, a shower, but she couldn't trust her ankle climbing in and out of that high claw-footed tub. She had to settle for a sponge bath, washing her hair clumsily over the tub. At least she wouldn't go to settlement today with dirty hair.

Grabbing clothing from the closet, she dressed in a clean pair of sweats and started back downstairs. The telephone shattered the stillness inside the house. Bessie, of course. Or J.D. She wasn't ready to talk to either of them. What could she say, after all? Why did you lie? Why didn't you believe me?

Crutches made cleaning hard, awkward work, but she felt better once she tidied the living room. When the phone rang again she decided to answer, but whoever it was disconnected as she lifted the receiver.

In the act of dialing Bessie's number, she hesitated. She still wasn't ready to talk to her friend, only the silence inside the house had become oppressive. She would go to the shop, instead. The shop represented safety despite the watcher. At least he hadn't been dressed as an elf.

With the walking cast, surely she could drive two blocks. The car was an automatic, after all. She headed for the hall, put on her coat and reached for her purse and keys.

Her car keys weren't there.

A quick search of her purse and her pockets didn't turn them up either, and they weren't on the floor.

Anxiety changed to anger, as she realized J.D. must have taken her car keys along with her house keys when he went to pick up her prescription. It meant another trip upstairs, but she did have a spare set tucked away in a drawer.

Thoroughly annoyed, Jackie found them and headed for the back door, carefully locking it behind her. The next time she saw J.D.—and she had no doubt that would happen soon—she would demand her car keys back.

Her car tended to be temperamental. It turned over when she started the engine, but the wipers couldn't clear the frost from the windshield.

Disgruntled, she turned off the car and stepped out. The scraper was in her trunk. A movement on her left sent her twisting in that direction. A young man moved toward the garage two houses down. She waved to be neighborly, almost thankful to see someone else moving about in this quiet neighborhood. He didn't see her, but it was enough to know she wasn't alone out here.

She picked her way to the back of the car and stopped. Silver keys dangled from the lock.

She fought against a suffocating sense of panic. There was a reasonable explanation for her missing car keys to be in the trunk. Not J.D., of course. He wouldn't have any reason to open her trunk.

Unless, maybe he'd been looking for the snow shovel?

The snow shovel that had been sitting on the front porch in plain sight?

Well, maybe he hadn't seen it right away. Maybe he'd checked her car and the garage before finding it on the porch. It was possible. Wasn't it?

Every instinct screamed at her to go back inside. She

looked around, searching for the neighbor she'd seen earlier. Nothing and no one moved.

Heart pounding, her hand snaked out and twisted the key. Without giving herself time to chicken out, she pulled the heavy trunk open.

The elf lay crumpled like a sack of old laundry. His distorted expression sent her reeling backward. Only a burlesquelike ballet kept her from landing in a heap on the icy ground.

Her ankle throbbed in protest. The contents of her stomach battled their way up her throat. Silent screams choked her mind. She twisted toward the house and somehow made it inside as far as the kitchen sink before her stomach purged itself.

Gripping the counter for support, she waited until the dry throat-wrenching spasms finally stopped. The police. She needed to call the police. One of her crutches had fallen. She ignored it, desperate to reach the telephone. Using the backs of the kitchen chairs, she crossed the room and grabbed the receiver.

It took her shaking finger two attempts before she stabbed out the 911 sequence and asked for the police.

"Police emergency."

"This...this is Jackie Neeley. You'd better send someone. The body's back." The room spun, growing darker at the edges of her vision. She fought against a need to surrender to that soothing blackness. The calm voice on the other end helped anchor her. She answered questions, trying to blot away the horror. Help was on its way. This time they would have to believe her.

The telephone rang the second she disconnected.

A familiar gravelly voice filled her ear. "Jackie, it's J.D. We need to talk."

She almost laughed, but the laughter would be too close to the hysteria laying in wait for her.

"Not now," she whispered. "I can't talk right now."

"Jackie, what's wrong?"

His concern cleared away the fog. Jackie shook her head and her voice came out stronger, more certain.

"You don't want to know, J.D. Don't worry. I won't bother you any more."

She heard his voice speaking low and urgently as she replaced the receiver. Using her other crutch, she pulled the dropped one across the floor until she could bend over and pick it up. Then she stood and headed for the front door.

Officer Thompkins stepped from his cruiser. She squared her shoulders and focused on his stern features.

"Officer Thompkins."

"Ms. Neeley. Dispatch said you found another body?"

He was good, she'd give him that. He kept every trace of disbelief out of his expression and his voice.

"No, it's the same body, just a different location. This time someone put him in the trunk of my car. You can't miss him. The car's parked right in front of yours."

He stopped moving toward her and turned back to the driveway. Then he turned her way again. His expression showed nothing.

"What car?"

Chapter Seven

Her heart slammed against the wall of her chest. She swung her way across the porch, fighting a horrible sense of panic. "Right there, in the drivewa..."

Her car was gone. Only an oil smear showed where it had sat just minutes earlier.

Jackie barely noticed the policeman rushing onto the porch, steadying her, guiding her back inside the house. Not until he tried to lead her to the chair inside the living room did she snap out of the shocked stupor that had taken hold.

"The kitchen," she demanded. She could never sit in that chair. Just thinking about the body resting there yesterday made her want to gag.

Hot and cold crashed through her system. She couldn't decide if she was more angry or scared, but she tried to hold onto the anger. Fear weakened her. She needed to be strong or the police would lock her away for sure.

How could the body be gone again? What had happened to her car?

She sat at the table, staring blindly at the clean wood surface, trying to make sense of the disappearance. "Someone must have driven it away when I came into the house."

She'd never heard the car start up. Never even sensed another presence outside. Yet, he had to have been close by. Waiting.

"How could he have known I'd go outside just then?" She lifted her head to Thompkins, whose face was a blur. Instead, she kept seeing the horrible expression on that contorted face and—

"Take a deep breath. Lower your head between your legs."

"I'm not going to faint," she protested. But she took a steadying breath, and some of the blackness receded. "I don't understand. Don't you see? Even I didn't know I was going out there. I decided to check on the store at the last minute. I wasn't even sure I could drive with this leg. *How could he have known?*"

Her voice broke as she battled terror.

"Take a sip of this, Ms. Neeley. It's water."

She needed two hands to hold the glass Thompkins extended. She took a sip to please him before setting the glass back down on the kitchen table. Her entire body quaked with cold.

"I'll be right back," Thompkins said. "Let me check your garage." He left the room and returned a few moments later, shaking his head.

"I know you think I'm crazy," Jackie said. "I know there is no earthly reason for you to believe me. But I'm not insane. Someone put the elf's body in the trunk of my car and left it there for me to find."

He scowled, but his eyes remained darkly unreadable. There was no way to determine if that scowl was directed at her or the circumstances.

"The car's gone," she hurried to add. "Surely that's proof of something!"

Thompkins didn't say a word, simply scratched at his jaw. Jackie took another deep breath.

"He's doing this to terrorize me. He likes terrorizing people."

"Who does?"

"My ex-husband. After I filed for divorce he used to break into my grandmother's house and leave things for me to find. Once, he put a dead bird on my bed." She shuddered. "Now it's dead elves."

Thompkins sounded gruff and angry as he demanded a description of her car. Calmly, she rattled off the particulars including the license-plate number. Maybe Thompkins would realize she couldn't have lost her mind if she could remember things like a license-plate number.

Thompkins lifted his radio and began speaking in a low, clear voice, repeating her description. Did he believe her? Dear God, she needed someone to believe her. If only J.D. had grabbed the right elf last night.

They both heard the pounding on the front door.

"You expecting someone?" Thompkins asked brusquely.

"No."

"Wait here."

She listened to the low rumble of masculine voices. Relief washed over her. She would recognize that gravelly voice anywhere. J.D. had finally arrived. Only now did she realize she'd been waiting for him, even though she'd told him to stay away.

Thompkins led him back to her kitchen. J.D. paused in the doorway, looking incredibly handsome and solidly reassuring. He wore another perfectly tailored suit beneath his open topcoat, but his hair stood at odd angles—as though he'd been running his fingers through the thick waves.

"You look like hell," he told her.

The surprising words nearly summoned a smile. "Thanks. Just what I needed to hear." But his calm, matter-of-fact approach was, indeed, exactly what she had needed to calm the horror in her mind.

He rocked back on his heels. "Ben says you're seeing elves again."

The words snapped her erect, dissipating her calm in an instant. "Get out of here!"

Then she noticed the way his right hand clenched and unclenched at his side. His studied nonchalance was just that—an act. He even admitted as much with his next words.

"Well, at least you've got some color in your cheeks now." He nodded as though satisfied. "Want to tell me what happened?"

The burst of anger warred with her pulsing need to be believed. "What's the point? You and your baseball buddy don't want to listen to the truth. You've already decided I'm crazy."

He hooked a chair, drew it out and straddled it backward, draping his arms across the back. The casual action might not have surprised her if he'd been wearing jeans, but coming from a man so formally dressed, she had to work to keep her surprise in check.

His expression softened and his lips curved upward just a tad. "Maybe," he stressed, "that's what someone wants us to think, Jackie."

She couldn't seem to breathe. Couldn't look away from those dark, intent eyes.

"I never once said I thought you were crazy," he continued in that slow, gravelly voice. "It's obvious that something is going on around here."

She blinked back sudden tears. If he offered her sympathy she'd cry for sure, and she mustn't cry. Larry liked it when she cried. She wouldn't give that bastard the satisfaction of making her cry ever again.

She sucked in a deep breath, squared her shoulders and gripped the edge of the tabletop, nearly knocking over the glass of water. "I'm not crazy."

He nodded. "Then tell me what happened."

"I came home, washed my hair, straightened the house and decided to see if I could drive to the shop."

He frowned. She frowned right back at him.

"It's only two blocks," she defended.

"On a sprained ankle."

"The car is automatic."

He shook his head. "Never mind. Go on."

"There isn't anything else. I went outside, found the keys sticking out of the trunk—"

"How'd they get there?" Thompkins interrupted.

"I thought J.D. put them there," Jackie told him. "Me?"

She nearly smiled at his stunned expression. "When you shoveled the snow the other morning I thought maybe you opened my trunk to look for the shovel."

"The shovel was on the porch," he said as though explaining something to a slow-witted child.

"I know that, but I thought you must not have seen it right away," she snapped back. "You did help yourself to my house key, so it seemed reasonable to assume you also lifted my car keys."

His expression was enough of a denial. "You left them on the hall table, didn't you?"

The vexed tone aggravated her. "I always leave my keys there, I told you that."

"And I told you it wasn't safe."

"It's a perfectly fine place if strangers would stay out of my house."

Thompkins shifted but didn't interrupt.

"Jackie," J.D. began and stopped. He finger-combed his hair, adding to his slightly rakish appearance. "Just go on with your story."

"My fairy tale, you mean?"

"I didn't say that."

"Okay, fine. I saw the keys, opened the trunk and..." She had to swallow then, because the memory caused her stomach to lurch.

"You saw a dead elf inside," J.D. supplied.

His words snapped her back from the brink of a precipice she didn't want to face again. "Not a dead elf. The same dead elf. He was stuffed inside like—"

"I get the picture," J.D. soothed. "Then what?"

"What do you mean, then what? I came inside, threw up and called the police. But by the time your friend got here, the car was gone."

"I was here four minutes after the call came through," Thompkins stated, moving away from the refrigerator he'd been leaning against. "I was on patrol at the other end of town when she called."

J.D. twisted to face him. "You didn't see anyone driving away?"

"No."

Frustration rose in Jackie like bile. "Elves are magical, aren't they? Maybe they sprinkled the car with reindeer dust and—"

"Stop it, Jackie," J.D. ordered.

"Well, why not? You already think—"

"That you've had a hell of a shock," he stated grimly. "Again."

His words deflated her.

"This wasn't the elf you thought you saw last night?" he asked.

"Thought I saw?" she demanded angrily. "Of course, it wasn't. This one is dead!"

"What elf last night?" Thompkins wanted to know.

Jackie glanced at him to explain as J.D. demanded, "So who was the elf you had me chasing at the mall?"

Her gaze riveted back on him. "I never once asked you to chase—"

"Jackie!"

"The man from the living room," she told him, too tired to argue any longer. "The one I tried to hit with my crutch."

Thompkins took a step closer. "Wait a minute. I thought the elf you saw in your living room was dead."

"He was! The other man wasn't dressed as an elf, then. The elf was on the chair. The man from last night was the one who was crouched down between the chair and the bed."

Thompkins glared at J.D. "We've got more than one elf?"

"Looks like it," J.D. agreed. Succinctly, he filled Thompkins in on the events at the mall. Jackie decided they sounded much less threatening the way J.D. told the story. "I nearly got arrested for assault," he concluded.

Thompkins muttered something pithy.

"If you'd listened to me," Jackie cut in, "we could have gone back to where they were taking pictures and found the right elf."

"Not a chance," J.D. argued. "You can bet he was long gone as soon as security hauled me away."

"You can't know that." Her fingers gripped the edge of the table.

"It only makes sense, Jackie. Wouldn't you run?"

About to argue, she suddenly grasped the lifeline he was offering. "Does that mean you believe me?"

J.D. closed his mouth on whatever he'd been going to say.

Thompkins scowled at both of them. "Ms. Neeley, how did you know the elf last night was the same man who'd been in your house the other day? You weren't even able to give me a description after it happened."

"I know, but I saw his eyes both times. They were blue."

Thompkins snorted; J.D. shook his head. "Jackie, do you know how many people in the United States have blue eyes?"

"You don't understand, we made eye contact both times. He recognized me at the mall just as I knew him. That's why he changed places with that girl."

Thompkins interrupted before J.D. could respond. "Let's back up here a minute before I get even more confused. Does your husband have blue eyes?"

Startled, Jackie shook her head. "No. Why—"

"So what does an elf at the local mall have to do with your ex-husband? That is who you thought was moving the dead elf around earlier," he reminded her.

Her heart slammed against her rib cage. "I don't know," she had to admit. "But there must be a connection."

J.D. drummed his fingers on the tabletop. "What's the word on her ex?"

"So far, we know he's remarried and the last report had him living in Ohio. The Akron police are still checking."

"Married?" Shock doubled her anxiety. "He married some other poor woman?"

Thompkins rocked to and fro on his heels. "So it appears.'' To J.D. he said, "There's no current wants or warrants. He does have a small pedigree—some drunk-and-disorderlies, two assaults and one aggravated assault, but those were in Indiana and the assault charges were all subsequently dropped.''

"Nice guy," J.D. muttered.

Thompkins shrugged. "I still don't see a connection to dead elves in Maryland.''

Neither did Jackie. "Then you at least believe that I saw a body?''

Thompkins lifted a shoulder. "Frankly, ma'am, I don't know what the hell to believe. There's not one shred of proof, you know.''

Jackie tried to stand, but dropped back down when she put weight on her bad foot. Ignoring the stabbing pain, she glared at him. "What do you call a missing car? You think I drove it away, walked back here on crutches and then called to report a dead body inside?''

"I didn't say that, Ms. Neeley.''

"Jackie—" J.D. rumbled in warning.

"Just what do you believe, Officer?''

Thompkins heaved a sigh. "Was anybody around who could verify your story?''

"No. I came back from Bessie's early this morning by cab. The driver might have noticed my car.... Wait! I'm not sure he saw me, but a young neighbor, two doors down on the left, was going to his garage when I went out to start the car. I waved, but he didn't see me—or at least he didn't wave back. Still,'' she hurried to add, "he might be able to verify that my car was in the driveway. Or maybe one of the other neighbors noticed.''

She looked from one doubting face to another. "Well, somebody might have seen me getting out of the cab! That can't be normal around here in the morning. You can check with the cab company to see when I got home. Besides, you can't get around the fact that my car is missing."

Thompkins's brow pleated more deeply. "Two doors down on the left, you say?"

"Yes. The gray house with the black trim."

He grunted in J.D.'s direction. "I'll go check it out. You staying?"

"Yeah." J.D. met her gaze. "I'm staying."

"MIND TELLING ME HOW you can get in so much trouble in just a matter of hours?"

Anger, then hurt flashed in her expressive eyes, but Jackie had a tight lid on her emotions. "Practice," she told him with droll humor.

"Have you eaten?"

She shuddered. "I'm not hungry."

"How about coffee?"

"I'm out until I get to a grocery store. Which I guess is going to take a while, now that I don't have a car. I don't imagine too many rental places will rent a car to a woman on crutches. That reminds me, I need to call my insurance company."

"Jackie, what's going on?"

She didn't pretend to misunderstand. She shook her head, her ponytail swinging from side to side. Her shiny hair was damp. Surely she hadn't taken a shower on that leg.

"I don't blame you for questioning my sanity. I'm beginning to wonder about it myself. Larry must be behind this. You saw the card he sent. He wants to terrorize me. He's crazy."

"Crazy enough to kill?"

"Oh, yes." She shuddered again. "I'm sure of it. He has a terrible temper."

J.D. hesitated. "Okay. Let's say he is crazy. Let's say he's so nuts he killed an elf and left him in your house to scare you. Why the games with the corpse? Thompkins assures me you don't just move a body around like a houseplant—his words, not mine. Is Zalewoski a big guy?"

He watched the tiny ripple of fear course through her. "Yes. He's big. And strong. He likes to lift weights." Her eyes focused on his face, demanding his belief. "Moving a body around is exactly the sort of thing his sick mind might come up with."

"But would he kill someone to create a body?" J.D. persisted. "That's premeditation, not anger."

She hesitated. "I...don't know. Somehow, that feels wrong. I can see him killing someone who got in his way or thwarted him somehow, but...premeditation...he's more an act-first-and-think-later sort of person."

She gnawed on her lower lip, drawing his focus to her pale complexion. Her quiet beauty had an almost translucent, fragile look to it this morning.

"He doesn't know anyone in Maryland," she stated softly. "Neither of us had any connections here. That's one reason I came here. I thought I'd be safe. I don't keep in touch with anyone back home except Brenda. She's my best friend and I promise you she wouldn't tell Larry the time of day. She never did like him, even when we were dating and he was pretending to be Mr. Wonderful."

"But you think he's here."

"You saw the Christmas card. He mailed it from downtown."

"Someone did," he corrected.

Her eyes clouded. "I suppose you think I sent it to myself."

"The thought did cross my mind."

Anger lit her face. "No matter what I say, I look foolish or like a liar. I'm not lying, J.D. And I'm not crazy. Not yet."

J.D. stood and prowled her kitchen. He couldn't shake the conviction that she was telling the truth—from her point of view. And who else would have a motive to terrorize her besides her ex-husband?

Thompkins returned looking morose.

"So?" J.D. demanded.

"Do you know any of your neighbors?" he asked Jackie instead of answering.

"No. I haven't been here long enough to meet anyone."

He nodded as if that was the answer he expected. "Two doors down on the left you have an elderly couple whose children live elsewhere. None of them was visiting this morning and Mr. Foster was still in bed when I knocked."

"The man was young, not elderly."

Thompkins nodded. "They have no idea who could have been in their yard. The Greysons live next door. They have three children, but the oldest one is ten. On the other side of the Fosters are a young couple—with no children—who travel extensively. Neither one is home at the moment."

"So, what you're saying—" she began.

"What I'm saying is you didn't see a neighbor and none of your neighbors saw you or your car."

"I can't believe this!"

J.D. reached out to press against her shoulder when she would have risen from the table. "All that says is Jackie probably saw the guy who stole the car."

They stared at him.

"Coincidence only goes so far," he told Thompkins. "Even you have to admit something is going on here. Her car is missing. And I doubt she drove it away to create this illusion."

The policeman turned his frown on Jackie. "Describe the guy you saw again. Could it have been your ex-husband?"

"No."

If she was lying, she should have said yes.

"He walked like a young person. You know, sort of loose-limbed? He was dressed in jeans and a black jacket. I didn't notice if he wore shoes or boots."

"Hair color?"

Jackie bit down on her lower lip. Her eyes stared past his shoulder as if conjuring the memory from the wall at his back. "Dark, probably more brown than black."

"Height? Weight?"

"I don't know, I wasn't paying all that much attention. At a guess, I'd say five ten or eleven, maybe a hundred forty, hundred fifty pounds." She sighed. "I know that isn't any help. I'm sorry."

"Look, Ms. Neeley, I don't know what's going on here. I'm being totally honest with you now. This is a small town with a small police force. We'll continue to check out your ex-husband and we'll look for your car. If there's a dead man inside, we'll have some sort of starting place for an investigation. But in the meantime, there isn't much we can do to protect you. My advice would be to call a friend—or better yet, a group of friends. Don't stay alone. You're vulnerable when you're alone. Maybe you could consider a trip someplace for a few weeks."

Jackie shook her head, her expression stubbornly independent. "He's not going to make me run away again.

I'm supposed to settle on this house today. Bessie is counting on me. I have a business to run and no money to take a trip. And I won't risk putting a friend in possible jeopardy. Whether you believe me or not, a man is dead.''

Thompkins scratched his jaw, but didn't look surprised. ''Okay then, this is how it will be. We'll do frequent drive-bys. You see anything suspicious, you call it in. I'll let dispatch know your calls are hot. They'll send a unit right away. Your vehicle description is out there. We'll have to wait for it to turn up. Then, we'll see.'' He looked at J.D. ''There isn't much more I can do.''

J.D. nodded. ''I know, Ben. I appreciate your help.''

''So do I,'' Jackie snapped.

J.D. squeezed her shoulder and felt her quiver.

''I'll walk you out,'' he offered. Jackie said nothing.

The two men descended to the cruiser in silence.

Thompkins raked him with a steady gaze. ''How come you're still involved here? Don't tell me you've developed a hero complex.''

''No, I—''

''Good, because you've got two kids to worry about,'' he pointed out. Then he stopped dead, staring at J.D. ''You're falling for her.''

''What—?''

''Don't shake your head, J.D. Nobody goes this far out on a limb unless they've got a stake. And I admit, if she fixed herself up some, she'd be a nice-looking lady.''

''Ben, get in the car.''

''I'm going.'' He made no move to get inside.

''Someone's going to a lot of effort to make her look crazy, don't you think?'' J.D. asked.

''Damned if I can tell. Like you, I'm beginning to wonder. I saw her face when she realized the car was gone. Honest to God, I thought she was going to pass out.''

"Then you believe her?"

"Hell, I don't know what to believe any more than you do. But it's like you said the night this all started. No way was she faking her reaction." He shook his head. "Just be careful, J.D. If there really is a body, then someone is willing to kill to make this lady look crazy." Ben slid inside and closed the door. He lowered the window and frowned up at J.D.

"Watch yourself. Don't take chances."

"I won't," J.D. promised. As the car pulled into the street, he remembered what he'd wanted to ask Thompkins.

This morning he'd read and reread the small article on the death of Oggie Korbel. The account implied the youth's murder was drug or gang related. Did the police know about the tenuous connection between Jackie and the dead man? The Lieberman kid had also died. Burned to death in a car accident. So many crazy events swirled around Jackie and this house.

He looked at the silent structure. Unimposing, taken by itself, but he decided it would be real easy to hate this place. What secrets did it hide?

That damn lock on her basement door kept gnawing at him. It was as out of place as all the other cockamamy things around here.

J.D. ran through a mental list of his appointments today and decided there was nothing that couldn't wait. He couldn't leave Jackie alone after what had happened.

Hell, at least he should be honest. He didn't want to leave Jackie alone, and not just because someone had stolen her car or because he'd acted like a jerk after that incident at the mall. He wanted to know the real woman who hid behind baggy clothes and fake glasses. He wanted to know if their strange attraction was merely that or if something deeper, more important was going on here.

Don't take chances, Thompkins had warned him.

J.D. pictured his children chatting freely over dinner last night, happily relating stories about the important things happening in their young lives. And Jackie, smiling and listening. Really listening to them, her face soft and beautiful, animated and filled with caring.

Life entailed all sorts of risks. Jackie was a chance worth taking.

J.D. mounted the porch steps and entered the front door. He heard Jackie talking on the telephone in the kitchen.

"Okay. No, that will be fine. Yes. Of course. All right, then."

"Problem?"

She replaced the receiver. "More like a reprieve. They had to postpone today's settlement. We've rescheduled for next Monday."

"I know I'm probably out of line here, but I don't think buying this place is a good idea."

Her eyes flashed. "I'm already committed."

"Not until you sign the papers."

"I promised Bessie."

"She can find another buyer."

Her gaze slid away from his.

"She can't find another buyer?"

Jackie frowned. "I'm sure she could, but she's my friend and I promised."

The phrase, "my friend," had a hollow sound to it. Something was wrong. Come to think of it, why had she left Bessie's so early this morning? Why hadn't Bessie or Frank brought her home?

"You take friendship seriously, don't you?" he asked gently.

Her eyes flashed. "Of course. Friendship is important."

"Does Bessie take it the same way?"

Bingo. Her troubled expression told him something had happened. Something that had put that all-important friendship at risk.

"What happened this morning, Jackie? How come you came home so early—and alone?"

"It's not important," she mumbled.

"I think it may be very important."

"Why? What difference does it make to you?"

J.D. picked his next words carefully. "Because I'd like to be your friend, too. I think you can use another friend, Jackie."

She turned to stare out the window. Her hands gripped the crutches like a lifeline. He waited several seconds.

"Want to talk about it?"

Her back tensed. She didn't turn around. J.D. waited silently, hoping she'd decide to trust him.

"Bessie lied to me."

The words were so softly uttered, it took a moment for them to register. "What about?"

Jackie turned back toward him. Pain shadowed her eyes. "All along she told me she didn't have the key to the basement lock, but I found it in her kitchen this morning with all her other spare keys. Why would she lie to me, J.D.?"

Her eyes pleaded for an answer, but he didn't have one to give her. "Does she know you found the key?"

"No. I... It's probably silly, but I felt betrayed. I mean, why would she lie? I needed to think, so I came here."

She looked deceptively fragile, but J.D. knew she wasn't. Only a strong woman could survive in the middle of this nightmare. He crossed the room until he stood within inches of her.

"What conclusions did you draw?"

Awareness glinted in her eyes. She tilted her head up and her lips parted. He had no business focusing on those lips. Definitely, no business remembering how soft and utterly kissable they were. Still, when she looked at him like that it was hard to think about anything else.

"Don't kiss me again," she whispered.

He cupped her face, feeling the satiny texture of her skin against his palms. "Why not?"

"Because."

"Not good enough," he told her. His mouth descended for another taste of her incredible softness.

Chapter Eight

She pulled back, her vulnerable eyes misted by desire. "We shouldn't do this."

Her mouth drew him inexorably back to her lips. He kissed her again more slowly, savoring the taste and texture of her, feeling the pliant sway of her body toward his. "Why not?" he whispered against her ear.

She turned her head in search of his mouth and her lips clung to his. She wanted him. The heady knowledge surged like a drug through his system, causing his body to harden against her slender form.

"I can't think when you kiss me," she murmured.

He kissed her again, this time tracing the fullness of her lips with his tongue. When her lips parted, J.D. refrained from accepting her unspoken invitation to delve inside the heat of her mouth. Instead he drew back a little, trying to control the escalating passion inside him.

"I can't think when I kiss you, either," he agreed. He pressed his lower body against hers.

Her mouth rounded in surprise and her eyes widened as she stared at him, defenseless in her own naked need.

J.D. groaned. "Don't look at me like that."

"Like what?"

"Like you're starving and I'm a feast."

His mouth closed over hers completely and his tongue began the ritual mating with hers. Jackie arched upward.

Kisses simply weren't enough. Gently, he rubbed her breasts through the sweatshirt. Her nipples puckered, straining for his caress. He pushed up the sweatshirt, sliding his hand across the soft bare skin of her abdomen, and she trembled sweetly.

Her right crutch clattered to the floor.

J.D. paused, shaken by the strength of his desire. Jackie stared up at him, her eyes dark with heady passion. He inhaled deeply, slipping his arms around her to hold her tightly against his chest.

When she attempted to withdraw, he released her, bending to pick up her crutch. It was better this way, he told himself. Another couple of minutes and he would have taken her right there against the wall.

"I'm sorry," he said, hearing the husky edge to his voice. "I've never lost control like that before."

"You're apologizing?" Jackie stared at him, annoyance mingled with traces of unfilled desire. "I don't know whether to be hurt or insulted."

He cupped the side of her face with aching tenderness. "When we make love, Jackie, it won't be against a kitchen wall. You're much too special for a quick tumble."

Her eyes widened and her lips parted, but no words came out. He felt the same way—astonished by the unexpected need that made him want to carry her upstairs and finish what they had started.

"Come on," he said softly. "We need to go."

"Go where?"

"I need some breakfast. We'll go to the pancake place over near the high school. Then we'll decide what to do."

He could almost follow the tumble of thoughts in her

changing expressions. "I have to check on my shop," she protested finally.

"We'll do that, too."

She hesitated, her uncertainty palpable.

"Come on, Jackie. You don't want to be alone right now. And if we stay here, I'm going to make love to you."

Her tiny gasp made him want to smile, but she recovered quickly.

"Has anyone ever told you that you have an arrogant, controlling streak?"

He did smile then. She was so incredibly tempting. "Are you going to deny what just happened?"

"A kiss," she insisted. "It was just a kiss."

"Just a kiss?" He stepped closer. Watched her eyes widen warily. The glimmer of answering excitement was all he needed to see.

Hard and hungry, his mouth descended on hers without restraint. He kissed her thoroughly, with a desperation that surprised even him. Wanting her was a fever that threatened to rage past his control.

She quivered beneath the onslaught, then opened for him, surging against his body with equal fervor.

Once again, her crutch struck the floor, acting as a brake on his raging hormones. She clung to him, breathing hard, her right arm wrapped around his neck, her expression startled, yet filled with desire.

He hugged her to his chest, inhaling the subtle scent of her shampoo while he tried to catch his breath. When she squirmed, he released her and bent to retrieve her crutch. His smile felt crooked as he handed her the piece of wood. "You do seem to have a problem holding on to these."

"Yes."

She wouldn't meet his eyes. A wash of color stained

her face a delicate pink. Her lips were puffy, looking thoroughly kissed and highly enticing. If he didn't stop staring at her, they were going to be right back up against the cabinets.

"We need to go somewhere public. You're a powerful temptation, lady."

The pink deepened to a soft rose. "But—"

"Trust me."

She stared at him in silence, then inhaled sharply and expelled her breath in a whoosh of air. A smile touched her lips. It was timid and a little cynical perhaps, but it was a smile. "Tell me something," she said. "Why do men think 'trust me' is an answer to anything?"

AN HOUR AND A HALF LATER, they decided it was much too late for anything resembling breakfast, so they sat inside a busy hamburger franchise finishing lunch with the rest of the noontime crowd. They hadn't talked much, but the silences that fell between them weren't strained.

J.D. was a comfortable man to be with despite what had happened between them earlier. Jackie didn't want to know if his thoughts were tracking along the same lines as hers because she couldn't stop thinking about what had happened in the kitchen.

Her reaction to his mind-boggling kisses shocked her. Should she be embarrassed, ashamed or annoyed? Larry had never stirred her senses the way J.D. did. But how did J.D. feel?

Women wanted intimacy. Men wanted sex.

The explosion of passion between Jackie and J.D. felt like so much more than lust. Beyond the desire had been a yearning she'd never experienced before. Did he feel it as well?

Oh, Lord, what if he just felt sorry for her?

"We'll need to get you a surge protector," J.D. said suddenly.

"What?"

"A surge protector. For the computer." He smiled and the smile lit his eyes, not just his mouth. "What were you thinking about?"

"Nothing," she said quickly. Too quickly, obviously. His expression turned knowing and she looked away, trying not to blush.

She changed the subject. "Thank you for bringing the computer over to the shop and for setting it up for me. I told Angel she could play with it when she isn't busy."

The brackets at the side of his mouth deepened into those hidden dimples that so captivated her.

"I heard you." His slow, sexy smile said he knew exactly what she was trying to do. "Angel seems extremely competent."

"She is."

"Are you finished eating?" he asked, looking at her plate.

"Yes." She pushed the remains of the meal to one side.

J.D. signaled for the check. "Then we should get going. I thought we'd pay a call on Teller's photography shop." The waitress smiled when he handed her a couple of bills and stood to reach for Jackie's crutches.

"Why are we going there?"

"Because they're the ones who supplied the elves."

Her heart clattered in her throat, while acid began to churn away at the food she'd just eaten. "Then you do believe me!"

"Jackie, even Ben Thompkins can't dismiss all the crazy things that have been happening to you. I just thought if we were discreet, we could ask a few questions and maybe give Ben something concrete to follow up on.''

She quickly swallowed the lump that clogged her throat, blinking away a shimmer of grateful tears. Until that moment, she hadn't realized how desperately she wanted him to believe her. If they went there and proved the elf existed...

A new and frightening thought suddenly struck her. ''What if he's there?''

J.D.'s lips formed a grim line as he led her outside. ''If the elf from the mall is there, we won't give him a chance to change places this time.''

About to get in his car, Jackie paused as she saw a police cruiser pick up speed and veer toward them. Instinctively, she knew who the driver would be.

Officer Thompkins pulled up, opened the door and placed one leg on the pavement. Half in and half out of his car, he didn't waste time on a greeting.

''Good thing I spotted the two of you. A neighbor just called in. Someone tried to get inside Ms. Neeley's house. You guys can follow me over there.''

''Right behind you,'' J.D. promised. Jackie practically fell inside as J.D. hurried around to the driver's seat. They raced behind the squad car until they reached her house, where another unit sat parked in the driveway.

Her neighbors must love seeing the police at her door on a daily basis, Jackie thought. A policeman came around the far corner of the house.

''It's secure,'' he told Thompkins.

Jackie recognized the policeman from the night the elf had reappeared in her living room.

''No sign anyone got inside. When the key didn't work, he tried to jimmy the door. That must have been when the neighbor spotted him. She called out to him and he jumped off the far side of the porch and took off running. I found this on the porch.''

He held up an evidence bag, and even from where Jackie stood she saw the small tarnished key inside. J.D. slid an arm around her shoulders and Jackie slumped against him, grateful for his presence. She didn't doubt the key would have fit her old locks.

''Ms. Neeley? You want to go inside and have a look around? Just to make sure everything's okay?'' the officer asked. ''There's no sign that anyone entered, but we should check to be sure.''

''Did the neighbor get a description?'' Thompkins asked.

His companion made a wry face. ''Average build, dark hair and dark clothing, that's all she noticed.''

''Figures.''

Jackie's hand shook as she delved for the bright new keys and handed them over. They entered the eerily silent house with care. Nothing appeared out of place downstairs. Jackie waited while Thompkins unlocked the basement door and the men descended for a look around.

Fear pulled at her mind. Would they find the body of the dead elf in some new and unexpected place? Part of her hoped so, even as she dreaded the idea. If only this nightmare would end.

Jackie and J.D. followed as they went from room to room. The officers were thorough this time around. More thorough than their searches in the past had been. This time they peered behind furniture and inside closets—to no avail.

Too bad her next-door neighbor hadn't also seen the dead elf. Obviously, she made a more credible witness than Jackie herself.

In the master bedroom, Thompkins checked the closet,

shut the door and suddenly snapped it open again. He stepped inside and stared at the ceiling. Without a word, he motioned them back and the other officer forward.

Jackie watched them pull down the rickety steps leading to the storage area in the attic overhead. She'd forgotten all about that space. Thompkins climbed warily, one hand on his weapon.

J.D. rubbed her back, a silent, supportive caress, but he barely took his gaze away as Thompkins disappeared from sight. The second man vanished to his waist, but went no farther. Their voices were muffled. Then, they came back down.

"Ms. Neeley, have you been in that overhead since you moved into the house?" Thompkins asked.

"No. Why? What's up there?"

Thompkins frowned. "Nothing at all except dust and cobwebs."

"But?" J.D. questioned.

"But…it doesn't mean anything since there's no way to tell when it happened." His shoulders lifted and dropped quickly. "But the dust has been disturbed."

"By a body?" J.D. asked.

Thompkins shrugged.

"But it could have been a body?" Jackie asked carefully. "A body someone might have hidden because they didn't want you to find it the first time I called?"

The men exchanged glances and Thompkins faced her squarely, his expression troubled. "Possible. Not likely, but possible."

Jackie closed her eyes. She couldn't decide whether to be relieved or angry. At last she had more "almost proof" that she wasn't insane. She opened her eyes and limped to the chair in the corner to sit down.

"She shouldn't stay here alone," Thompkins told J.D. sotto voce.

"She isn't going to," he responded gruffly.

"Good. Ms. Neeley?"

Jackie raised her face, marveling at the tiredness tugging at her.

"Who else had keys to your house?"

That didn't take any thought. "Bessie, her husband, Frank, and her son, Donnie," she rattled off. "He lived here before me and may have given keys to any number of people."

Thompkins scowled. "That's a dead end. Half the town could have had access."

Jackie started thinking about the house keys hanging in Bessie's kitchen...the ones she had taken this morning...the ones Bessie claimed to have lost. Should she mention them?

Why had Bessie lied to her?

Jackie shut her eyes again, letting the men's voices rumble above her. Lack of sleep and the constant state of anxiety were trying to suck her down into a yawning pit of exhaustion.

"Jackie? Come on, love. You don't want to sleep in that chair. Wake up."

Her eyes fluttered open and focused on J.D.'s face. His concern was so loving. She reached out and touched his face, running her fingers down his smoothly shaven cheeks.

"J.D."

"You fell asleep. The police left."

She nodded, still feeling half-asleep. "I like the aftershave you wear."

His chuckle was husky. "You do, huh?"

"Mmm. Sexy."

His lips brushed hers, then returned to linger in a long, soft kiss. He held her face gently between his palms. "I'll bet you aren't a morning person, are you?"

"No, why?"

"I can tell."

Her breath caught as J.D. lowered his face and kissed her so tenderly, her defenses melted away leaving behind an ache only he could fill. He drew back watching her.

"Wh-why are you looking at me like that?"

"I like looking at you. You're very beautiful."

The intensity of his expression caused her body to tighten. "I'm really not, J.D."

He shook his head. "Beneath those baggy outfits lies a beautiful woman."

Her breathing quickened. "You have no idea what my body looks like."

"I have a wonderful imagination," he teased gently.

So did she and she was imagining all sorts of possibilities right now.

"I want to spend some time getting to know you."

A low, slow heat stirred to life. "Me? Or my body?"

J.D. rubbed his thumb softly against her lower lip. "Both."

She began to tremble. No man had ever unsettled her like this.

"Just for a couple of hours, can we be friends?" he murmured. "No elves. No children. Nobody and nothing but a man called J.D. and a woman called Jackie."

Larry had looked at her like that once, but it had been only another illusion. One of the many masks Larry used to convince the world what a nice person he was.

Years of caution sent the words tumbling past her lips before she could stop them. "Does that line usually work?"

Hurt came and went, leaving his features totally masked and unreadable. "You have more lines of defense than the military," he said sadly.

She closed her eyes. "I'm scared, J.D."

"I know. With all that's been happening—"

"No." Her eyes opened and she shook her head, willing him to understand. "I mean here. Right now. The way you make me feel."

"How do I make you feel?"

"Giddy. Like I'm riding a rocket into space with no idea where I'll land or what will happen."

His features relaxed. "Nothing will happen you don't want to happen."

"I...I think maybe that's my problem. I have a good imagination, too."

The corners of his lips tugged upward. "I think I like the sound of that. Do I haunt your dreams, Jackie? The way you haunt mine?"

She gripped the arms of the chair, remembering the erotic dream in which he'd recently starred.

He chuckled. "I'll take that as a yes."

"We really need to talk about your arrogance," she told him. But she found herself smiling, reaching out to caress his chest.

"I don't think we really need to talk, at all." He leaned forward, but instead of kissing her he nipped at the vulnerable tip of her earlobe.

Jackie gasped. Shivers of anticipation raced along her nerve endings. His lips feathered kisses down her cheek until he kissed, then gently sucked at the sensitive skin of her neck.

The coil of heat tightened inside her. Jackie nearly surged off the chair.

"What are you doing to me?"

"Whatever you like," he promised huskily.

"Oh."

His eyes glittered, a deep smoky gray that seemed to envelop her in a passionate haze. "I'd really like to see if my imagination did you justice. May I?"

He didn't wait for an answer, but knelt to remove her sock and cast. He stroked the bottom of her foot, rubbing sensually.

"J.D...." She couldn't find words. The sensations were too staggering as his hands drifted upward, caressing her ankle, gliding up her calf.

"We can't."

His fingers stopped moving. "Why not?"

She didn't want his fingers to stop moving. She didn't ever want him to stop this slow seduction. "I need...I want...I haven't even had a bath today."

Merriment danced across his face. "What a wonderful idea."

He stood and walked into her bathroom. Water began to run in the tub. The sound mingled with the cascading thud of her heartbeat. All the reasons why she shouldn't do this suddenly seemed unimportant. She wanted this moment out of time with him.

J.D. strode into the bedroom trailing the scent of her bubble bath. The image of him sitting in a tub full of bubbles made her smile. J.D. was a large man. Tall. Big. Strong.

"Our bath awaits." And with that one wicked grin, he banished her remaining fears. J.D. was not Larry.

"Our bath?"

"Well, you didn't think I'd let you have all the fun, now, did you? I wash your back and you wash mine."

The idea of the two of them crowded into her bathtub

tightened that knot of anticipation into unbearable pressure. "We won't both fit," she warned him weakly.

His eyes darkened. "We'll fit just fine."

Unbelievably, he proved to be right.

She helped him tug at the elastic of her sweats, wishing she owned sexy satin underwear instead of plain white cotton. But J.D. didn't seem to mind. His own white briefs clung to his hips like a lover's caress, barely concealing the strength of his arousal.

His chest was broad, powerful. Masculine. With her eyes, she traced the scattering of hair that arrowed downward until it disappeared below the waistband of his briefs.

He reached around her, unhooking the bra, sliding the straps off her arms in a slow striptease. Her nipples tightened, puckering beneath his gaze.

"I knew you had a lovely body."

"So do you." And it was true. All hard planes and rippling muscles, but not the kind that bulged and threatened.

He lifted her gently, as he carried her into the bathroom.

He set her down, supporting her with one hand, while he slid his other fingers inside the elastic of her panties. "Let's see the rest."

She stood before him naked and curiously unashamed.

"Beautiful."

His look truly made her feel beautiful.

He helped her into the warm water heaped with bubbles, mindful of her sore ankle. When she was settled, he waggled his eyebrows in a bad Groucho Marx imitation. "Now for the fun part. I get to wash all that lovely skin."

The words sent up a tingling everywhere. "What do I get to wash?" she demanded.

His eyes glittered. "Anything you desire."

"Your knees," she said promptly. "I've always had a thing for knees," she teased.

"Damn. And I only have two."

"Well, maybe I can find something else of interest."

His fingers went to the waistband of his briefs. "I hope so," he said, lowering them with deliberate slowness. "I certainly hope so."

A happy, light feeling bubbled inside her. Loving this man would be so easy. J.D. was nothing like Larry. And she was no longer a naive twenty-two-year-old girl.

He urged her to scoot forward, then slid in behind her. Water sloshed unheeded on the bathroom floor. She'd never felt anything like the sensation of his body pressed against hers. Until he squirted soap into his bare hands, rubbing them together to form a lather and began to caress her breasts. He touched her everywhere, rubbing and stroking until she feared she'd dissolve under the intensity of the sensations.

She gripped his hands, stilling their exploration. "J.D., please! I need to touch you, too."

"All right." He stood, dripping water, and reached for a towel.

"What are you doing?"

He dropped the towel on the floor, stepped from the tub and told her to slide back. Instantly, she complied and he got back in as they switched places.

Rubbing soap across his chest and back was every bit as erotic as having him touch her. She moved lower, then around the sides, to find him wickedly erect. She slid her soapy hands up and down, savoring the feel until he stood abruptly, sloshing water, and turned toward her, his face tight with passion. Bubbles dripped down his body.

He looked magnificent.

J.D. added more bubble bath to the water and turned

on the tap for a few minutes. This time, he settled her in front, facing him.

"Can we go back to the kissing part for a minute?" she asked. "You're very good at that."

His chuckle rumbled as he took her mouth.

The kiss tantalized, stirring all the warm, building urgency within her. She kissed him back, running her hands over his slick skin.

She was more than ready when he positioned her carefully onto his lap. The warm, soapy water and the tight confines of the bathtub added an incredible element of excitement as she fitted her body to his, feeling stretched and wonderfully alive.

"J.D.!"

"I know. Let it happen, love." His mouth took her breast, sending the waves of excitement rushing to overwhelm her. Water slapped against the sides of the tub unheeded as she clung to his shoulders, meeting each thrust of his body. Incredible sensations sent her spiraling higher and higher, until she cried out in sheer pleasure, only faintly hearing his own rumble of satisfaction.

He held her tightly against his chest, rubbing her back in soothing comfort until their breathing steadied.

"That was...unbelievable," she told him.

J.D. grinned in satisfaction. "I told you we'd fit." He kissed the tip of her nose.

"So you did."

"The water's getting cold."

Jackie laughed. "I hadn't noticed."

"I love your laugh. You need to do that more often."

Her smile faltered. "There hasn't been much to laugh about lately."

"We'll change that," he promised. He lifted her gently and stepped from the tub, reaching for more towels.

A moment out of time, she thought wistfully. One glorious moment. She sat, toweling herself, while J.D. went to gather their clothing.

"You need to pack some clothing," he told her a few minutes later.

"What for?"

"To take to my house."

"I can't go to your house."

"Jackie, we aren't going to start that all over again, are we? Ben says it isn't safe for you to stay here, and I agree."

"Well, good for you. What are you going to do if Larry finds me at your house? The children and Aunt Dottie could be in danger."

Grim lines replaced all trace of humor. "I won't let that happen."

"You might not have any choice."

"Have a little faith in me, Jackie," he said softly.

"God, you're stubborn. And—"

"I'm stubborn?"

"You're missing the point. I know Larry. He's dangerous, J.D. I tried to tell the police that back in Indiana. No one listened to me then, either."

He cupped her face. "We're listening to you now, Jackie. Ben circulated the man's description and put out a pickup call on him. Kylerston isn't that big. If he's staying anywhere in the vicinity, they'll find him. Now throw some stuff in a bag and let's get out of here. Unless you'd rather stay with Bessie."

"No!" Her objection came out sharper than she'd intended. J.D. cocked his head. "I could go to a hotel," she suggested weakly.

"Sure. You'd be real safe in a hotel where people come and go at all hours." He handed her the crutches.

He was right and she knew it. She moved to the closet, pulling down outfits at random and wishing again that she had something nice to wear. Her current wardrobe consisted mainly of sweat suits.

She turned to hand J.D. another pair of sweats, when she realized he no longer stood at her shoulder. He was clear across the room near her dresser, holding a large, ornate picture frame in his hand.

"What have you got there?"

"You tell me."

Jackie swung to his side, the sweats forgotten on the closet floor. Mutely, he handed her the picture.

Jackie caught her breath as Larry's face beamed back at her. The camera had captured his handsome features in a wide, gloating smile. Why had she never noticed the cruel twist to those lips? Or the fact that his smile stopped there, never reaching those sinister dark eyes?

Oh, his tuxedo appeared tailor-made and his looks were as striking as ever as he posed with his arm around his heartbreakingly young bride. She beamed at him with a radiant expression, her beauty augmented by an innocence the camera was happy to display.

Jackie's blood chilled all the way to the marrow of her bones. The shaking started somewhere inside and spread until she trembled so hard it was difficult to stand up. "Where did this come from?"

"On the wall next to the mirror."

Words were so hard to form with the tiny voice inside her head screaming in terror. "This isn't mine."

"You didn't hang it there?"

"I've never seen it before." She was cold. So cold her teeth chattered.

J.D. set the offending picture on the dresser and led her over to the chair. "Sit down." Her body collapsed like so much wet pasta. J.D. dropped to one knee beside the chair. "You didn't hang that picture on the wall?"

"No! God, no. There was a seascape there." She heard the explanation tumbling from her lips and shuddered. Who cared about the seascape? She didn't. Oh, God, Larry had been here. Right here in her bedroom. Now she had proof.

"I'm going to call Thompkins." J.D. rose.

"But he said no one got inside."

"Obviously, he was wrong. Someone switched the seascape for your wedding picture."

"That's not my wedding picture!"

J.D. frowned. He turned back to the obscenity, lifting it from the dresser to study the people. Jackie could almost hear his thoughts.

"This isn't your wedding picture?"

"No!"

"Then when was it taken?"

"How would I know?" She could hear the shrill rise in her voice and was helpless to control it. "I told you, I never saw that thing before."

Chapter Nine

J.D. stared from her to the picture and back again. "Are you saying this woman isn't you?"

Jackie fought against the tears determined to push past her eyes and run unchecked down her face. She would not cry. But oh, God, the woman in the picture looked just like her.

"You said you don't have a younger sister, right?"

Jackie shook her head, unable to speak.

"A cousin who looks like you?"

She pushed a single word past the barricade of horror lodged in her throat. "No."

"How old were you when you married him?"

Despair washed through her. "Twenty-two."

He studied the picture again. "Do you know who this woman is?"

"I've never seen her before in my life." A tear slipped past her guard and trickled down her face. She brushed at it angrily.

J.D. crossed the room, lifted the telephone by her bed and punched in some numbers. "This is J.D. Frost. I'm at 2137 Maple Drive. Officers Thompkins and Barker just left here. I'd like one of them to return. We've found something they should take a look at."

He hung up and turned to her, his face hard and expressionless. "Jackie, you need to take a closer look around. See what else has been disturbed."

"We looked before. I didn't even notice the picture. How could I not have noticed something like that?"

"You weren't looking for anything subtle before. Now we will."

"But, J.D., don't you see? I can't be sure when he changed the picture. It could have been there for days."

"Maybe. Come on. I'll help you—" He paused, turning back to stare down at the nightstand that housed the telephone. Jackie struggled to her feet as he drew an object from the table.

"What is it?"

J.D. extended his palm. The rings were distinctive, of white gold and diamonds with ruby chips on either side of the center stones.

Jackie went numb all over. Finding an inscription would be anticlimactic. She knew J.D. held her wedding rings. Larry liked her to wear rubies. Jackie pulled back when J.D. would have handed them to her.

J.D. replaced them on the nightstand and crossed to the picture on her wall. Jackie stayed put, her stomach rising and plunging with each breath, threatening to disgorge its contents at any moment. She knew what J.D. would see. The woman in the picture would be wearing these rings.

J.D. KEPT A TIGHT REIN on the anger in his chest as Ben Thompkins stared at the picture, looked at Jackie and shook his head. J.D. understood his disbelief. The woman in the picture looked as Jackie must have looked several years ago. Without a magnifying glass, he could only make an educated guess that the rings on the woman's finger were identical to the rings sitting at Jackie's bedside. They appeared to be the same, ruby chips and all. Yet Jackie claimed she wasn't the woman in the picture.

Jackie closed the last of her dresser drawers and lifted lifeless eyes to Thompkins. "Nothing else is out of place."

Thompkins didn't seem surprised. J.D. knew what he was thinking. Would anyone really go to all this trouble just to make her look insane? Particularly an ex-husband she hadn't seen in years?

J.D. clenched his fist. He was no psychologist, but someone around here was crazy.

He stared hard at the picture. There were subtle differences, he decided. The woman in the photograph had much lighter brown hair and her face was insulated by a soft layer of baby fat. Still, any way he looked at the picture, it looked like it was Jackie's face that beamed fatuously up at her groom.

Larry looked straight into the camera while his bride's head angled slightly upward to gaze adoringly at her husband. J.D. grimaced. His gaze shifted to the damning rings on the hand that rested against the black lapel of Larry's jacket. Rings that appeared identical to the ones on Jackie's nightstand.

He peered closer. Wasn't that the heart necklace she'd mentioned Larry giving her? Of course, she'd said he gave it to her after they were married, not before.

"We can try dusting for prints, Ms. Neeley, but I seriously doubt we'll get anything at this point since both you and J.D. already handled the frame."

"What about the rings?" J.D. asked.

Thompkins shook his head. "Even if you hadn't picked them up, we couldn't get anything usable from an object like that."

Jackie turned away with a shake of her head. J.D.

watched helplessly. He didn't want to believe she was crazy or a liar, but those damnable rings...

"And you admit these are your wedding rings?" Thompkins asked.

"I think so."

She could hardly deny it when the inscription gave the date and her initials.

"When was the last time you saw them?" Thompkins continued.

"The day I left." Jackie answered without emotion. It was the lack of expression in her voice and on her face that caused J.D. another pang of indecision.

Was she telling the truth?

More than anything, he wanted to believe her.

"The only things I took from our house were my clothing and some personal items that I owned before we were married. I left the rings on the nightstand next to our bed."

J.D.'s glance drifted to the nightstand where he'd discovered the rings. They glittered obscenely.

Had she been playing them for a fool all along? Listening to Thompkins's questions and Jackie's listless answers, J.D. realized she fully expected them to disbelieve her. Shouldn't she be trying to convince them she was telling the truth instead of staring at them with dejection written in every line of her body?

"Walk me downstairs, J.D.?"

"I'll be right back, Jackie." She didn't even look at him.

"Damn it, what's going on here?" J.D. demanded as they stepped onto the porch.

"You know her better than I do."

No. J.D. wasn't sure he knew her, at all. "What does she gain by planting this stuff and lying?"

Thompkins scratched at his jaw. "Your sympathy?"
He scowled.

"Now, don't jump down my throat," Thompkins protested. "Think it through. No one got inside this house today unless Luke handed out one of the new keys."

"No way," J.D. snarled.

"Agreed. And those are good locks, J.D. Not a mark on them."

"I know that, but what if her neighbor actually saw the guy leaving the house instead of trying to get inside?"

"Only the back door's been tampered with. The old house key implies someone attempted to enter through the back door."

J.D. made a disgusted sound low in his throat. "Anyone could have dropped that key at any time."

"Maybe. And maybe she's so besotted by her ex-husband that she hung their wedding picture where she could see it each night and dream about what might have been."

The thought gnawed at him. "That doesn't exactly go with a restraining order," J.D. responded.

Thompkins shrugged. "As a cop, I've seen stranger things."

J.D. rubbed his jaw wearily. "I'd swear her fear is real."

"If she's mentally unbalanced, she doesn't have to fake the fear. I'm no psychiatrist, but there are some disturbingly real things happening here that may be pushing her over some edge. The neighbor did see someone on her porch earlier. It's possible with all the local burglaries, our perp was trying what he thought would be an easy target. He could have read the kid's obituary and decided to take a chance that this house might be empty and easy pickings."

"Do you really believe that?"

Thompkins shifted uncomfortably. "No. Our thief has been real particular lately. This isn't the sort of neighborhood he's been hitting. He's going for the big estates. The expensive-looking places."

And this was a family-oriented neighborhood.

"Her car is missing," J.D. pointed out.

"Unless she moved it herself." Thompkins raised a hand to ward off J.D.'s instant protest. "And she does have a restraining order against her ex-husband. I know. Those are facts. The dead elf and the rest of these things?" He spread his hands. "Truth or fantasy, who can tell? Maybe her ex is playing some sort of mind game with her. If so, the guy's nuts and probably dangerous." His expression hardened in warning. "No telling what he'll do to another man involved with her."

"Or what he'll do to her if there isn't one," J.D. added darkly.

"True. On the other hand, if she isn't playing with a full deck…I'm not discounting what she's said, but a little concrete evidence would be nice. I don't buy this wedding picture appearing out of thin air. A picture that she didn't notice hanging on her wall until you picked it up."

Yeah, that bothered him, too.

"And let's not forget the rings."

As if he could.

"I mean, come on, J.D., they're sitting there like she just forgot to put them back on."

J.D. didn't want to hear his own thoughts expressed so clearly.

"And," Thompkins added, "let's not forget the disappearing, reappearing dead elf or the missing teddy bear with his eyes pulled off—both of which only she ever saw."

"And an unsigned Christmas card," J.D. mumbled.

"What?"

He explained about the Christmas card, and Ben scratched at his jaw. "You say it was mailed here in town?"

"I saw the postmark," he admitted glumly.

Thompkins's expression came close to pity. "Tell me something, J.D., other than the fact that you're a nice guy and she's an attractive woman, why are you hanging around here? Call one of your other women friends. Enjoy an active evening for two—or something."

Thompkins indicated the partially open front door. "Whatever's going on here, the lady inside is pulling your chain."

"And if she's not?"

Grim lines bracketed his mouth. "Watch your back, okay? We'll keep an eye on the house."

"Thanks, Ben."

He watched Thompkins head down the sidewalk before stepping back inside. Jackie stood at the bottom of the staircase. From her stricken expression, he realized that she'd heard every word.

He noted her stiff carriage and the way she wouldn't quite meet his eyes. Embarrassed, he said, "We need to finish packing."

"Go home, J.D."

Her words tightened his stomach. "Look, Jackie, nothing has changed. You—"

"I said go home."

Her voice could frost glass.

"Jackie, Ben's a cop, and cops—"

"Are you going to leave or am I going to—"

"—are trained to be suspicious," he finished weakly.

"—have to have you removed?"

Angry determination lifted her chin and gleamed in the haughty depths of her dark eyes. Two tiny spots of color high on her cheekbones accentuated the stark whiteness of her skin.

"Jackie, don't do this."

Without a word, she spun and swung her way down the hall toward the kitchen. Heart pounding, he followed her after a moment to find her lifting the telephone with a steady hand.

"Put it down. If you really want me to go I'll leave."

She stared at him, regal and in perfect control, her finger poised to push buttons. And in that moment, he wondered again if she hadn't been telling him the truth.

"Go home to your children." Contempt laced her words. "They need you."

Damn. "What about you?"

"I don't need you, at all."

J.D. sat in his car staring at her house for several long minutes, his mind in turmoil. Why did he feel as if he'd just lost something special?

Because he'd made love to her.

The memory of the way she gave herself so sweetly, so completely, was a dull ache in his mind. He'd had relationships with other women, but today had been different. Jackie was different.

Part of him wanted to go back inside and reassure her. The other part told him to be grateful that he was no longer involved in this impossible situation. He started the car, trying to soothe away his guilt.

He wasn't leaving her friendless and alone. She had Bessie and Frank. Yet, he couldn't help feeling he was making a terrible mistake as he drove away.

"Damn." He slammed the heel of his hand against the

steering wheel. Jackie Neeley had thrown his well-ordered life into chaos.

He gripped the steering wheel in frustration. He should go to the office for an hour or so, except he was in no mood to work right now. Instead, he drove home.

The television rumbled in the living room, but there were none of the sounds associated with two active children. J.D. found his aunt asleep in her chair, a talk show keeping her company. Where were the kids?

A sudden thought assailed him. Surely they wouldn't go to the shopping center after his talk with them the other night. His heart rate increased. They must be outside playing. Any minute now they'd spot his car and come bursting through the door.

In the kitchen, he found glasses in the sink and plates with brownie crumbs. He helped himself to one from the cookie jar, aimlessly chewing until he spotted their coats on hooks by the back door. They were home. Tension drained from him and J.D. headed for the staircase.

Whenever the two of them were this quiet, they were usually up to something. He mounted the steps, avoiding the two that had a tendency to creak.

Todd's door gaped open to reveal schoolbooks tossed carelessly and a pile of items scattered across his desk. An empty piggy bank lay discarded on the bed. Behind Heather's partially closed door, came the distinct babble of childish voices.

"Jackie's going to be so surprised," Todd said gleefully. "That came out good, Heather."

"Yeah, but I should have bought the smaller buttons."

"Huh-uh. The smaller ones would've been too small. Besides, I like these green ones better than the black ones."

J.D. heard shuffling sounds, then Heather's voice came clearly. "Oh, no. It doesn't fit in the box. It's too big."

"Here, let me try."

J.D. nudged the door carefully and peered inside. A sewing kit sat on the floor along with a tube of Christmas wrapping paper, a length of ribbon, scissors and tape. The children huddled over a shoe box on the bed. Todd held something yellow that he kept trying to cram inside the battered box.

"Can I help?" J.D. asked.

The two whirled, guilt stamped across both faces. Todd quickly concealed the yellow object behind his back.

"Daddy, what are you doing home?"

"Yeah, Dad," Todd seconded. "Is Jackie with you?"

His heart sank a little at their expectant faces. How was he going to explain about Jackie?

"What are you guys doing?" he temporized.

"Nothing, Dad," Todd was quick to assure him.

Heather knew better. "It's a surprise for Jackie," she told him.

"May I see?"

They exchanged glances. "Okay, but you won't tell Jackie, will you?"

"That all depends," he answered.

"It's a surprise, Dad."

Heather pulled a stuffed yellow teddy bear from her brother's hands and held it out. Cold and sick, he stared at the ludicrous toy. Two bright green buttons had been sewn with an inexpert hand where the eyes should have been. A matching length of green ribbon had been tied awkwardly around the bear's neck in a tiny bow.

"Someone tied a teddy bear to the door of my store yesterday morning... A garish yellow teddy bear... Larry

won one just like it...except...the eyes had been pulled off this one."

"Where is this bear now?"

"I don't know. I can't find it."

Breathing became difficult. J.D. struggled to keep the incipient panic from his voice. He hunkered down at eye level with the kids, striving for control. "Where did you get this, Heather?"

The children fidgeted, looking small and a little scared. Heather flushed guiltily as she cast a look at her brother.

"We didn't steal it, Dad," Todd said quickly. "We just borrowed it."

"Yeah, Dad. When we found it the other day, Jackie said it was her old toy. But I could tell she was upset because somebody pulled the eyes off and ruined the ribbon."

"Yeah. And she said she was gonna throw it out," Todd put in. "But she looked real funny and she put it in a drawer. We just rescued it, is all."

"We wanted to get Jackie something special for Christmas," Heather cut in, "but we didn't have enough money, so I thought we could fix her bear."

Two anxious faces peered at him, tearing a hole in his heart.

"And we didn't go to the shopping center by ourselves. Aunt Dottie took us to the drugstore to get the buttons. She even gave us the wrapping paper," Todd offered.

"We didn't want Jackie to be sad any more. Is it okay, Dad?" Heather asked timidly.

J.D. reached out and drew the children against his chest, blinking back the moisture that threatened his eyes. He'd never been so proud of his kids.

"You're not mad at us?" Heather asked, her voice muffled against his coat.

"No, sweetheart, I'm not mad." He hugged them tightly then set them back from him and lifted the teddy bear, examining the work Heather had done. "I think Jackie will be very surprised."

Heather beamed with pleasure.

"I picked out the eyes," Todd said proudly.

"But the box is too small. Do you have a bigger box we could use?"

"I'll tell you what—how about if I take you to the mall later on and we'll buy a bigger box to put this in?"

"We don't have much money," Heather warned.

"It'll be my contribution to your gift."

Todd beamed. "Great. Can we go now?"

"No, not right now. There's something I have to do first. I love you guys, you know that?"

"We know, Dad."

"We love you, too," Heather agreed.

He knew Jackie would forgive them for taking the bear. He just wondered if she would forgive him.

"Look, guys, I might not get back home in time tonight to put you to bed. I need to run over to Jackie's and help her with something."

Heather smiled widely. "That's okay, Dad." And he saw her thumbs-up motion to her brother as she turned away.

Were his children playing matchmaker? He couldn't believe it, but excitement glittered in Todd's expression.

Never one to let an opportunity slide past, Todd asked, "Can we order pizza for dinner tonight?"

Distracted by the idea that they accepted Jackie and him as a couple, J.D. nodded absently. "That's fine."

He'd have to sit the children down and explain his relationship with Jackie—but first, he'd have to work it out for himself.

Remembering the way he'd left her, he amended that thought. At the moment, they didn't have a relationship. In fact, he'd be lucky if Jackie would let him back inside her house.

JACKIE COULDN'T EVEN CRY. Her eyes burned with unshed tears when J.D. closed the front door. She stood in the doorway between the kitchen and the dining room and watched him cross the lawn to his car.

She'd expected too much of him. But oh, God, it hurt to watch him leave. She'd wanted him to believe her. Needed him to believe her. Couldn't he have trusted her just a little?

No, of course he couldn't. Once again, Larry had proved his resourceful intelligence. He'd always hidden his madness so that few ever saw past his friendly, clever mask. Hadn't it taken her over a year to realize his fixation on her wasn't love? She'd been a possession, and Larry jealously guarded his possessions.

Jackie entered the dining room, slumping into the nearest chair. She'd never felt so alone in her life.

What should she do? The police weren't going to help. Not without proof. And J.D.... She took a gulping deep breath, willing herself not to cry. J.D. needed to keep his family safe. He could do nothing to help her now.

Bessie? Jackie visualized the basement key hanging from the hook in her kitchen. It didn't matter why Bessie had lied about something so trivial. Bessie had been her friend and confidante for years. And Bessie was distraught over her son's death. She probably—honestly—hadn't noticed the key on the chain with the other two. Jackie couldn't put her at risk. She couldn't put anyone at risk. Larry wanted to torment her, and if he'd killed the elf and left him for her to find, he wouldn't hesitate to hurt someone close to her.

Run.

Jackie closed her eyes. She refused to give in to the building panic. Run where? There was no one to turn to. And how far was she going to get on crutches? They certainly made her invisible and hard to find, she thought with self-mockery.

She opened her eyes, focusing on the Christmas card from Larry—only inches from her fingertips. With a sweep of her arm, she angrily brushed it to the floor. The action disturbed the rest of her mail, which also fluttered to her feet. Brenda's unopened letter landed on top.

Brenda. Childhood friend, matron of honor at Jackie's wedding and mother of her only godchild. Jackie reached for the letter. Brenda had always hated Larry. Brenda hated writing letters. And Brenda was the only person left in Indiana who knew where Jackie lived.

Renewed trepidation made Jackie's hand shake as she ripped open the envelope and removed the short note.

Jackie,
I don't want to scare you, but something happened you should know about. Someone broke into my house, but nothing appeared to be taken. Much later, I discovered two things missing. That's when I got worried. The picture of you and me and Billy (the one Brian took at the christening) is gone. So is my address book. The only thing these items have in common is you. Your new address was in that book. What if Larry is the one who broke in here? I tried to call, but your phone's been disconnected. I've got a bad feeling about this. Call me, okay?

Brenda.

The lines of ink blurred. Jackie let the note fall to the tabletop. She picked up the envelope, proud that her hands were now steady. Brenda had sent this to the apartment over a week ago. Jackie wondered what she would have done if she'd received the warning sooner. Would she have given up her life here and run away?

Isn't that what she contemplated doing right now?

She lifted the letter, skimming the contents again quickly. Her future stretched before her, a series of lonely days and nights as she waited for Larry to find her again. She could not live in fear forever. There was only one way to end this. The police needed proof before they would help her. Somehow, she had to get them something irrefutable. The bear would help, but what she needed was the dead elf.

"Yeah, right," she muttered.

Okay, failing that, she needed to at least show that the elf existed. A connection between Larry and the elf wouldn't hurt, either.

Her gaze darted to the dining-room window as a car turned into her driveway. She was on her feet, heart lunging against her chest, when the heavy footsteps reached the porch.

In the early dusk, his features were hard to discern, but Jackie recognized J.D. at once. She entered the hall, even before he began pounding on her front door.

"Jackie!"

She opened the door wide enough to stare at him and shiver at the blast of icy air. "What are you doing here, J.D.? I told you to go home."

He laid his palm along the door. Now she wouldn't be able to close it unless he let her.

"I did. I'm back."

"Why?"

He started to answer and stopped. His solemn expression slowly changed, replaced by something very different. Something subtle and inexplicable.

"You forgot to wash my knees."

He pressed gently on the door, forcing her back a step. "What?"

J.D. stepped inside. There was something mildly intimidating in the way he stood there, filling her hall. He was such a large man. So tall and overwhelming.

"I don't do one-night stands, Jackie," he said mildly. "Or I guess in our case I should have said one-afternoon stands. And I don't walk away from someone I care about—even when she throws a temper tantrum."

He stepped closer. Jackie backed up, bumping into the hall table. She shivered, telling herself it was from the cold air drifting in through the open door. Quickly, she straightened and gave him her best glare. Shaking the hand that still clutched Brenda's letter, she said, "I did not throw a temper tantrum."

"Could have fooled me."

Baffled by his presence and the gentle teasing in his tone, Jackie shook her head. "What are you doing here, J.D.?"

"If you're done being mad at me, I came to take you home."

"I am not going to your house. I'm going to a motel."

He tipped his head as if considering that. "Not a bad idea, actually. If we rent a room, I won't have to worry about the kids catching me in your bed in the morning."

Flabbergasted, she gaped at him. "Why, you arrogant—"

She dodged the finger he would have pressed against her lips, but saw the laughter in his eyes. That only confused her further.

"You rile faster than Aunt Dottie when someone interrupts one of her soaps."

Jackie knocked his hand away, feeling horribly off center and unsure of herself. "I don't understand you."

The amusement faded instantly. "I know. I shouldn't tease you, but sometimes it's hard to resist."

He shut the door, giving her a moment to regroup.

"Larry is obviously dangerous, Jackie. We need to find some hard evidence the police can use. Right now, we're fighting shadows."

"We?"

"Yeah, you know, like in you and me—together."

The image that evoked didn't belong in her mind.

"What do you have there?" he asked.

Brenda's letter was still in her hand, but she couldn't focus on that. J.D. was lobbing too many curves her way. "You didn't believe me."

"You didn't give me much of a chance. Are you confused right now?"

"Yes!"

"Good. Then you know exactly how I felt seeing those damn rings sitting next to your bed after we made love. Confused, angry, upset."

She hadn't thought about the situation from his perspective. The horror had cloaked itself around her from the moment she saw that picture. It must have been twice as hard for him. After all, he didn't know the woman wasn't her.

"Ben's a cop. He needs proof, Jackie."

His serious expression soothed something fragile and broken inside her. "And what do you need, J.D.?"

"To help you find that proof."

"What if I really am crazy?"

His grin came slowly, but it widened to reveal the hidden dimples. "You are at times irritating, sexy, maddening and stubborn. But you are not crazy."

As her heart took wing, fluttering madly about her chest, he reached out and took the letter from her fingers. "May I?"

She watched him scan the contents quickly, waiting for his reaction. "So that's how he found you initially. Come on. Let's get your things together and get out of here. This place isn't safe any more—even with the new locks."

"J.D., I told you. I can't go back to your house. We have to protect the children. He's dangerous."

Grim again, J.D. nodded. "I know. Let's do like you planned. We'll rent a hotel room for the night. It's time we start taking the offensive."

Thoughts of the two of them in a hotel room were pushed aside by his second remark. "How?"

"While you pack a bag, I'll look up Teller Photography. With a little luck, maybe we can track down one of Santa's elves before he causes any more mischief."

Chapter Ten

Outside, the wind began to sweep harshly through the branches of the large maple tree. Jackie finished packing while J.D. located Teller Photography in the phone book. They had an address off Main Street.

J.D. replaced the phone book and a finger of apprehension traced its way up his spine. The windows rattled noisily as the wind gusted. He hoped it didn't storm again.

"All set?" he asked as Jackie entered the kitchen.

"Yes." Her gaze whipped to the window. "Listen to that wind."

J.D. quickly moved forward to rest his hand on her arm. "It'll be okay. I promise. Let me run up and get your bag."

She stared at him for a second and then relaxed. "I need to stop by the store for a minute."

"No problem. I'll be right back." The upstairs hall had a dark, almost sinister feel. Spooky damn house. Jackie didn't belong here. He didn't like this place one bit.

He lifted the case from her bed and his gaze drifted to the nightstand. The rings still sat where he'd seen them last, an uneasy reminder of all the weirdness that surrounded Jackie.

He knew it was irrational, but he hated those rings and

what they represented. Still, he reasoned more cheerfully, if they'd held any meaning at all for her, Jackie wouldn't have left them sitting on the nightstand like a discarded tissue.

She'd been telling the truth. All of it. Seeing the bear had convinced him. Of course, Ben would be the first to tell him that Jackie could easily have plucked the eyes off the teddy bear herself, but J.D. shook his head ruefully. Some things you just have to take on faith.

Jackie stood at the bottom of the stairs.

"Wait here while I put this in the trunk and I'll come back and help you down the steps outside."

"I'm not helpless, J.D."

He smiled, thinking she was the least helpless female he knew. "Believe me, I know. But humor me, okay? Aunt Dottie takes me to task unless I'm a perfect gentleman."

Clouds gathered overhead, pushed by the icy breeze. Sleet or snow again. He could almost feel it in the pregnant air.

At the shopping center, a parking place stood vacant in front of the store, almost where he'd parked the night he first met her. A fat raindrop splattered against his windshield as he turned off the engine.

Wind lashed the cold, stinging rain against his cheek as he helped Jackie from the car. His gaze swept the busy lot, abruptly landing on something that immediately caught his attention.

A lone figure stood at the tree line near the road. His utter stillness drew J.D.'s attention. A hunter, waiting for prey. And from that vantage point, the person had a clear view of the brightly lit shop at J.D.'s back.

Hadn't Jackie mentioned a watcher?

Adrenaline kick-started his heart. The person could be

there for any number of reasons—all of them innocent. But there was something ominous, almost threatening in the quiet way this person stood.

"Is something wrong?" Jackie asked.

He quickly lowered his eyes to stare at the back of his car. There was no sense spooking her. "Yeah. The car felt funny. I need to take a look at the back tire. Why don't you go on inside while I make sure I didn't pick up a nail or something."

"There's a gas station across the street."

"Convenient, if I need them. Go ahead and talk to Angel. I'll be right in."

"Okay."

J.D. waited until she entered the shop, then he started across the parking lot. Immediately, the figure turned and disappeared behind one of the trees. J.D. began to run.

A car horn blared on his right. He jumped and slid in a puddle, almost falling. He'd run right in front of the oncoming car. If the driver hadn't been paying attention, he'd be making a puddle of a whole different sort on the asphalt.

J.D. waved an apology and kept going more attentively. He couldn't see the watcher any more. By the time he reached the tree line, J.D. knew he'd wasted his time.

Parked cars lined the street, but all of them appeared as empty as the sidewalk in both directions. The person could have headed left into the housing complex or right onto the main street.

At the corner, a bus stopped for a cluster of people. The watcher might have been waiting in the shelter of the trees for the bus to come. He could be any of the wet huddled figures boarding at this moment. Or he might have been waiting for a ride that picked him up.

Or maybe he'd been watching Jackie and was hiding somewhere nearby right this minute.

Wet, cold and frustrated, J.D. trudged back to the store. Jackie was nowhere to be seen. Angel manned the counter, chatting with two young men as she handed them their order. She smiled in recognition when J.D. approached.

"Jackie's tearing her office apart looking for something," Angel said.

J.D. stepped back to let the two customers pass. "Angel, have you noticed anyone hanging around outside, watching the store?"

Her smile faltered. "No. Why?"

"Look, I don't want to spook you, but someone was standing by the trees when we pulled up. It may have been coincidence, but when I headed in that direction the person took off."

"Really? No wonder Jackie insisted I have Juan come over to keep me company."

As though summoned, the bell over the door rang and a young Hispanic youth sauntered in. Broad shouldered and muscular, he assessed J.D. before smiling possessively at Angel.

"Juan, this is J.D., he's a friend of Jackie's."

Some of the posturing went out of the youth.

"Hey, man," he greeted.

"J.D. said someone was lurking in the trees across the way when he pulled up."

Instantly, Juan bristled. "No foolin'? Where?"

J.D. explained, adding, "Look, it was probably just someone waiting for a ride, but Jackie has an ex-husband who may be dangerous."

"She told me," Angel said. "No wonder she's been so tense and nervous lately. That's not like her, at all."

"No?" J.D. asked.

"Oh, no. She's always relaxed and friendly. She kinda keeps people at a distance, if you know what I mean, but she's great once you get to know her. And she really loves your kids. She always plans little chores for them to help with and stuff. Sometimes I think she's a little lonely, you know?"

No, but he wanted to know everything he could about Jackie Neeley. Angel's words confirmed his own first impression of a carefully controlled person—not someone given to hysteria and wild tales. Not someone who would see imaginary dead elves on her bed.

"Uh, let's not mention the watcher to Jackie," he suggested. "She's had a rough couple of days and I could have been mistaken."

"Sure. Okay. She does seem pretty uptight tonight."

"Who seems uptight?"

Jackie came around the corner from the back of the store. Stress had etched tired lines in her face. He was doing the right thing not telling her about the watcher.

"Hi, Juan." She turned to J.D. "Is the tire okay?"

"Yeah. It's fine. Must have been my imagination. Are you all set?"

"Just about. Angel, I really think we ought to close early. It's already starting to sleet out there and I don't want the two of you driving on slippery roads."

"You're the boss, but I don't mind staying. How about if I give it another hour and close at seven?"

Jackie frowned, looking toward the glass front door. "Okay, but keep an eye on the weather."

"Don't worry, Jackie," Juan said, "I'll take care of Angel."

She smiled. "I'm sure you will."

J.D. took her arm and guided her toward the door before she decided to stay and lock up herself. With a hasty good-night, he hustled her outside, scanning the area carefully while Jackie was getting back in the car. If the watcher still lurked, he was well-hidden.

Sleet now peppered the car as J.D. steered in the direction of Main Street. "We need to come up with an approach to ask questions at the photography studio," J.D. said. "The owner isn't likely to give information to strangers."

"How about if we tell them we want some pictures of your children?" Jackie suggested. "We can tell them we liked the elf who took the Santa picture this year and wondered if he was available."

His grin widened along with his admiration. "Simple and perfect. You're brilliant. That's a great idea."

He saw her shyly pleased smile when they passed under a street lamp. J.D. reached for her hand. After a startled second, she squeezed his fingers and he sensed her relax. Good. Nobody was going to terrorize her again if he could help it.

The photography studio was housed in an old building on a side street around the corner from Seth Bislow's mortgage company. Darkness shrouded the area despite the lighted stores on either side. The nearest street lamp glowed dully, too far away to do much good. Naturally, there were no open parking spaces anywhere.

"I'll pull up near that alley and drop you off. I'm going to have to go back to Main Street to find a place to park." He pulled the car over and went around to help Jackie out. Unfortunately, he'd pulled so close to a fire hydrant that she barely had enough room to open the door.

"Sorry. I didn't see it."

"That's okay, I can manage."

Wind whipped icy rain against their bodies. J.D. shivered, feeling curiously exposed. He sent a quick glance around.

"Go park the car," Jackie said. "I can make it inside without help." She started toward the shop.

J.D. couldn't explain the unease that had him scanning every doorway around them. He waited until she got inside, and then went in search of a parking place. He was thoroughly chilled before he reached the photography shop.

Despite the shabby outside, a comfortable waiting room showcased a series of brilliant photographs on the walls inside. Jackie was alone when he entered, but seconds later a pretty young woman appeared from a back room, a smile lighting her pleasant face.

"I'll be right with you, sir." She turned to Jackie. "Sorry to keep you waiting. I'm short staffed today. May I help you?"

"I hope so. Is the owner around?"

"You're looking at her. I'm Susan Teller."

Her smile remained steady as though prepared for Jackie's surprise. She did look awfully young to be running her own studio. Early twenties, J.D. decided.

"Ms. Teller, I'm Jackie Neeley and this is J.D. Frost. We were wondering about having some pictures taken."

"What sort of pictures?"

"Portraits," J.D. told her. "We were at the mall the other night and I was very impressed by a young man who was doing the Santa pictures."

"Which night was this?"

"Last night, around eight or so."

Susan Teller frowned. "You say it was a young man? That would have been Steve." She seemed surprised that they were interested in him.

"Steve?" Jackie echoed faintly. Her expression grew troubled. Did the name mean something to her?

"Yes, he's one of the temps I hired to fill in at the mall during Christmas."

"Then he doesn't work for you on a regular basis?" J.D. asked.

"No. Until I get better established, I only have a couple of permanent employees. But, I think I can help you. The work on the walls is my own."

"Very nice."

"Steve's last name wouldn't be Pinta, by any chance?" Jackie asked.

J.D. tensed. Susan Teller frowned.

"Uh, yes, as a matter of fact. Do you know him?"

No doubt about it, Jackie was upset and trying to hide the fact. J.D. felt a bit upset himself. Who the hell was Steve Pinta?

"I don't actually know him." Jackie's troubled eyes flashed to J.D., then turned to Susan Teller. "But we did meet once. He was a good friend of my partner's son."

Damn. Another friend of Donnie Lieberman? No wonder Jackie was upset. What the devil was going on here? Donnie Lieberman was dead. His good friend Oggie something-or-other had just been killed. Now some other friend of Donnie's just happened to work for a photographer and dress as an elf?

The telephone on the desk in front of Ms. Teller trilled loudly. "Excuse me a minute," she said.

"Teller Photog— Betty? What do you mean he didn't show?" Her voice raised in vexation. "No, he didn't call in.... I don't believe this! How am I supposed to get my work done if I have to substitute at the mall?"

Jackie stared up at J.D. with a frightened expression.

"No, no, it isn't your problem. Let me call his place…

You did?.... Of course there was no answer. Why am I not surprised? I knew those two were trouble.... Okay, do the best you can and I'll come right away." She tapped a nail against the countertop. "I don't care, Betty. As far as I'm concerned, they're both fired."

J.D. stepped closer to Jackie, laying a reassuring arm across her shoulders. She jumped in reaction and J.D. rubbed her shoulder lightly.

Ms. Teller replaced the phone with a decisive clatter. Her left hand balled in frustration. "Look, I'm sorry, but I can't help you right now," she said. "I've got an emergency and I have to close the shop immediately."

"I understand," Jackie said quickly. "Just tell me one thing. Does Brad Volmer also work for you?"

Was this another of Donnie's friends?

Susan Teller stiffened. "Who are you?"

"My name's Jackie Neeley. My partner and I own Sundae Delights over on Mclarin Street."

Suspicion pinched the photographer's features.

"Steve Pinta and Brad Volmer were friends of my partner's son, Donnie Lieberman," Jackie added hurriedly.

"Wait a minute, wasn't he the kid that got killed in that car crash out on Interstate 70?"

"Yes."

All pretense of friendliness disappeared. "You didn't come here for pictures, did you?"

"Uh, no, not really. You see—"

"Sorry, but I'm going to have to ask you to leave."

Jackie persisted. "It's just that my partner and I are trying to sort through Donnie's belongings, and Brad or Steve may be able to help us."

The woman's expression turned bitter. "I don't discuss my employees. But you can do me a favor. When you find Brad and Steve, let them know I'm really ticked off over their disappearing act, okay? And I want my elf costumes back.''

"When did they disappear?" J.D. asked.

"I'm sorry, but you need to leave."

J.D. released Jackie and stepped forward. "This could be important, Ms. Teller."

"I don't have time for this," she said. "I need to get over to the mall right now. Pinta didn't show up tonight. Volmer pulled the same disappearing act on Monday."

"What do you mean, disappearing act?"

"Just what I said. Gone. Poof. No call. Nothing. He didn't report for work and no one knows where he is. I knew those two were trouble. I should never have hired them. Look, I really have to go."

From her shuttered look, he'd gotten as much as he was going to tonight.

"Thank you, Ms. Teller. Come on, Jackie."

"But..." Jackie swallowed back her protest. "Okay. Thanks for your time."

With a curt nod, Susan Teller followed them to the door, clicking the lock shut behind them and quickly turning the sign to Closed.

Sleet battered the street. J.D. would have sworn the temperature had dropped another several degrees. He turned to see Jackie's excited expression.

"Did you hear what she said? Brad's been missing since Monday. The day I saw the body on the bed! And she wants their elf costumes back!"

"Whoa, don't go jumping to any conclusions."

"What do you mean? Donnie and Oggie are dead and Brad and Steve are missing. Brad has to be the dead elf."

J.D. pulled his coat more tightly around his body as wind ripped at him. "Jackie, if you know them, why didn't you recognize the body?"

"I don't know them. I only met them once, at the funeral, and my attention centered on Bessie, not the mourners. But Bessie used to talk about Donnie's 'gang.' Don't you see, J.D.? We finally have some proof. The elves do exist and two of them are missing. It's enough to take to Thompkins, isn't it?"

His mind was still reeling, trying to sort through the surprising information. "Yeah. We'll tell Ben."

Jackie's crutch skidded on a patch of hidden ice and she nearly fell.

"Hey, easy. You okay?"

"I'm fine."

"Look, I'm parked clear around the corner. Why don't you wait here and let me get the car? The sidewalk is too slippery with you on crutches."

"I'll be fine, J.D." And she slid, dropping the crutch and grabbing for the light pole in an effort to keep from falling.

"Yeah, right." Retrieving the crutch she dropped, J.D. slid as well. "Wait here. Don't move. I'll be right back."

"Good idea."

She offered up a tremulous smile and J.D. found himself grinning back before picking his way carefully down the sidewalk. Now, of course, there were parking spots galore. The street was as empty as a dawn morning. He only hoped the street wasn't as icy as the sidewalks.

JACKIE STOOD WHERE he left her, fighting a building cloud of euphoria. They finally had something to take to the police. The elves not only existed but Brad's disappearance coincided with the body on her bed.

But would the police believe she didn't recognize them? Even now, she only had a dim recollection of meeting the three young men, and that image kept being superimposed by a face badly distorted in death.

Jackie shuddered. The young men, and Donnie, had all been of a size and shape. Tall, lean, dark haired—indistinguishable in her memory. If one of them had had bright blue eyes, she hadn't noticed at the time.

Snowflakes began to flay her bared face. Jackie grimaced and huddled more tightly into her coat. She wished J.D. would hurry. All of a sudden she felt dangerously exposed and vulnerable on the darkened sidewalk. Nothing moved except traffic on Main Street, half a block away, but she couldn't shake her sense of unease.

What did Donnie's friends have to do with her? They couldn't have anything in common with her ex-husband, yet this wasn't a coincidence, either.

One of them could have sent the Christmas card. For certain, at least two of them had been inside her house after Donnie died. But how would they know the significance of a yellow teddy bear or a Chinese menu?

Bessie.

Jackie shook her head at the answer, but her heart pounded quickly. Bessie knew a lot about Jackie's former life. And Bessie had lied about the key to the basement.

"No," she whispered to the falling snowflakes. Bessie was her friend. Besides, Bessie wouldn't have access to her former wedding rings or a picture of Larry.

None of this made any sense.

Jackie stared at the deserted street while the wind tore between the buildings to tug at her clothing. Where was J.D.? Her breath formed a mist, which the wind instantly whisked away. She was freezing.

Running footsteps brought her head back around in time to see a dark figure plunge out of the alley. He ran straight at her. Before she could move, a gloved hand snaked out to yank her purse from her shoulder. A burly body smashed against her left side. Jackie toppled back against the fire hydrant and tripped.

A belated scream wrenched from her throat. She tried to use her crutches to maintain her balance, but the right crutch slipped off the edge of the curb. She fell in slow motion, helpless to stop herself.

She caught a heart-stopping glimpse of a taxi cab barreling down the street. The vehicle suddenly spun sideways as the driver made a desperate effort to stop. Then the pavement rushed up to meet her, knocking the air from her lungs. A loud bang shattered the quiet night. Water exploded, cascading over her with terrible force.

SHE WASN'T DEAD.

It took her stunned mind several seconds to absorb that fact. From somewhere, she found the strength to open her eyes. The force of the geyser blurred her vision. The fire hydrant, she realized. The cab had taken out the fire hydrant instead of her.

"Jackie! Don't move. Can you hear me? Where are you hurt?"

"J.D.?" Jackie struggled to sit up.

"Don't move." He pressed her into stillness against the cold, wet street, unmindful that he was getting soaked himself. "Where are you hurt?"

"I'm not." She realized that was mostly true. "Except maybe my ankle. It's really throbbing."

"Okay. Stay still while I call an ambulance."

"I already had the dispatcher call one," the cabbie announced, running up to them. "How bad is she hurt?"

"I'm not hurt," Jackie told him. She strained against J.D.'s hands, trying to get out of the path of the water. "I don't need an ambulance."

"It wasn't my fault," the driver said. "I tried to stop. She just fell right in front of me."

"I'm fine," she said, trying to reassure both of them. "Just help me up. Where's my other crutch?"

"Don't move until the paramedics get here," J.D. insisted. He cradled her head tenderly, bending over her body to shield her from the water.

"We'll drown," she pointed out, amazed at how shaky her voice sounded.

"I won't let that happen," he promised.

From nowhere, a crowd gathered. Jackie shivered. She lay perpendicular to the cab, scant inches from the front tire. J.D.'s expression looked more bleak than she had ever seen. He closed his eyes, holding her close and rocking her against his chest.

Abruptly two paramedics pushed aside onlookers as a familiar voice told people to step back. Great. Doubting Thompkins had arrived to witness another event-filled moment in her life.

J.D. reluctantly allowed himself to be replaced by the attendants. But the concern in his expression warmed her despite the cold.

"Lie still, ma'am. Where are you hurt?"

"I'm fine," she tried to explain.

She was still trying to convince them in the ambulance minutes later. In truth, Jackie felt weak and numb with cold. She was so grateful for the warmth of the car and the blanket put over her, she decided not to argue any further.

"Where's J.D.?" She'd lost him in the commotion.

"The guy you were with?"

"Yes."

"He's going to follow in his car," the attendant promised. The doors clanged shut and they were off with sirens blaring and a sliding, slipping lurch as the back tires spun in the widening ice slick caused by the fire hydrant.

A hydrant whose existence had saved her life, she reminded herself again.

At the hospital, a familiar intern greeted her with a shake of his head. "Back again?"

"Not by choice," she muttered.

Dressed in a ridiculous hospital gown, she answered medical questions, interspersed by questions from a young police officer she'd never seen before. Reluctantly, she submitted to poking and prodding and another session with the X-ray machine, but only because her ankle throbbed like mad.

Her patience, however, fled once she finally warmed up and knew that the ankle was still just sprained. "I'm fine," she told everyone who would listen. "I want to talk to J.D."

When the curtain parted once more, annoyance sent words tumbling past her lips even before her eyes lifted to the newest visitor. "I want my clothes right now."

Thompkins raised both hands defensively. "I didn't take them."

Embarrassed, she dropped her pointing finger to her lap. "I thought you were the nurse," she mumbled.

"Not even on my good days," he assured her.

Jackie realized Thompkins wasn't in uniform. His heavy winter coat was dark, but definitely not police issue. He also wasn't alone.

J.D. came forward, his intense gaze raking her from top to bottom. Not for the first time, she was reminded of a predator, despite his current, rumpled condition. His outer clothing was sopping wet. Bristles shadowed his jaw and his hair had that finger-combed look again. Yet, he still managed to appear dark and disturbingly sexy.

"You sure you're okay?" he demanded huskily.

"Fine. I've even got the tests to prove it." But his obvious concern soothed something ragged in her chest.

"You scared the hell out of me." And he kissed her full on the mouth right there in front of Thompkins.

"J.D.!"

"Don't ever scare me like that again!"

"It wasn't my fault! I was attacked."

"I know." His expression shuttered, that bleak look returning. "It was my fault. I should never have left you there. I thought I'd die when I saw him push you in front of that cab."

The intensity behind his words had her reaching for his hand. "No. It wasn't your fault. I was just in the wrong place at the right time. It could have happened to anyone."

"You do lead an exciting life, Ms. Neeley," Thompkins interrupted. "Want to tell me what happened?"

"I already told you," J.D. said. He never took his eyes from her face.

"And I already talked to another officer," Jackie pointed out. "Besides, what's the point? You don't believe a word I tell you, anyhow."

"Jackie..." J.D. squeezed her fingers warningly.

"Be quiet, J.D." Thompkins said sternly. "Please, Ms. Neeley. Humor me. Take your time and tell me in your own words exactly what happened."

Jackie lifted her chin and sent him a glare. "I was waiting for J.D., when someone ran out of the alley behind me. He tore my purse from my shoulder and knocked me into the street."

"Can you describe him?"

"Sure. He was big and he wore something dark that

covered his face. That's all I saw. The streetlight was out, and the wind was blowing snow in my face."

Thompkins rubbed at his jaw. "Okay. Can you describe your purse?"

"Down to the tissue inside," she assured him and proceeded to do just that.

"I suppose those keys you just mentioned included your new house keys?" Thompkins said.

She glared at him. "All my keys were in my purse." She spared a wry glance at J.D. "J.D. thought it was dangerous for me to leave them on the table in my hall."

He winced, but didn't release her hand. How could he look so incredibly sexy to her? And why was she even thinking about sex right now?

"Ms. Neeley—"

"Look, I'm tired and I'm hungry. I've been assaulted, flash frozen and examined. I have no desire to sit here all night in this dinky gown answering any more questions. I've told you what happened. The cab driver is blameless. If anything, he should get a medal. I still don't see how he missed me."

"Me either," J.D. muttered.

"No charges will be filed," Thompkins promised. "I'm just doing my job, Ms. Neeley."

"Well in case J.D. didn't fill you in, let me give you something interesting to think about tonight. We spoke to the woman who owns Teller Photography. It seems she's missing a couple of elves."

Thompkins gave J.D. a sharp look. "What do you mean she's missing some elves?" he demanded.

J.D. released her then. Feeling righteously smug over what they had learned, Jackie explained. "One of her elves disappeared sometime after work on Sunday. Another one failed to show up tonight. Both young. Both male. And both just happen to be friends of Donnie Lieberman and Oggie Korbel.''

Thompkins's surprise was all she could have hoped for and more.

"Oggie Korbel was murdered,'' he muttered. He looked at J.D., who nodded.

"I know,'' Jackie agreed. "Now, you may think I'm crazy, but even you will have to pay attention to three dead men, Officer Thompkins.''

"Three?''

"Trust me,'' she said sarcastically. "At least one of those missing elves is dead.''

Chapter Eleven

J.D. almost smiled. His relief was indescribable. Jackie really was okay. In fact, other than a few bruises, Jackie didn't look or act like a victim. Despite what she'd been through, she was giving them hell in a tart, refined manner. He wanted to hug her as Thompkins pursued his questioning. Instead, J.D. slipped out of the cubicle and cornered the doctor.

"Okay to take Ms. Neeley home?"

"Sure. We were just waiting for you guys to finish with your questions."

The doctor obviously believed J.D. was with the police since he'd trailed behind Thompkins from the moment they entered the hospital. J.D. thanked him and went out to move his car to the curb. Nothing had ever scared him as badly as seeing Jackie fall in front of that taxi and knowing there wasn't a thing he could do to save her. He still couldn't believe she was all right.

Thompkins came through the pneumatic doors before J.D. could reenter the hospital.

"They're releasing her. Don't let her go back to the house."

"Not a chance," he agreed.

"Why didn't you tell me about the elves?"

J.D. shrugged. "I forgot." It was the truth. He hadn't been able to think of a thing beyond Jackie's safety.

Ben rubbed at his jaw, his expression troubled. "I don't like this. Her mugging is too coincidental."

Thompkins wasn't doubting any more.

"You think it had something to do with our visit to the photographer?"

"Frankly, I don't know what the hell to think. Just be real careful until we find out what's going on, J.D."

"Can I assume you're going to the mall?"

"Yeah. They'll be closing in a few minutes. I want to have a chat with Ms. Teller before she leaves."

"You'll let me know what she says?"

Thompkins frowned, but nodded. "Yeah."

J.D. grabbed Jackie's case from the trunk of the car, thankful he'd put an entire change of clean clothing inside his gym bag only yesterday. He'd already changed his own wet jacket for a spare sweat jacket.

He heard her before he parted the curtains.

"You must have a clothes dryer somewhere in the hospital," she complained. "I can't leave here in sopping wet clothing."

J.D. entered the cubicle, smiled sympathetically at a nurse who held a sodden bundle of clothing, then handed Jackie her bag.

"Here you go. I have the car waiting at the door, so you won't need a coat. Yours wouldn't do you much good anyhow. The buttons are gone and the shoulder tore out of it completely." He took the wet bundle from the nurse and allowed her to precede him into the hall, ignoring Jackie's protests.

The nurse offered him a warm smile. "You've got your hands full with that one."

J.D. grinned back. "Yeah. I do, don't I?" He felt good. Wonderful. Jackie was going to be fine.

He hummed tunelessly, in relief, as he put her wet belongings in the trunk of his car and cleared the windshield of new snow. She had come close to dying tonight. The horror still hadn't left him.

He used the car phone to call home and check on the kids, noticing for the first time the way snow blanketed the grassy areas and had begun to cling to the asphalt, as well.

"I know it's a school night, but the kids aren't here, J.D.," his aunt informed him. "Joan Honnrue invited them to spend the night. They're predicting several inches of snow tonight and the schools already announced delayed openings for tomorrow."

J.D. studied the swirling snowfall. If his children were at the neighbor's down the street, his responsibilities for the rest of the evening were nonexistent. "That's fine, Aunt Dottie. Do you think you can stand the peace and quiet all night?"

"I'll manage," his aunt said with a chuckle. "You just go tend to your love life. I like that girl," she told him. "Jackie has spunk."

Was his entire family playing matchmaker? He looked up and saw Jackie heading toward the glass doors. Aunt Dottie didn't know the half of it.

"You're a wonder, Aunt Dottie. See you tomorrow."

He disconnected and climbed out to hold the car door for Jackie.

"I could have called a cab, you know," she stated grumpily when he slipped behind the wheel.

He wanted to laugh in sheer relief, but she probably wouldn't take it the right way. And she was entitled to be grumpy after tonight's events.

"No money, remember?"

"Oh, no! How am I going to pay for my motel room?"

"I have money. And credit cards," he told her.

"I can't let you pay for my room!"

"Okay, I'll pay for my own and we can share."

Jackie stopped fidgeting and stared at him. "What about the kids and Aunt Dottie?"

"The kids are staying the night with the neighbor down the street." And he would send Joan Honnrue a dozen roses in the morning. "I just talked to Aunt Dottie. She's already in bed watching television."

"Oh."

What was she thinking? "Are you still hungry?"

"Yes."

"They have a decent restaurant across the street. I'm buying since I haven't had dinner yet, either."

Her silence hung in the air. "I'm tired, J.D."

"You have to eat," he cajoled.

"Not dressed like this, I don't."

He grinned in relief. It wasn't him she was objecting to. "The hotel probably has room service."

He let the words linger in the silent car. The remembered taste and feel of her teased his libido. Was she also remembering the sweet way she had given herself to him this afternoon? Was she regretting her actions? Or looking forward to a repeat?

"I've been thinking about that attacker, J.D. What if he wasn't some random mugger? I mean, Steve Pinta could have seen us go inside Teller's. Maybe he thinks I'm a threat to him."

"Thompkins is already looking into that possibility."

"Oh." She settled back in her seat, somewhat deflated. "I still don't see how there can be a connection between Donnie and Larry. It doesn't make sense."

The car lost traction as J.D. turned a corner. Snow clung to the roads making driving treacherous.

"It's really coming down out here."

"Yeah. Aunt Dottie says we're going to have several inches before the night's over."

Jackie twisted to face him as he drove past the state police barracks and pulled into the parking lot of a chain motel. He parked the car, turned off the ignition, then reached over and cupped the side of her face with his hand.

"Is this okay?"

"Yes."

At her soft response, he claimed her lips. She trembled beneath him, alive. Blessedly alive. The thought of how close he'd come to losing her made him pull back. "I'm glad you weren't seriously hurt tonight."

"Me, too." Her hand on his upper arm quivered just the tiniest bit. Passion, rather than rejection dominated her expression.

She was so unique. So unbearably special.

"I can get two rooms if you'd rather," he offered.

She drew in a shaky breath and raised her chin. "Seems like a waste of money to me."

J.D. chuckled. He kissed her again, a hot, demanding kiss, gratified when she responded in kind. "Hold that thought," he whispered. He pulled away and opened the car door. The biting wind and snow cooled more than his ardor.

He checked them in, grateful that the clerk seemed too preoccupied by the football game on his small television set to ask any questions about their bedraggled state. Jackie hovered silently.

He imagined she hadn't spent a lot of time in hotels in her life. He'd bet there were a lot of things she hadn't had time or money to do since her disastrous marriage. Including spending a night with a man who wasn't her husband.

Jackie was endearingly nervous as she eyed the king-size bed. J.D. called room service for a meal while she excused herself to use the bathroom and change clothes. He knew better than to fantasize about her changing into some slinky, seductive outfit. After all, he'd seen her wardrobe.

He stripped out of his sodden dress pants and pulled his own sweats on.

After setting his wet shoes near the heating unit and hanging his socks and wet pants to dry, J.D. prowled the room listening to her hair dryer. Finally, he flipped on the television to catch the last part of the nightly news.

The food arrived before Jackie came out. J.D. realized he was the nervous one now as he arranged their dinner and poured them each a glass of wine. He wished the motel had had a flower shop.

When she stepped into the room, J.D. flicked off the sports. She'd brushed her hair until it gleamed in the soft light, pulling it away from her face with a small clip. Despite the bruised look beneath her eyes and the wary way she surveyed the room, she carried herself with an aura of grace and dignity.

When had he fallen in love with her?

"Good, the food came. I'm starving," she said.

"Me, too. Dig in. I'm ready to eat yours and mine and call for seconds. I hope you like Chablis."

"I don't know. I don't drink much."

"It'll help you relax."

Jackie peered at him from beneath a fall of hair. "Do I need to relax?"

"After that fall you took," he said lightly, "I think so."

She hesitated, then lifted her fork. They ate in a strangely companionable silence, looking out over the parking lot and the falling snow.

"I'm not sure this is a good idea, J.D.," Jackie said in a quiet tone.

He swallowed and cocked his head to one side, deciding to keep his tone light. "What isn't?"

"You and me."

He studied her face and saw years of self-abasement reflected there. "Then nothing will happen, Jackie. We'll finish eating, watch a movie on television and go to sleep. Married couples do it all the time."

"We aren't married."

"For tonight, we're whatever we want to be. If you're tired, we'll sleep. No pressure and no demands." He wanted to destroy the apprehension lurking in her eyes.

Apparently, it worked. She took several more bites before slanting a glance in his direction.

"And if I want to make demands?"

He almost laughed at the mercurial flux of her mood. "Oh, I'll suffer through somehow."

"You're a tease, Mr. Frost."

"Thank you."

"No," she said, suddenly serious again. "Thank you."

"For what?"

"For caring. For just being you."

J.D. set down his glass, no longer interested in food or the wine. "You've intrigued me from the moment we met over that ice pick in your store. Every time you sent me away, I found myself looking for reasons to come back."

"You aren't just feeling sorry for me?"

J.D. leaned closer, brushing her knee with his own. Jackie's lips parted, but she didn't draw her leg away.

"I might feel sorry for Ben Thompkins or the nurses and doctors you were taking to task, but not for you. You're the strongest person I know." He covered her hand with his own, feeling her tremble.

Jackie pushed her plate aside. "I'm not strong."

He slid his hand along the material covering her arm. "Oh yeah, in every way that counts, you're solid steel." His hand rounded her shoulder, soothing the delicate tremors. "But you're also sexy as hell." He pushed back a fall of hair that had worked its way loose from the clip. "Very sexy." And he leaned forward until he could kiss the side of her neck. Jackie quivered in reaction.

"Sensitive."

"I..."

His lips covered hers, tasting the flavor of the wine in her sigh of pleasure. "Tempting."

THE REALITY OF HIS KISS created a tide of yearning so strong she quaked from the force of the emotion. The taste of man and wine made a heady combination.

Her arms sought his neck, drawing them closer together as the strange mix of emotions spread to aching womanly places. She wanted him.

Jackie squeaked in surprise when J.D. lifted her without warning and carried her to the bed. He dropped her gently with a wicked grin and lay back against a pillow alongside her, hands cradled behind his head. "Take me, I'm yours."

Delighted by his playfulness, she leaned over him and tentatively ran her fingers across the hard planes of his chest. His muscles contracted beneath his dress shirt and the amused expression in his eyes suddenly sobered as she tentatively toyed with a button.

"Are you going to undo that or just tease me to death?"

Now, anticipation gleamed in his eyes. She released the button from its hole, suddenly anxious to bare his chest and touch the tempting flesh beneath. Fascinated, she ran her hands lightly over his exposed skin, pausing briefly when her finger crossed his nipple and his body reacted.

Excitement tingled in every pore. Jackie inhaled his scent. Her tongue flicked over his flat nipple and his chest rose as she sucked gently on the tiny nub.

He tenderly pushed her aside, his expression smoky with passion. "My turn."

He raised the hem of her sweatshirt and she remembered she wasn't wearing a bra. Then she forgot everything as his mouth closed over one exposed nipple and suckled.

Self-restraint shattered. Jackie cried out in sheer joy.

J.D. withdrew the clip holding back her hair. His hands cupped her scalp, massaging and pausing to rub strands of her hair between his fingers.

"So soft," he murmured.

She shook her hair so the mass fell free, and bent to trace butterfly kisses down his chest. His indrawn breath pleased her. She fumbled with the drawstring of his sweatpants. J.D.'s fingers eased hers aside to loosen the knot her fingers had made.

Daringly, she slid her finger just inside, touching the crisp whorls of hair hidden from view. He looked at her with such love, her heart contracted. She laid her other hand along the pronounced bulge beneath the fabric.

"You're playing with fire," he warned teasingly.

"Is that what you call this?"

"Can't you feel the heat?"

Oh yes, she could feel him all right. She stroked his length, watching him twitch beneath her ministrations. A heady sense of power nearly overwhelmed her. He made no effort to stop her fingers as she inched the sweatpants down with one hand, while the other stroked his velvety soft skin.

"Jackie."

Her name came out a gasp, somewhere between a plea and a moan. She lowered her head then, her mouth closing over the pulsating shaft right through the soft material.

"Hell," he muttered, coming halfway to a sitting position. He pushed her down beside him, capturing her mouth with greedy lips. He stripped away her baggy pants, careful not to reinjure her ankle. Then his mouth closed over the nearest breast, drawing the air from her lungs. His other hand plucked her free nipple until her back bowed. She couldn't stop a moan of sensual pleasure. Her body was on fire.

He drew her against his chest. Her nipples tightened when they brushed his skin, electrifying her with unexpected sensations.

He palmed her stomach, which quivered in reaction. Then, his hand moved lower, brushing the curls at the apex of her thighs.

"Oh!" His gentle touch was indescribable.

"I like the tiny sounds you make," he told her. His hand continued to rest there, and Jackie squirmed in anticipation. Nothing had ever felt like this.

Jackie pulled his face closer, trying to convey her emotions in the silent kisses she placed against his jaw and down his throat. Her hands skimmed down his arms and shoulders, delighting in the feel of him.

She reached his waist and realized he still wore his sweatpants.

"Roll over," she commanded.

A smile lurked at the corner of his lips. "If you tell me to fetch I'm going to be very disappointed." But he rolled over, taking her with him.

Determined to repay the pleasure he had given her, she tugged his pants and shorts over his hips, setting him free and planting feathery kisses along his strong thigh, amazed when he seemed to grow larger and harder before her eyes.

He was so utterly male.

Her hair brushed against his erection and he groaned.

"You're killing me," he told her.

He kicked free of his pants and positioned her across him carefully. Slowly, sensually, she slid down over him. She paused, sitting astride him, savoring the feeling. Exquisite agony. Then slowly she tightened her muscles around him.

"Jackie!"

They moved together in an ageless rhythm, building the pleasure until she thought she would die from the unbearable excitement. She reveled in his power and in hers. And when he took her hand and positioned her finger so they both touched the spot where they joined, all thoughts ceased as pleasure cascaded through her. J.D. drove himself to release inside her a moment later.

Jackie collapsed against his sweat-slicked chest, not certain she would ever move again. Sure that she didn't ever want to move.

A long time later, J.D. settled her against his side. He tugged the blanket from beneath them, to cover them instead. Wind rattled past their window.

"Sounds cold," he said.

"Uh-hmm," she agreed around a yawn and nestled closer to his body. Her eyes fluttered closed. She felt his lips brush her hair, but exhaustion pulled her further and further down a long, dark tunnel.

THE SCENT OF COFFEE woke her. Jackie opened one bleary eye to find J.D. perched on the edge of the bed, slowly waving a cup near her nose. The room was alive with brilliant sunlight that streamed through the sheer curtains covering the windows.

"Good morning."

"What time is it?" she muttered.

"Nine-oh-five."

"It can't be!" Jackie sat up quickly, wincing as her body protested. She had some new aches, and a few were in places that made her want to blush. She tugged the covers up, suddenly conscious of J.D. staring appreciatively.

His grin was sexy as sin and twice as naughty. "Here." He offered her a sip from the cup in his hand. J.D., she noticed, was fully dressed in yesterday's rumpled clothing. His hair was damp from a shower and he had even shaved.

"Hope you don't mind. I borrowed one of your pink plastic razors."

"I never even heard you get up," she muttered.

"I know. I'd have let you sleep some more, but room service will be here with breakfast shortly."

"I never sleep this late." Heat suffused her cheeks, when she thought about the reason she had slept so long. "Has it stopped snowing?"

"Yep."

She swung her legs off the bed a bit gingerly, feeling self-conscious in the extreme. As if sensing her discomfort, J.D. walked to the window. "While you get dressed, I'll call home and check on Aunt Dottie and the kids. They canceled school today."

"Oh." Jackie couldn't think of anything to say to that.

J.D. had left Jackie's crutches near the bed, so she crossed the room and pulled clothing at random from the suitcase. His voice stopped her as she started for the bathroom door.

"Has anyone ever told you what a delectable backside you have?"

His teasing sent scalding heat to stain her cheeks.

"Of course, the front side is even better," he added evilly.

Jackie suddenly found a smile on her lips. She threw back her head and tossed her hair from her face. Slowly, she turned her head to peruse him from top to bottom, settling her gaze just below his belt buckle.

"You aren't so bad, either," she said seductively.

J.D.'s startled expression was priceless. Then, his low, guttural laughter spilled forth to follow her into the bathroom. She had never felt more gloriously alive in all her life.

He was watching a local television news station when she reentered the bedroom. He immediately switched it off and smiled at her. Room service had delivered breakfast, including a fresh pot of coffee.

"How is everything at home?"

"The kids and Aunt Dottie are fine. There's several inches of snow outside and the entire neighborhood is out there playing in it."

"Several inches! You're kidding." She moved to the window overlooking the parking lot. Cars were buried under mounds of sparkling snow. "You aren't kidding. They weren't calling for this much snow last night."

"Didn't you know Mother Nature has no respect for weathermen? Come on and eat. I'll even share the paper—as long as I get first dibs on the sports page."

"Naturally."

They grinned at one another and ate in contented silence. Jackie was just finishing her second cup of coffee when the telephone rang, startling her.

J.D. didn't seem surprised. He crossed the room before Jackie could move. "Hello? Good morning to you, too." Light sarcasm laced his tone. His gaze flashed to her, his face suddenly serious. "No one does. That was the whole point." He listened for several long seconds, then uttered an expletive and dropped his gaze to the nightstand.

Thompkins. She knew it as surely as if she heard the officer's voice. The coffee turned to bitter acid in her mouth. She replaced the cup in its saucer and waited.

"No. She's in the bathroom," J.D. lied.

Time had caught up with them. Time and reality.

"Yeah. Okay. I'll tell her."

Jackie waited, watching him replace the receiver and knowing she wasn't going to like whatever he had to say.

"That was Thompkins. Sorry, but this morning I told Aunt Dottie it was okay to give him this number. He was annoyed we didn't check in last night. They found your car."

Her stomach clenched around the breakfast she'd just consumed. "And the elf?"

"He was in the trunk, Jackie. Just like you said."

J.D. ARGUED, BUT THE state police insisted Jackie view the body. They did let him go along, and it wasn't a pretty sight.

"Strangled," she whispered. "That explains his distorted expression."

"Jackie, don't."

"I'm okay, J.D. You have to remember, this isn't the first time I've seen him."

His nails bit into his palm, and he forced himself to relax. Jackie stayed remarkably calm during questioning. Her story never once deviated from her original statement. The police admitted the elf was almost certainly Brad Volmer, based on the identification in his pocket.

Volmer had over five hundred dollars in his wallet. Robbery obviously wasn't a motive. J.D. wondered how much cash Oggie Korbel and Donnie Lieberman had been carrying.

"Rather a lot of cash for a kid that age," J.D. pointed out. His thoughts suddenly stretched in a strange new direction. "Look, I know you guys know your job and everything, but I'm just wondering...how sure are you that Donnie Lieberman is dead?"

Jackie's eyes widened in shock. The officer stopped in the act of rising from his chair.

"What makes you ask that, Mr. Frost?"

J.D. shrugged, giving Jackie an apologetic look. "I'm not sure, exactly. Jackie said Lieberman's body was burned beyond recognition. It was supposed to be an accident, but what if it wasn't? Or what if he isn't the one who was killed? You read about this kind of thing all the time."

The officer sat back down.

"We're talking reality here, Mr. Frost, not fiction. Forensics is an exacting science. If they ruled the body belonged to Donnie Lieberman, you can be pretty certain there was compelling evidence to that effect." He paused before adding, "We'll be taking another look into the Lieberman car accident."

"Good. There has to be some sort of connection here."

The officer was noncommittal. "Thank you for your help. We'll be in touch."

J.D. and Jackie walked in silence to J.D.'s car. Unbelievably, they'd spent most of the afternoon with the police.

"Do you really think Donnie might still be alive?" she asked.

"Probably not, but who knows?" He opened the door and helped her inside. "I just want to make sure they take this seriously. Pinta was in your house at least once moving that body. And he did try to burn the place down," J.D. reminded her grimly.

"Unless I knocked that candle over myself when I fell."

J.D. waved that aside. "If he didn't kill Volmer, why move the body?"

"To get it out of the house?"

"Why? Let's say they had a fight, Pinta kills Volmer and you show up unexpectedly. He hides the body in the overhead to cover the crime. Why not just leave it there? Why come back and try to get it out of the house?"

"I don't know, J.D. Maybe he wanted to cover the murder completely by dumping the body where it wouldn't be found."

"Then why leave it in the trunk of your car? And how the hell does this tie in to Zalewoski?"

Fear lurked in her expression. "I don't know. Larry was there. How else do you explain the wedding picture or the rings? Even Bessie couldn't have known what my wedding rings looked like."

Frustrated, J.D. closed the car door and walked around to the driver's side. He still found it amazing that the woman in the wedding picture could look so much like Jackie.

"Well," he said, sliding behind the wheel, "you'll have more new locks for the house after today. Luke's meeting Ben Thompkins over there right now."

"I should be there."

He shot her a stern glare. "You shouldn't be anywhere near that place! Everything centers around that damn house."

"Why?"

He started the engine and shook his head. "I wish to hell I knew."

They drove in silence. The main roads were in good shape this late in the afternoon, but some of the side streets were still impassable.

"Can we stop by the shop, J.D.?" Jackie asked suddenly.

About to protest, he decided she probably needed a distraction. The store would be safe enough in broad daylight.

Inside, Angel contended with an amazing number of customers. Among them, Joan Honnrue sat at a table, surrounded by what appeared to be half the children in their neighborhood.

"Daddy!" Todd launched himself out of his seat and straight into J.D.'s arms. J.D. hugged his son tightly, pleased by the glow on that small, round face. Heather approached with more dignity, but her happiness at seeing Jackie and him together was just as obvious.

"Hi, Dad! Hi, Jackie!"

"Hi, yourself," Jackie greeted. "What have you guys been up to?"

Her face automatically softened as she talked to J.D.'s children. She genuinely listened and in minutes she was surrounded by kids clamoring to describe snow forts and snowball fights.

Joan came to stand beside him, a smile lighting her pleasant features.

"Thanks, Joan. I owe you one."

"Don't worry, I'll collect. Actually, I've hardly seen anything of the kids since this morning. They headed outside to play as soon as school was called off. I walked up here for some milk and everyone insisted on coming along."

"The entire neighborhood?"

"Only half." She grinned back at him.

The bell jingled as the door behind them opened and more people crowded inside. Before he could introduce them, Jackie excused herself to give Angel a hand.

"Looks like everyone in walking distance had the same idea. You would have thought it would be too cold for ice cream, wouldn't you?" Joan asked.

"It's never too cold for ice cream," J.D. assured her. He watched Heather begin to collect empty containers from the table where she'd been sitting. After a minute, Todd joined her. Soon all the kids were picking up their trash and depositing it in the nearest receptacle.

"Amazing. Your Jackie certainly has a good influence on the children around here," Joan said.

His Jackie. J.D. liked the sound of that.

Heather rushed over to him. "I need to help Jackie. The floor needs sweeping and the tables need to be washed. Can we stay? Is it okay?"

He looked from her to the woman behind the counter braced on one crutch, scooping ice cream into a dish.

Had there really been a day when Jackie wasn't part of their lives?

"You'd better get to work," he told her. "Looks like Jackie needs a lot of help."

"Thanks, Dad!" He returned her hug and watched fondly as she set off for the counter.

Joan smiled as she gathered up the other children and their belongings and herded them toward the door.

"Joan, thanks again."

"Any time. I'll talk to you later."

As more people entered the store, J.D. realized Jackie couldn't be safer. No one would approach her with all these people inside.

"Jackie, I'm going to run home for a minute. Will you be okay?" he asked, crowding up to the counter. She never missed a scoop as she glanced in his direction.

"Fine. Go ahead."

"The kids plan to stay and work."

Surprise crossed her features, but J.D. waved and headed for the door.

Dottie looked up from her television show in surprise when he walked in the house a few minutes later. "I've got to shovel the driveway to get my car off the street," he told her. "And Jackie will be spending the night here."

"Good." She said. "I like that girl," she told him again.

"So do I," he replied.

The snow was wet and heavy, so it took him more time than he planned. When he finished, he called his office to check in. He'd left a message earlier to let Carol know he wouldn't be in. Now she reported briskly. Two things had come up, but she'd handled both with her usual competency.

Relieved, J.D. headed upstairs for a quick shower and a change of clothing. Pulling on a sweater, he looked toward the window. The sky grew darker even as he watched. He hadn't meant to leave Jackie alone this long.

J.D. smelled the stew Aunt Dottie had cooking on the

stove before he reached the kitchen. "I'm going to pick up Jackie and the kids. Do you need anything?"

"Nope. Dinner'll be ready in an hour."

"We'll be here."

Full dark descended even as he kissed her wrinkled cheek. According to his watch it was only four-thirty. He hoped that didn't mean another storm rolling in. Although, a storm might make it easier to convince Jackie to spend the night at his place. He couldn't leave Dottie and the kids tonight, and he wasn't about to leave Jackie, either.

He mulled over his best approach as he pulled into the shopping center.

A police car was parked right in front of the store.

Chapter Twelve

Fear tightened his gut. He shouldn't have left her. Not even for a few minutes. The kids were in there. If something had happened...

He drew every eye as he burst inside. Thompkins sat at a table near the door. Angel looked up from behind the counter where she was taking money from a customer. Jackie and the kids were nowhere in sight.

"Heather? Todd?"

Thompkins came out of his seat. "What's the matter?"

"Where are Jackie and the kids?"

"In the office on the computer. What is it? What's wrong?"

Tension drained from him, leaving him feeling foolish. "I saw the police car and thought..."

"Sorry." Ben Thompkins shook his head and slowly sat back down. "I came to give Jackie her new house keys."

Jackie appeared from the office, pleasure softening her face when she spotted him. She came around the counter quickly and crossed to them. J.D. pulled out a chair and waited for her to sit down.

"I'm glad you're both here. I have some information."

J.D. sank onto the nearest chair. "Now what?"

"We just got the report back on Ms. Neeley's ex-husband."

J.D. unbuttoned his coat. "What is it, Ben?"

"Zalewoski's in-laws haven't been able to reach their daughter in a couple of weeks. According to neighbors, he claimed they were leaving on vacation, but no one saw them go."

J.D. tensed.

"They found the wife in the bathroom—beaten to death."

Jackie gasped, her face going deathly white.

"It gets worse," he told them apologetically. "The second wife? She's a dead ringer for Ms. Neeley."

J.D. felt like he'd been sucker punched. "The wedding picture," he muttered.

"Exactly. The picture in Ms. Neeley's bedroom puts Zalewoski right here in town."

"It puts him in her bedroom!"

JACKIE SAT QUIETLY, imagining the young woman in the picture, bloody and dead on a bathroom floor. A woman who could have been her. Her fears and insecurities bubbled to the surface. Then J.D. reached out and captured her hand. His touch imparted more than warmth. Comfort and a strange sense of security came with the gentle squeeze of her fingers.

Only hours ago, she'd made passionate love to this man, discovering a sensuality she'd never suspected. Larry couldn't take that from her. No one could.

A stream of customers entered the store just then. Jackie excused herself to help Angel with the crowd, aware of J.D.'s worried gaze but thankful to have something to take her mind from the horror of this living nightmare. She forced a smile and chatted with customers. Eventually, she saw J.D. walk Thompkins outside.

"Jackie, can you come here a minute?" Heather asked.

The child stood beside the counter looking puzzled but faintly excited. Since there were only two people left in line, Angel immediately waved Jackie off.

"What is it, Heather?"

"Todd found some hidden files on your computer."

"Hidden files?" Jackie followed her back toward the office. "What are they?"

"You know, ones that don't show on the directory."

The children's knowledge amazed her. Just turning on a computer intimidated Jackie. "Why would anyone want a file that doesn't show?" she asked.

Todd looked up, his face glowing with excitement. "It's sort of a game," he explained. "No one can see your files, but you can call them up as long as you know what you called them. Only, these files are dumb. Mostly just numbers and stuff, see?"

He hopped out of the desk chair so she could sit behind the terminal. On the screen was a file with a series of numbers and letters.

"L(3)107R(2)64L(1)4RtoS. What does that mean?"

"Beats me." The small shoulders shrugged expressively.

Jackie frowned. "Is that all there is?"

"Yeah, in that file. But there's a whole list in this other one."

Todd reached around her and tapped away at the keyboard, disclosing another file. Jackie scanned the entries. Obviously, an inventory of some sort. Most items were abbreviated, but words like CD and TV appeared several times, along with numbers. Periodically, initials and dates interrupted the list. The dates, if that's what they were, all fell within the past four months. The exact length of time the thieves had been striking.

"Show me how you found this," Jackie requested trying to keep her voice calm.

Todd obliged, chatting away as he went through the steps, almost too quickly for her to follow.

"That's impressive, Todd. How did you learn this?"

"Jerry showed me."

"He's our friend Billy's older brother," Heather explained.

"Is there anything else hidden?" Jackie asked.

"Just some—"

Angel burst into the office. "Jackie! Someone's in the parking lot shooting a gun!"

Heather and Todd leaped to their feet. So did Jackie. "No! Sit down! Both of you!"

The children halted.

"Angel, get in here and close the door!"

"But—" Todd began.

Jackie stared hard at him. "Listen to me. You stay right here. Do not go near that door."

"But Dad's out there," Heather protested, wide-eyed with fright.

"And he'll skin you alive if you move from this room." Panic gripped her, but she had to protect them. "Angel, call the police. Heather, lock this door behind me."

"How come we can't come, too?" Todd demanded as fear warred with excitement on his small face.

Jackie fell back on the quickest reason she could think of. "Because I'm the boss," she told them sternly. "Don't step one foot out of this room until I tell you it's safe."

Maybe they'd be safe if Larry didn't see them.

A quick glance showed the shop was empty. Jackie

limped to the back room to check that the rear door was secured. J.D. and Ben Thompkins were out front in the parking lot. Assuming Larry got past them, he'd have to come in through the front door.

As she came around the counter, a tall, dark figure filled the front entrance. Instinctively, she grabbed for the ice pick.

J.D. stepped inside and Jackie's heart stopped trying to climb out her throat. The ice pick clattered back on the counter. He strode swiftly up the aisle like the sleek predator he had reminded her of the first time she ever saw him.

"Where are the kids?" he asked.

"I had Angel lock them in the office with her."

"Good thinking."

"Larry?"

J.D. shook his head. "No, love. I was afraid you'd think that. Some idiot tried to hold up a man using the money machine two doors down despite Ben's cruiser parked right out front."

Stunned, she stared at him, her lips parted in shock. "Not Larry?" For just a second, she knew what it meant to go weak-kneed with relief. J.D. reached for her and she pressed herself against him, seeking the comfort of his arms.

"I'm sorry you were scared, Jackie. This was just some punk kid with a handgun that went off and shattered the plate-glass window at the furniture store. The idiot was so shocked he dropped the gun and ran straight toward Ben. It was all over in seconds."

J.D. rubbed her back with his cold hands.

"You're shaking."

She couldn't respond, her relief was so great.

"Come on. We've had enough excitement for one day. Let's get the kids and go home."

She met his eyes. "I can't go home with you."

J.D. tilted his head to one side. "Why not?"

"Because Larry's out there somewhere, and he's already killed once."

J.D.'s look of gentle concern nearly undid her completely. "And the last place he'll look for you is my house. Zalewoski will expect you to go home or to Bessie's or to a hotel. Ben says police are covering your house and mine. You'll be safe with me."

You'll be safe with me.

How was it he could impart such certainty in those words? Was it desperation that made her want to believe him?

"J.D...." Words of protest faltered on her lips.

"It'll be all right, Jackie. I promise." He released her and headed for the office. "Angel, it's J.D. Open the door."

Jackie didn't listen to the excited questions or J.D.'s calm explanations. She was still pondering her options when J.D. helped her on with her coat.

"Angel, would you like me to follow you home?" J.D. offered.

"No, I'll stay. Juan's here." She pointed and Jackie saw Angel's boyfriend standing on the fringes of the crowd gathered outside. "We'll probably do a lot more business after all the excitement dies down."

J.D. nodded. "Okay, if you're sure."

Jackie suddenly snapped out of the stupor that seemed to be holding her. "Excuse me, but I think this is still my shop," she reminded them gently. Angel blinked in surprise. J.D. stared at her.

"I'm not sure your staying here is a good idea," she

told Angel. "I think we should close the store for a few days."

"You can't do that, Jackie. The holiday promotion on those ice-cream cakes starts Sunday. The shipment comes in tomorrow, remember?"

No. She could barely remember her own name at the moment.

"The ads start in the local papers tomorrow. But don't worry. Juan's finals are over. If it's okay, he can stay here with me. I can really use the money, and we'll be careful—I promise."

Jackie hesitated. Was it safe?

"Oh, and Bessie's called here at least four times today. She sounded upset. We were so busy I forgot to tell you earlier."

Bessie.

Friend or foe?

"I'll call her tonight," she promised.

"Are you ready to leave?" J.D. questioned.

Everyone stared at her expectantly. "Yes. I'll call you in the morning," she told Angel. "But don't take any chances and be sure the bolt is on the back door when you leave."

Angel's head bobbed in obvious relief. "No problem. See you tomorrow. Bye, kids."

"Bye, Angel," they chorused.

The children chatted all the way home, excited and disappointed to be so close to a real, live burglary attempt and not see anything. They did, of course, take childish delight in ogling the shattered window of the furniture store as J.D. drove past. And they regaled Aunt Dottie with the tale as soon as they hit the front door.

The comforting hubbub of family life swirled around Jackie all evening, until J.D. insisted the children head for bed. They put up only token resistance, tired after a hard day's play in the snow.

While J.D. supervised bedtime, Jackie said good-night to Aunt Dottie and entered J.D.'s messy office. The phone sat half buried under a pile of papers that she lifted carefully. Bessie answered on the second ring.

"Oh, child, I've been so worried," her friend chided. "Where have you been? The police were here and they told us the most outrageous stories. Why did you disappear like that? I've been worried sick."

Bessie as a foe? How could she have thought Bessie was anything other than the kind, supportive friend she'd always been? Jackie felt ashamed. "I was afraid I might be putting you in jeopardy by staying," she fibbed.

"Good heavens. This building has so much security you couldn't be safer. Where are you? We'll come and get you."

"That's okay, Bessie. I took a hotel room in Frederick."

Now why had she said that? Why hadn't she told her friend the truth?

There was a low-pitched rumble as someone else spoke to Bessie. Frank, Jackie surmised.

"She's in a hotel up in Frederick," Bessie related. "Frank wants to know if you're okay."

"I'm fine. A little scared, but otherwise okay."

"What's that?" Bessie asked another voice at her end. "No. I don't think so." She spoke to Jackie again. "Seth just reminded me to tell you that settlement has been postponed again."

Settlement. Jackie gripped the receiver tightly and twisted around to stare at the computer terminal on the work table behind J.D.'s desk. She couldn't go through with the purchase of the house. Not now. "Bessie, about the settlement," she began.

"Hush. I don't even want you to think about that right now. With that maniac ex-husband of yours on the loose, that house is absolutely the last thing you need to be thinking about. Besides, as Seth pointed out, I'm not so sure you should buy the place, after all."

Relief coursed through her.

"Now you just hush, Frank. We aren't moving to Florida until the spring. We can find another buyer. Jackie, you tell me which hotel you're in and I'll send Frank and Seth to bring you back here."

"Thanks, Bessie, but I'd just as soon stay where I am."

Bessie's immediate silence conveyed her surprise and hurt. Jackie hurried to soothe away the unintentional wound.

"I'm pretty sure Larry has been stalking me," she explained. "If so, he knows about my relationship with you and Frank and that's the first place he'll look for me. I couldn't stand to put you at risk."

"But—"

"The police are guarding me, so I think it's best if I stay here tonight. By the way," she added quickly, "I want to tell you what just happened."

As intended, Bessie was quickly diverted by the tale of the foiled robbery attempt.

"So Angel's going to open the store in the morning," she concluded. "I'll join her to get the stock checked in and the signs up for the sale."

J.D. entered the den, his quiet presence immediately soothing some of the jangled tension knotting the back of her neck.

"Do you think that's wise, Jackie?" Bessie asked. "I mean, Larry can find you if you go to the store."

"Don't worry. I have police protection now."

J.D. came forward and bent to kiss her hair. "And me," he whispered against her hair.

"I know," Bessie protested, "but I worry about you."

"I'll be fine," she promised rashly.

J.D. smiled, a slow, sexy smile that started a tingle down low in her body. "I'll see to it, personally," he murmured.

"I could send Frank over to give you and Angel a hand tomorrow," Bessie offered.

J.D. carelessly pushed aside the stack of papers so he could perch on the edge of the desk. He ran a knuckle lightly down her cheek. Dark promise glinted in his eyes and Jackie struggled against an arousing sense of excitement. What had Bessie just said? Something about Frank coming over?

"Jackie, are you still there?"

Jackie forced her attention back to the telephone. "Yes, I'm sorry, Bessie. I'm so tired I think I'm falling asleep sitting here." She faked a yawn and J.D. gave her his little-boy naughty grin, which exposed both dimples.

"Will you promise to call me tomorrow?" Bessie asked.

"Absolutely."

"If you need anything, anything at all, you just call me, you hear?"

"I will, Bessie. And thanks."

Unable to maintain a conversation with J.D. tracing paths up and down the hand holding the phone, Jackie said a quick good-night and hung up.

"Stop that," she told him.

"Stop what?"

"Touching me."

His smile deepened. "You like it when I touch you."

"Arrogant male. Not when I'm on the phone."

"You aren't on the phone any more," he pointed out. "What did Bessie want?" His hand began to knead her shoulder.

"She invited me to stay with Frank and her."

"Turn around." Before she could ask why, he spun the chair so her back was to him. His strong fingers began to knead the muscles at the back of her neck.

"Oh. That feels wonderful. Where did you learn how to do that?"

"My mother used to get tense when she sewed for long periods of time. She used to say I had magic fingers."

"Ohh, yes. I agree. That's marvelous. Yes, right there. Ohh."

"Have you forgotten what else I can do with these fingers?" he murmured, nipping at her ear.

Jackie stiffened. "J.D., I can't sleep with you tonight." His fingers stilled.

"I wouldn't feel right with your aunt and the children here in the house."

J.D. rotated the chair. "I already made up the spare room," he told her, unperturbed. His eyes sparkled with sudden mischief. "But how do you feel about a quickie on the desk?"

"J.D.!" Desire flooded her. His lips were feathery soft as they captured hers in a kiss of sweet yearning.

Her hands clasped his neck, pulling him closer. "J.D...."

"Is that a yes?" he growled in her ear.

A light tapping at the door caused them to pull apart only seconds before Heather appeared. "Daddy?"

"What are you doing out of bed?" J.D. barked at her. Heather hesitated, then stepped fully into the room.

"There's somebody outside. In the backyard. I saw him from my window."

Jackie's gaze flew across the room to the windows along the wall. Light spilled across patches of glittery snow, except one area which was blocked by the shadow of someone standing outside the window.

"Into the hall," J.D. yelled. He lifted Jackie against his chest and plunged for the door and Heather's retreating shape.

"Where's Todd?" he demanded.

"Asleep." Heather's lips quivered.

"Go to your room," he commanded, setting Jackie on her feet. "And stay away from the windows." He started toward the kitchen, fury radiating from every pore on his body.

"Daddy, don't go out there!"

Jackie pulled Heather's quaking body against her own. "She's right, J.D. What if he breaks in through a window while you're outside?"

J.D. hesitated. Frustration clouded his face.

"I thought the police were watching the house." How had Larry gotten this close? "Maybe it isn't Larry," she added quickly. "Maybe we saw the policeman prowling around."

J.D. shook his head, but fury faded, replaced by thoughtful contemplation. "Upstairs. We're too vulnerable down here."

Jackie couldn't argue with that, but the telephone suddenly rang, making all of them jump. "Wait here," J.D. ordered.

"Hello," he growled. "Yeah. We're fine, but there's someone—" He paused to listen. "Okay."

Jackie shivered. Heather clung to her waist. She stroked the girl's silky hair in mindless comfort, hating the idea that she'd brought fear into the child's life. The house was so quiet she could hear the grandfather clock ticking in the living room.

"Fine. Sing out or we won't open the door. Right." J.D. cradled the phone. "That was an Officer Lannigan. He's outside. Wait here while I let him in."

"J.D., wait! Are you sure?" Jackie tried to keep her voice calm, conscious of Heather clinging to her. "You've never heard Larry's voice."

J.D. stopped in his tracks. "Damn." He hesitated a second. "But I've seen the bastard's face. I won't let him in until I'm sure. Wait here."

Jackie didn't wait. "Is Aunt Dottie asleep?" she asked Heather.

"Uh-huh. I went to her room first."

"Do you think you can go upstairs and wake her? Tell her what's going on?"

"Is it a burglar?" Heather asked in a tiny shaken voice.

"Maybe. Hurry, sweetheart." As Heather scooted up the stairs and J.D. headed for the front door, Jackie hurried toward the kitchen. She found the sharp knives in a rack on the counter and withdrew the largest one as J.D. called out through the closed front door.

"Step back, into the light where I can see your face." She heard him order.

There was a pause, then J.D. opened the front door. A large figure stepped through. Jackie moved to stand in front of the steps, the knife at her side, its wicked blade glinting in the hall light.

"Mr. Frost? I'm Officer Lannigan." Dark brown eyes in a face as dark as the night itself, swept the hall, pinning her where she stood. "Ms. Neeley?"

Jackie trembled with relief. J.D. turned around and saw her for the first time. "What the hell? What did you think you were going to do with that knife?'' he demanded, striding forward and taking it from her limp fingers.

"Whatever I had to," she responded, raising her chin a notch.

"You're both all right?" the officer asked.

"Yes," J.D. answered tersely. "What about Zalewoski?"

"The prowler got away, I'm afraid, sir. I gave chase, but he had a vehicle on the next street over. I got the tag number. He won't get far."

"Then it was Larry?" Jackie asked.

"I couldn't say, ma'am. I never got a good look at the guy."

"J.D.?" Aunt Dottie stood at the head of the staircase, clutching a loose housecoat around her bony frame. Heather peered at them from beside her. "What's going on down there?"

It took almost four hours to get the house quieted back down. Only Todd slept through the commotion. Jackie slid into bed, huddled under the blanket in the spare room and knew she wouldn't sleep a wink.

Morning brought renewed determination and an Officer Smith to replace Officer Lannigan. Officer Smith was svelte, dark haired and exceptionally pretty. She had a tough, no-nonsense attitude that marked her as a policewoman despite the street clothes she wore.

"I don't like this," J.D. told them.

"Larry has to be stopped, J.D."

"Well, why the hell can't the cops find him? We don't have that many motels or hotels in this area. Lannigan even got the license number of his car last night. How difficult can this be?" he demanded of the officer.

"I couldn't say, sir. My job is to protect Ms. Neeley. I assure you, I intend to do just that."

Aunt Dottie bustled into the room, took one look around and hurried for the stove. "I'll fix some breakfast."

"No, thank you, Aunt Dottie. I have to get to the shop," Jackie told her.

"I'm going with you," J.D. announced.

Jackie stood, ignoring the twinge from her ankle when she forgot to use the crutches. "Don't you have a business to run, J.D.?"

"Damn it—"

Heather and Todd appeared in the doorway behind him. "Stop cursing," she told him. "It sets a bad example for the children."

"They're upstairs."

"No, we're not, Daddy, we're right here," Todd announced. "Who're you?"

Jackie sat back down, grateful for their timing. Part of her thrilled to the idea that J.D. cared enough to want to protect her. But facing Larry was something she would have to do sooner or later, and J.D.'s presence in her store might put him at risk.

In the end, a disgruntled J.D. watched her leave with her new escort.

Officer Smith—Freddie, as she asked to be called without a flicker of an eyelash—proved a godsend. Posing as an employee, she pitched in to help. And she wasn't half bad, Jackie decided. The crutches made climbing and lifting impossible, so Angel and Freddie took care of hanging the signs while Jackie checked off the new inventory and caught up on paperwork between customers.

By midafternoon, things quieted down enough for Angel to take a lunch break with Juan. Seeing the two together, brought her thoughts to J.D. Why hadn't he called to check on her? Was he angry? Having second thoughts?

"Jackie? I need to use the rest room," Freddie told her a few minutes later. "I'd prefer it if you'd come back with me and wait in the office for a minute."

That seemed to be carrying the togetherness a bit far, but Jackie nodded. The bell over the door would alert her if anyone entered the shop. She gathered the newspapers and went back to her office.

The computer reminded her of Todd's discovery. She'd forgotten all about it until now. She'd show Freddie the files and see if the officer thought they might be related to the burglaries.

Jackie spread open the paper. The first two ads were in good, prominent spots in the local daily and the Frederick paper. In the third paper, a weekly, the ad was smaller than it should have been and faced the obituary columns.

"Great. Just great." She was frowning over the placement when her eye was snagged by the heading in the first obituary. "Local Businesswoman Dies." Jackie read the headline, but it was the picture that sent waves of pure fear rolling through her.

Jackie dropped the paper, heart pounding. Before she could call out to Freddie, the telephone rang sharply. Trembling, she reached for the instrument. "Sundae Delights," she managed to say.

"Jackie?" J.D.'s growly rumble filled her ear.

"J.D." His name came out on a sigh of relief.

"What is it? What's wrong?"

"The paper. I was checking on the ad for the holiday sale. They put it next to the obituaries."

"Is that all?" His voice sounded amused. "For a minute I thought something was really wrong."

"It is, J.D. Do you have a copy of the paper?"

"No." Caution entered his tone. "What's wrong?"

"The lead obituary. It's mine."

Chapter Thirteen

For a moment there was silence. Jackie heard loud noises coming from the storeroom. What was Freddie doing? Why had she gone back there? Then J.D. said quietly, "Where are you? Where's Officer Smith?"

"I'm in my office. She went to the bathroom, but I can hear her in the storeroom."

"Show her the ad. I'm on my way."

"No. Wait, J.D." But she was talking to an empty line. Jackie hung up, her eyes carefully averted from the newspaper picture. It had been taken without her knowledge right outside the shop.

She tried to stay calm. Fear was her enemy. Larry liked to see the fear. She mustn't give him that pleasure. But reading the words, seeing her picture underneath that heading, she tried to stop shaking and couldn't.

"Freddie?"

There was a muffled sound, but Freddie didn't answer her. Jackie rose, unable to sit a moment longer with that awful article staring up at her. "Freddie? You need to see what I just found."

The bathroom door stood open and empty.

"Freddie?"

She heard no movement now from the storeroom. A new fear pricked her heart. Why hadn't Freddie answered?

The back door!

No, the door was locked. They might not have put the bolt down after the last delivery, but the lock was on. She'd made sure each time the door had been opened, and Freddie had double-checked.

"Freddie?"

This time, she heard a muffled but distinct groan. The lights in the storeroom left no dark corners. They clearly revealed Officer Freddie Smith, crumpled on the floor, her bloody face resting against a crate.

"Freddie!"

Jackie stopped, fighting her instinct to rush forward. She expected to see Larry standing there grinning, but the room was empty. No one had passed her office to get to the storeroom. How had anyone gotten inside?

Freddie groaned.

Jackie pivoted, heading for the telephone.

There was no sound, but the sudden blast of icy air gave her an instant's warning as the freezer door opened. It was enough. She dropped the left crutch even as she spun around, the right crutch raised in both hands as a weapon.

He lunged at her.

Jackie smashed the crutch across his face. There was a distinct crack as his nose broke. Larry yelled. Blood spurted. Jackie ran for the front of the store.

Larry swore viciously as he came after her.

She wouldn't make it around the counter, she realized. A meaty hand closed over her shoulder. Jackie felt her sweatshirt tear. She ducked her head instinctively as he spun her around. His fist bounced off her shoulder. She reeled back against the waist-high freezer.

Jackie drew a deep breath and screamed. Larry yanked her forward and her bad ankle twisted.

"You can't run," he snarled.

His breath was a foul stench against her face. His once handsome face was unshaven and ugly with rage. He shook her until her teeth clacked together.

"Let her go, Zalewoski!"

Though startled, Jackie didn't turn at the sound of J.D.'s voice. Instead, she groped for the ice pick behind her.

Abruptly, Larry shoved her back against the counter, a well-remembered fury gleaming in his eyes.

"If it isn't the lover," Larry sneered. "You just saved me the trouble of coming after you next."

"No! J.D., go get help!" Her fingers closed over the ice pick.

"Yeah, J.D., get some help. You're going to need it."

Murder shone in his eyes. He raised his fist and Jackie stabbed upward with all her strength.

The point plunged through his heavy winter coat and buried itself to the hilt. For a stunned second, neither of them moved. She couldn't tell if she'd hurt him or not. Larry's expression was nothing short of incredulous.

He yanked the ice pick from his coat and twisted to face J.D. who barreled around the counter, hitting him in a tackle that sent all three of them crashing to the floor. The ice pick flew from Larry's hand. Jackie rolled clear as the two men traded blows. She scrambled to her feet, searching for another weapon.

Larry slammed J.D.'s head back against the freezer. He reached for the ice pick and got to his feet.

"J.D.! Look out!"

"Police," Freddie yelled from the doorway. "Drop the weapon." Blood ran down her face, matting her hair.

Most of one eye was closed, yet the gun in her two hands held steady, pointed right at Larry's chest.

Larry twisted to face this new threat. Lurching forward, he raised the ice pick in his meaty fist. The gun exploded in a volley of shots and Larry collapsed against the policewoman.

"THERE'S STILL A LOT of unanswered questions, Ben," J.D. told his friend the next morning.

Thompkins set his coffee cup on the kitchen table and rubbed at the stubble on his unshaven chin. "Yeah. We know. He had keys," Thompkins told him. "We were so fixated on the house we looked right past the obvious."

"Zalewoski was the one who mugged Jackie that night?"

"So it appears. They recovered her purse from his car this morning. Apparently, he'd been living out of the car for several days now. There was a camera and lots of pictures. He'd been stalking her for at least a week. There were pictures of the two of you and even some of your kids."

J.D. felt sick.

"He waited until after the last delivery," Thompkins continued, "and unlocked the back door. Smith was in the bathroom when she remembered they hadn't put the bar down. She wasn't particularly worried since she knew the door was locked. Hell, none of us expected him to attack at the store in broad daylight."

J.D. managed a curse. "I should have thought of the store keys when she said all her keys were in her purse."

"If you think you've cornered the market on self-recrimination, get in line. It was Smith's job to protect her. That oversight nearly cost both their lives."

"How is she doing?"

"Serious, but stable."

"Have they questioned him yet?"

"He's dead, J.D. Six o'clock this morning. He never regained consciousness." Thompkins made a sound of frustration. "Bastard should have died on the spot."

"But he is dead."

Both men whirled at the sound of Jackie's voice. Framed in J.D.'s kitchen doorway, she appeared small and fragile. J.D. stood, but something in the proud lift of her head kept him from rushing across the room.

"About time you got up," he said instead.

Gratitude flashed in Jackie's eyes and J.D. knew he'd made the right decision. She didn't need fussing over. She needed to feel in control again after what had happened.

"Coffee?" he asked.

Jackie nodded and limped to the nearest chair. She hadn't bothered with crutches today, he noticed.

"How are you feeling, Ms. Neeley?" Thompkins asked.

"Bruised. And logy." She gave J.D. a meaningful glare. "Like someone drugged me."

He spread his hands. "Hey, the doctor recommended you take those pills since you wouldn't stay at the hospital last night. They were just mild sleeping pills and they worked. You slept." He picked up the fresh mug of coffee and set it down carefully in front of her.

"Yeah, all night and half the day."

"It's not eleven-thirty yet," he pointed out, trying to tease her a little.

Jackie made a face and turned to Thompkins. "I suppose you're here with more questions."

"No, ma'am, I'm not here officially, at all. This case belongs to the state boys now, though they've been kind enough to keep us local folks updated. I was just passing along the latest information.''

Jackie took in his frayed checkered shirt and jeans and visibly relaxed.

"Well, I have some questions, if you don't," she said.

"Yes, ma'—"

"Do you think you can stop calling me ma'am? I mean, since you aren't here officially?"

J.D. had never seen his friend look embarrassed before. Ben nodded.

"Why did he come after me now? It's been six years."

"They're still putting it together, but it looks like he snapped completely after he killed his second wife."

"The girl in the wedding picture?" J.D. asked.

"Yeah. She would have been twenty tomorrow."

Jackie inhaled sharply. "And now she's just dead."

"There's a real good chance you two weren't his first victims," Thompkins told her sympathetically. "They're checking his past, looking for other wives or ex-girlfriends."

"Still," J.D. protested, "once Jackie left Indiana, why did he wait so long before looking for her?"

Thompkins shrugged. "Who's to say he waited? Maybe it took him this long to find her. Or maybe killing his second wife just pushed him over some edge. We may never know." Thompkins took a swallow of his coffee and eyed Jackie. "But if he'd managed to kill you yesterday, it's a safe bet he would have gone hunting for another woman who looked like you."

Jackie shuddered. "Why did he kill Brad Volmer?"

Again, Thompkins rubbed at the light stubble on his chin. "We don't know that he did. Volmer was strangled, remember? Zalewoski liked to use his fists."

"And Oggie Korbel was shot," J.D. said thoughtfully.

Thompkins nodded. "Zalewoski didn't carry any weapons that we can find. And what would be the motive?"

J.D. frowned. "You're telling us it's coincidence that three men connected with Jackie's house are dead?"

"I didn't say that."

"Come on, Ben, what's going on? What aren't you telling us?"

Thompkins drummed his fingers on the table. Jackie sipped her coffee, never taking her eyes from his face.

"Okay," he said finally, "but this doesn't leave this room, all right? We're building a case around the supposition that Lieberman and his three pals were the burglars we've been looking for. Not one house has been hit since Lieberman died. We're theorizing that there was a falling out among thieves."

Jackie suddenly straightened in her chair. "The basement lock!"

J.D. nodded. "Makes sense."

"What about that basement lock? You keep harping on that damn basement lock," Ben said irritably.

"Why would Lieberman put a dead-bolt lock on an inside door? He didn't have kids that he wanted to protect from falling down the stairs—"

"But how convenient if he wanted to keep people from going down there when he had a basement full of stolen goods," Jackie finished. "It all makes sense!"

J.D. smiled, glad to see a sparkle back in her sad eyes.

Jackie went on excitedly. "The house only stood empty for a couple of days after Donnie's death. Bessie and Frank were in and out during much of that time, so the boys couldn't get anything out of the house until after the funeral. They probably didn't know Bessie asked me to move in right away." She paused, more thoughtfully.

"Only, why would Steve Pinta kill Brad in my bedroom if they were just getting stuff out of the basement?"

"Maybe there were some things up there," J.D. suggested. "Donnie's personal belongings, for example. Do you have any leads on Pinta?"

Thompkins shook his head. "We figure he's probably three states away by now. And—" he held up a palm "—we don't know for sure that Pinta killed anyone, either." He smiled apologetically at Jackie. "I'm afraid as a cop I still need evidence to proceed. We don't even have proof the boys were the burglars."

Jackie's mouth parted, her expression filled with new excitement. "Yes, we do. At least, I think we do. What would you say to some hard evidence?"

"I'd say you'd make my boss a happy man," Ben replied cautiously.

"Well then, get ready for a promotion. And you have J.D.'s kids to thank." She turned to J.D. "Remember the computer you brought to the shop? Your son found two hidden files on it. One contains a list of dates, initials and abbreviated items. Compare the dates and the list and I'll bet you'll find they match the burglaries and stolen items. I didn't examine the information, but I think there are dollar amounts next to each item. You might even be able to learn who they sold the things to."

Ben uttered a low expletive. "J.D., can I use your phone?"

"Be my guest." He beamed at Jackie and found her grinning back. "Want some breakfast?"

Jackie laughed. "I'd love some. Suddenly, I'm starving."

J.D. was pulling out ingredients for an omelet when Ben got off the phone. "I'm afraid we're going to have to impound your computer," he told her.

"Impound away. It was Donnie's computer."

"Thanks. My boss is most grateful. Catch you guys later." He grabbed his jacket from the back of the chair and headed for the door.

"Looks like it's finally over," J.D. said. He instantly regretted his words when her expression darkened.

"I can't believe Larry's finally dead."

"Believe it." He hunkered down next to her chair. "Look, my timing probably stinks here, but—"

"Hey, Dad! Is Jackie up yet? Oh, hi, Jackie! You've got to come see our cool snowman."

J.D. jumped as his offspring burst through the kitchen door bringing with them a bitter blast of cold air and loose snow that tumbled from their clothing to the floor. Jackie's unexpected giggle got his full attention.

"If you could just see your face, J.D.," she told him around choked laughter. "Priceless."

"Hey, Dad, what were you doing practically kneeling on the floor?"

J.D. closed his eyes and prayed for patience. Then he opened them and found himself staring into Jackie's laughing eyes and knew it didn't matter. There'd be a better time for what he wanted to ask her.

JACKIE EYED THE SILENT house with even more trepidation than she'd felt going back into her shop earlier this morning. Between the police, reporters and everyone else, she felt as though she hadn't had a moment to herself in the past two days. Nor, unfortunately, had she and J.D. had any time alone together. There always seemed to be someone around with another question.

Bessie was devastated to learn her son might have been a thief, while Frank didn't seem the least bit surprised.

"Knew the kid was up to something," she'd heard him

telling Thompkins. "I told Seth months ago that Donnie suddenly had way too much money to spend. I figured he was selling drugs or something, you know?"

Jackie had to bite back her annoyance, hoping Frank wasn't saying things like that in Bessie's hearing.

"You sure you don't want us to go in with you?" Angel asked, bringing her thoughts back to the present.

Jackie offered up a smile, aware that she'd been sitting in Juan's car for several seconds without moving. "No, that's fine. Thanks for bringing me over."

"J.D. isn't going to like you coming here alone," Juan warned.

"No, probably not, but I need to pick up some more things. I called J.D.'s office before we left the shop. Carol will tell him to meet me here."

Angel frowned. "Looks kinda spooky to me. And it's getting dark."

Jackie agreed with both points. "All the more reason for you two to get moving. There's nothing left to fear. It's just an empty old house with expensive new locks. Thanks for helping me clean up today."

"Hey, no problem," Juan assured her. "I'll go in with Angel to open in the morning."

Jackie smiled at the pair and stepped from the car. J.D. had been reluctant to give up his hovering and go back to work today, particularly when he learned she planned to get the store ready to reopen.

"Thanks for the lift. I'll see you tomorrow."

As much as she didn't want to go inside the house, it was time to put the past behind her for good. Besides, she was running out of clean clothing. Maybe it was also time to go shopping for something besides sweat suits.

Jackie entered the silent house and stood in the hall listening. The threat was over. Larry was dead. She had nothing to fear any more. So why did she still feel the house watched her with evil intent?

The dark staircase seemed to mock her. Jackie knew she didn't want to climb those stairs.

Delaying the inevitable, she turned toward the living room and flipped on the light. The charred carpet and missing drape would have to be replaced before Bessie could show the house to prospective buyers. Jackie made a mental note to call about that in the morning.

She shivered as she crossed the hall and stepped into the dining room. The bitter cold outside seemed to be seeping into the house itself, but at least everything appeared normal. The police had gone through Donnie's personal items looking for more evidence, but this afternoon Ben had told her they were finished.

In the hall, Jackie paused. Her gaze drifted to the basement door. Closed but no longer locked, the door drew her like a magnet.

Had the basement really been used to store all the stolen items? There was no proof. Ben said they'd gone through the boxes stored down there, but it was all Christmas stuff like the markings said.

Impulsively, she turned down the hall instead of going upstairs. No doubt J.D. would be here shortly, and there might be some decorations she could use for the store. Bessie kept saying she didn't want anything from the house, that Jackie should take whatever she wanted.

Jackie opened the door and turned on the light. As she started carefully down the steps, she saw the police had opened the boxes and left many of the contents scattered on the floor.

Jackie frowned, surprised Thompkins would leave such a mess. Then she saw the two metal shelves that had al-

ways rested against the far wall. They were pulled away
to reveal something built into the wall.

Jackie moved forward hesitantly. A safe? Ben hadn't
mentioned anything about finding a safe. But that first file
Todd had shown her could very easily have been a safe
combination.

A floorboard creaked above her.

Jackie lifted her head in shock. She was not alone in
the house! Someone moved quietly overhead. Bessie?
She'd given her friend the new keys to the house yesterday.

The footsteps entered the dining room. Too heavy for
a woman. Jackie turned back toward the stairs and something moved on the floor near the stack of boxes to her
left.

A scream rose in her throat, trapped by the horror that
prevented her from drawing a breath. Two blue eyes
stared up at her. Wide. Imploring.

Steve Pinta lay trussed on the floor, bound hand and
foot, tape running across his mouth. Terror gripped her.
The footsteps crossed into the kitchen.

Jackie scanned the Christmas items, looking for a
weapon. A can of spray snow lay almost at her feet. She
lifted it, decided it wasn't heavy enough and stuffed it in
her coat pocket. She reached instead for the heavy ceramic
snowman.

Steve squirmed. He made frantic sounds behind his gag.
The footsteps reached the basement door. Jackie ran to
the wall behind the stairs. There was no place to hide.
Whoever was up there would see her as soon as he came
down the stairs.

Fear threatened to choke her as a man's lower body
came into view.

"J.D., I'M GLAD YOU CALLED in," Carol's voice said in his ear. "Jackie called a few minutes ago. She wants you to meet her at her house."

Fear crawled through his belly. Larry was dead, but the police still hadn't located Steve Pinta.

"Carol, see if you can get hold of Ben Thompkins. Tell him…just tell him Jackie's alone in her house. Ask him to drive by, to be sure everything's okay. I'm on my way."

J.D. accelerated as he pulled onto the interstate. No doubt his imagination had become fanciful. After all, why would Steve Pinta return to the house?

Unless there was still something inside of value. Something the police had missed.

Grateful for the light traffic, J.D. soon turned onto Main Street. There, however, traffic came to a sudden stop. Fire blazed from a row of old buildings and shops. It took him a moment to realize both the mortgage company and Teller Photography were located on that block.

J.D. whipped his car down the nearest side street.

Ben hadn't driven by the house. He'd be busy with the fire. In a town this size, everyone's attention would be focused on the fire.

Minutes later, J.D. pulled in front of Jackie's house. As he stepped from the car, the first snowflake drifted from the ash gray sky overhead.

JACKIE SHOOK, WAITING for him to turn and spot her. Seth Bislow obliged.

"Hello, Jackie." As he came around the staircase, she saw the gun in his left hand.

Jackie threw the snowman. Seth dodged and ceramic shards splintered harmlessly against the concrete.

"That wasn't very friendly. But then, you never have liked me, have you?"

Jackie sidestepped, frantically searching for another weapon.

"You aren't going anywhere, my dear. Not yet, at least. My mood isn't particularly good at the moment, I'm afraid, so I really wouldn't do anything else that might make me pull this trigger. I'm on a tight schedule, you see. Stand still!"

His barked command stopped her inching progress away from him.

"Good. Now let's see if you can be more cooperative than Mr. Pinta over there. What is the safe combination?"

Jackie stared at him. "How did you get in here?"

Seth grinned. "Why, Jackie, as Frank's best friend, I found it a simple matter to lift the new keys from Bessie's kitchen—just like I took the old ones."

"You had her key to the basement lock! The one she couldn't find."

"Of course. I needed to search the house after that fool, Donnie, killed himself. Then you made a production out of needing the basement key, so I had to make a copy and replace it." His beady, little eyes narrowed. "Only you went and had all the locks changed again," he accused.

Jackie took a step back.

"Come now—I told you I don't have much time. The fire won't keep the police occupied for long. Mr. Pinta said the combination was on Donnie's computer. Unfortunately for him, he lied."

Cold fear snaked its way up her back. Seth Bislow planned to kill her.

"You were behind the burglaries?" she asked.

Impatience drew his mouth into a tight line across his

face. "Hardly, my dear. Petty burglary doesn't appeal to me. No, I plan on a much grander scheme, but those stupid boys nearly ruined everything when they chose my house to rob."

Fear pounded a staccato in her head. Keep him talking, she thought. Stall for time. It was her only hope. "Bessie never said anything about your house being robbed."

"Of course not. I could hardly report the burglary, now could I? Not when the bonds they stole from me were already stolen."

Jackie shook her head. "I don't understand."

"Bearer bonds, a veritable fortune in bearer bonds, payable to the holder. And the fools didn't even realize what they had. They took them along with my coin collection. Tomorrow, when the auditors arrive, those bonds will turn up missing—and so will I." He glared at Steve Pinta, whose expression of hopelessness only added a new layer to her fear.

"But the police searched the house," she protested.

"Yes, but they never found the safe where the boys kept all the small items. Little Donnie was quite creative. The shelves have a false back. The police probably examined the contents, but no one thought to move shelves that pressed up against a stone wall. If Donnie hadn't panicked and driven himself off a cliff, I'd congratulate him. He really did show moments of brilliance."

"But if you have Steve—"

"Unfortunately for him, he's convinced me that only Donnie had the combination. And now, you do."

The hidden files.

"Ah, I see you know exactly what I'm talking about. Open it!"

She cringed at his snarled demand. "I can't. I don't know the combination!"

He pushed against the thick glasses resting on the bridge of his nose, considering. "But you know where it is."

Time. She needed time.

"I assure you, unlike your ex-husband, my dear, I'm not the least bit crazy. A bit greedy, perhaps, but not crazy. The pain I inflict will be very deliberate."

Before she could speak, he turned and aimed the gun at the youth lying on the floor.

"Don't!" Jackie screamed.

"Then I suggest you show me where to find that combination."

Jackie lifted her gaze from the writhing youth. "At—at the shop. I t-took the spare computer to the store."

"Spare computer? There were two? No wonder I couldn't find it on the one upstairs. Shall we go?"

Numb with dread, Jackie turned and headed for the steps. The police had the computer, but obviously Seth didn't know that. She had to stall for time. "Did you kill Donnie and his friends?" she managed to ask.

"Donnie killed himself, I'm afraid. The Volmer boy was looking for the safe combination and unfortunately caught me inside the house searching for the bonds. I had no choice but to kill him," Seth told her nonchalantly. "I didn't realize Pinta was inside, as well."

His careless shrug implied he would have killed Steve, too. Jackie tried to control her trembling.

"I followed you out into the storm that night. Pinta apparently had the presence of mind to stay behind and hide the body to keep a police investigation away from the house. I admit, I didn't think to do that. But I was most grateful, as you can imagine. And it was rather amusing, the way you kept showing up every time he tried to get the body away from the house."

Jackie had almost reached the hallway when she saw a flash of movement just inside the kitchen. Someone else was inside the house?

She prayed for it to be Ben Thompkins and twisted in the doorway, blocking Seth from coming all the way up. "And Oggie Korbel?" she asked.

"A young man with an attitude, I'm afraid. He recognized me, of course. We'd met several times at Frank's place. And he was most uncooperative when I demanded my property."

"You killed him."

"Yes, I'm afraid he made me angry and left me little choice."

"Like me?"

His cold stare moved up and down her body. "A shame, actually. At one point, I had rather hoped you might want to come with me. Those bonds are worth quite a bit of money, you see. And there is probably a handsome amount of cash and portable items still inside that safe."

Jackie braced her hand against the doorjamb and lashed out with her weak foot. Seth easily blocked the kick but his glasses dislodged, falling from his face and bouncing down the steps to the concrete below.

"Bitch!" He grabbed her soft cast and yanked. Jackie fell to the hall floor, landing on the can of snow spray.

"Bislow!"

J.D.'s voice jerked her head around.

Seth stopped, two steps from the top. "I have a gun, Mr. Frost," he yelled. Anger made his oily voice shrill and grating. "Step out where I can see you or she dies."

J.D. came around the corner, lowering a kitchen chair. Tension radiated from him.

''If you had just let him step into the hall,'' he told Jackie, ''I'd have clobbered him.''

She swallowed past her terror. ''How was I supposed to know?''

Jackie fingered the lid off the can inside her pocket, as Seth stared myopically at J.D.

''That's the problem with modern women,'' J.D. said. ''They never wait to be rescued any more.''

She yanked the can out of her pocket and depressed the nozzle. White foam struck Seth full in the eyes as J.D. threw the chair. The gun roared harmlessly. Seth toppled backward down the stairs.

With a crash, the front door burst open.

''Police! Freeze.''

Epilogue

Scents of roasting turkey and fresh pine mingled in the air, with a hint of wood smoke coming from the fireplace. Jackie smoothed her kelly green skirt and watched Todd open a computer game with glee.

She still found it hard to accept that she was entitled to this mind-boggling sense of euphoria. The horror was truly over. Seth Bislow lay paralyzed from the neck down awaiting trial. Steve Pinta also awaited trial on burglary charges plus several other charges that stemmed from moving Brad Volmer's body.

Frank had taken Bessie to Florida to visit friends and look at property. He seemed subdued and more attentive with Seth Bislow out of their lives.

Heather opened her telescope with a shout of glee. Jackie smiled at J.D. and he grinned back at her.

"Here, Jackie. It's your turn to open a present."

Jackie accepted the much-taped box from Todd and plucked away the piece of tinsel hanging from his hair. Todd laughed, but both children watched anxiously as she undid the wrappings and finally removed the lid.

The yellow teddy bear nested inside a bed of tissue paper.

Her gaze flashed to J.D. He watched her almost as anxiously as the two children.

She examined the uneven stitches and the implausible wide green button eyes. A matching green ribbon was now tied around its neck. The children, of course. She'd forgotten all about them finding the bear at the shop that day. This was why it had disappeared.

With hands that trembled she lifted it, knowing she didn't have to be afraid of a stuffed teddy bear any more. As the bear came free of the tissue paper, a bright red ribbon tied around its arm made her catch her breath. A diamond ring hung suspended from that bit of ribbon.

Jackie stared. Her heart filled with such love she thought she might burst. A tear spilled from one eye. Heather, who'd moved to sit at her side, wrapped her arms around Jackie. "We didn't want you to be sad any more," she said.

Todd nodded agreement.

"I'm not sad. I'm happy. It's wonderful. *You're* wonderful."

"Daddy, too?" Heather asked.

Jackie met his gaze, seeing her love reflected there. "Especially Daddy."

Aunt Dottie coughed and reached for a handkerchief to blot her eyes. J.D. left his chair to kneel in front of her. "I'm glad you think so. We're a package deal, you know, so this is a package proposal. Will you marry us?"

"You have to say yes," Todd told her. "It's Christmas."

She wasn't sure she could get anything past her emotion-clogged throat.

"But if I marry you, I'll be Jackie Frost," she managed to tease finally.

"That's okay, Jackie," Heather assured her. "That's Daddy's name, too."

"What?" Startled, she stared at him.

J.D. nodded, a wry expression on his face. "You'd better know the worst up front. Jack Daniel Frost. My father has a warped sense of humor. You'll see that when you meet him this afternoon."

"Jack and Jackie Frost?" she asked faintly.

"What could be more appropriate?" Aunt Dottie asked, clearing her throat. "I can't imagine two people better suited to keeping Christmas in their hearts all year, can you?"

Jackie looked at each face, lingering on J.D.'s. "No, Aunt Dottie. I can't. Merry Christmas, darling."

DEBBIE MACOMBER

invites you to the

HEART OF TEXAS

Join Debbie Macomber as she brings you the lives and loves of the folks in the ranching community of Promise, Texas.

If you loved Midnight Sons—don't miss Heart of Texas! A brand-new six-book series from Debbie Macomber.

Available in February 1998 at your favorite retail store.

Heart of Texas by Debbie Macomber

Lonesome Cowboy	February '98
Texas Two-Step	March '98
Caroline's Child	April '98
Dr. Texas	May '98
Nell's Cowboy	June '98
Lone Star Baby	July '98

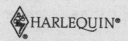

HARLEQUIN®

HPHRT1

HARLEQUIN®

I N T R I G U E®

In the mountains of Colorado, the snow comes in on a gust of wind, reaching blizzard conditions in a matter of minutes. Here, the Rampart Mountain Rescue Team is never lonely. But this year there's even more activity than usual for the team, as not only Mother Nature but mystery is swirling in their midst.

Rocky Mtn. RESCUE

Join three of your favorite Intrigue authors
for an intimate look at the lives and loves of the
men and women of one of America's highest
mountain rescue teams. It's the place to be
for thrills, chills and adventure!

Don't miss

#449 FORGET ME NOT by Cassie Miles
January 1998

#454 WATCH OVER ME by Carly Bishop
February 1998

#459 FOLLOW ME HOME by Leona Karr
March 1998

HARLEQUIN®

I N T R I G U E®

Seven Sins

Seven men and women

Seven flaws that keep them from safety...
from love...from their destiny...

Seven chances to win it all...
or lose everything...

Patricia Rosemoor and Harlequin Intrigue bring you
Seven Sins—a new series based on heroes and heroines
with fatal flaws...and the courage to rise above them.

Join us for the first two books:

**#439 BEFORE THE FALL
coming in October 1997**

**#451 AFTER THE DARK
coming in January 1998**

And watch for more SEVEN SINS books in the months to
come—only from Patricia Rosemoor and Harlequin Intrigue!

HARLEQUIN WOMEN KNOW ROMANCE WHEN THEY SEE IT.

And they'll see it on **ROMANCE CLASSICS**, the new 24-hour TV channel devoted to romantic movies and original programs like the special **Romantically Speaking—Harlequin™ Goes Prime Time.**

Romantically Speaking—Harlequin™ Goes Prime Time introduces you to many of your favorite romance authors in a program developed exclusively for Harlequin® readers.

Watch for **Romantically Speaking—Harlequin™ Goes Prime Time** beginning in the summer of 1997.

If you're not receiving ROMANCE CLASSICS, call your local cable operator or satellite provider and ask for it today!

Escape to the network of your dreams.

See Ingrid Bergman and Gregory Peck in *Spellbound* on Romance Classics.

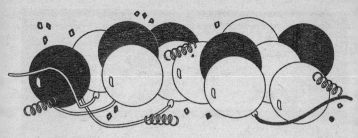

Ring in the New Year with

New Year's Resolution:

FAMILY

This heartwarming collection of three contemporary stories rings in the New Year with babies, families and the best of holiday romance.

Add a dash of romance to your holiday celebrations with this exciting new collection, featuring bestselling authors **Barbara Bretton, Anne McAllister** and **Leandra Logan.**

Available in December,
wherever Harlequin books are sold.